Highland Sky

Highland Outcasts
Book 3

By
Elizabeth Rose

© Copyright 2022 by Elizabeth Rose
Text by Elizabeth Rose
Cover by Dar Albert
Edited by Scott Moreland

Dragonblade Publishing, Inc. is an imprint of Kathryn Le Veque Novels, Inc.
P.O. Box 23
Moreno Valley, CA 92556
ceo@dragonbladepublishing.com

Produced in the United States of America

First Edition May 2022
Trade Paperback Edition

Reproduction of any kind except where it pertains to short quotes in relation to advertising or promotion is strictly prohibited.

All Rights Reserved.

The characters and events portrayed in this book are fictitious. Any similarity to real persons, living or dead, is purely coincidental and not intended by the author.

ARE YOU SIGNED UP FOR DRAGONBLADE'S BLOG?

You'll get the latest news and information on exclusive giveaways, exclusive excerpts, coming releases, sales, free books, cover reveals and more.

Check out our complete list of authors, too!

No spam, no junk. That's a promise!

Sign Up Here

www.dragonbladepublishing.com

Dearest Reader;

Thank you for your support of a small press. At Dragonblade Publishing, we strive to bring you the highest quality Historical Romance from some of the best authors in the business. Without your support, there is no 'us', so we sincerely hope you adore these stories and find some new favorite authors along the way.

Happy Reading!

CEO, Dragonblade Publishing

ADDITIONAL DRAGONBLADE BOOKS BY
AUTHOR ELIZABETH ROSE

Highland Outcasts Series
Highland Soul (Book 1)
Highland Flame (Book 2)
Highland Sky (Book 3)
Highland Silver (Book 4)

Author's Note

*(The **Highland Outcasts Series** features secondary characters from my MacKeefe Clan. The stories about the characters who are making guest appearances can be found in some of my other series, such as **Legacy of the Blade, Madman MacKeefe, Seasons of Fortitude, Legendary Bastards of the Crown,** and **The Highland Chronicles,** amongst others.)*

Some of the MacKeefe Clan heroes, heroines, and secondary characters seen in this book are:

Old Callum MacKeefe (Oldest living man in Scotland)

Ian MacKeefe (Callum's son – MacKeefe Clan chieftain)

Storm MacKeefe (Ian's son – also a MacKeefe Clan chieftain since they have holdings in both the Highlands and the Lowlands)

Heroes of the Highland Outcasts Series:

Gavin MacKeefe – hero of *Highland Soul*

Cam MacKeefe – hero of *Highland Flame*

Nash MacKeefe – hero of *Highland Sky*

North MacKeefe – twin brother of Nash, and hero of *Highland Silver*

◆◆◇◆◆

CHAPTER ONE

Glasgow, Medieval Scotland

RETURNING TO THE scene of the crime was never a good idea. Then again, no real crime was ever committed at the Horn and Hoof Tavern as far as Nash MacKeefe was concerned. Breaking Old Callum MacKeefe's silly tavern rules wasn't even deserving of a sentence. But as far as Old Callum was concerned, Nash and his friends were all guilty of what he considered crimes. Because of this, Nash, his twin brother, North, and their good friends Gavin and Cam had all been made outcasts of the clan until they served their time.

Gavin and Cam had already completed their punishments and were no longer outcasts. Nash and North, on the other hand, still had a long way to go.

"Och, nay," complained Nash, dismounting his horse as their traveling party reached the tavern. Right now, this was the last place he wanted to be. "Why couldna we have received our sentences at Hermitage Castle like Gavin and Cam, instead of here of all places?"

The MacKeefes were a Highland clan, with their camp near Oban. However, they had holdings in the Lowlands as well and ruled over Hermitage Castle.

"Stop yer doitit chatter," spat his twin brother, North, dismounting his horse as well. They were twins but not identical in looks. They both had long, brown hair, but Nash had hazel eyes, while North's eyes were silver. Nash was a little shorter than his brother, and North had more chiseled features. Nash was more outgoing, and sometimes a little reckless, but he didn't care. "I dinna mind stoppin' for some Mountain Magic before we're sent out on another of Old Callum's stupid missions."

Mountain Magic was the strongest whisky in all of Scotland and England, too. It was brewed by Callum MacKeefe, the oldest man in Scotland. Nash didn't believe Callum should have so much power over their fates, but he did. It was because he was the father of their laird, Ian, and the grandfather of their second laird, Storm. Plus, most of the clan's income came from his secret recipe of Mountain Magic. Old Callum swore he'd go to his grave never telling a one of them how he made the golden brew. Since he was so tight-lipped about it, the MacKeefes could only hope he truly did live forever, or the recipe would die with him, as well as their earnings.

"Ye two arena afraid to go in there, are ye?" Cam, their blond-haired friend, helped his new wife, Yvaine, out of the wagon. He and Yvaine, the widow of a chandler, had just been married at Hermitage Castle. Cam was a lucky dog to have his punishment already completed.

"Of course, they're no' afraid," said Yvaine, reaching up to get Cam's four-year-old daughter, Avianca, from the cart. "They're Highland warriors, just like ye, Cam. Highlanders are the bravest people I've ever met."

"I'll get Avianca, love." Cam scooped the little girl up, holding her tightly in his arms. For just finding out he even had a daughter, Cam was already proving to be a good father.

The door to the tavern opened, and their friend, Gavin, stood there with his arm around his new wife, Davita, who was the cordwainer's daughter. He held a tankard in his other hand. "About time ye got here," Gavin called out. "Callum is already gripin' that ye're late and the busy hour for drinkin' will be startin' soon."

"What's the matter?" asked Nash. "Is bein' late now one of his tavern rules we canna break either?"

"Whatever ye do, be careful," warned his brother as they headed into the establishment. "We dinna want to anger Callum more, or our sentences are goin' to be twice as bad and much longer than Cam's and Gavin's."

"What difference does it make?" complained Nash. "After all, we lived through their punishments already, as if they were ours. It doesna seem fair that we still await our sentences. We should no' be outcasts this long." Nash pushed past his brother and headed right over to the drink board where Callum was pouring a tankard of whisky for one of their lairds, Storm MacKeefe.

"Ah, there ye are," said Storm, taking a deep draw and thunking his tankard down on the board. "I suppose ye're wonderin' whose punishment is next. Well, I guess we should get started."

"I'll take a drink first," said Nash, reaching for the bottle on the drink board.

"Nay, ye willna," spat Callum, snatching the bottle away from him. "Ye are late! Because of yer dallyin', now ye're goin' to put me behind schedule. The busy hour is approachin', and this tavern will be packed to the gills."

North snuck up behind Callum, snitching a bottle of whisky from under the drink board, taking a swig before the old man even noticed. North didn't like asking for permission. When he wanted something, he just took it. That was one of his many downfalls.

"Get yer filthy hands off of that!" Callum yanked the bottle away as North was drinking, and a little spilled.

Dead silence, as they all looked at the spilled whisky atop the drink board waiting for Callum to explode.

"North, what did ye do?" Nash's eyes opened wide. "Ye ken Callum's number one rule of the tavern is to never waste Mountain Magic."

Their friend, Gavin, had learned this the hard way. Part of his punishment had to do with breaking Callum's number one rule.

This wasn't going to bode well for North, even if the spill was the old man's fault.

"I dinna spill it," protested North, raising his palms in front of him.

"We're no' blind. We see it right there." Callum pointed one bony finger to the spill. "Ye are wastin' my Mountain Magic, North MacKeefe. Ye ken my number one rule!" Just to prove his point, Callum walked over and pulled down the end of a parchment that was rolled up and attached to the back of the kitchen door. It listed all his rules, one by one. The first, of course, being that no one ever waste his precious Mountain Magic. "There!" he said, tapping the first rule with his finger.

"Nay." North shook his head, looking back at Nash. They all felt the tension in the room. North hadn't even been given his sentence yet. But this was going to only add salt to the wound.

"Too late now. The damage is done," said Nash, shrugging his shoulders. "I'm sorry, Brathair."

"Nay, I tell ye. It's no' wasted." North dove to the drink board, lapping up the spill of whisky with his tongue, much like a dog drinking water.

Laughing was heard from across the tavern, and Gavin and Cam roamed over to watch their friend make a fool of himself.

"There," said North, licking his lips, pointing down at the board. "The whisky is gone and no' wasted in the least."

"That it is," said Storm with a chuckle. "Well, Grandda, I guess North hasna broken yer number one rule after all."

"Mmmph," grumbled Callum, yanking at the end of the rule list, and letting go. It rolled up with a snap and made a full circle. Callum hobbled back to the drink board. "All right then. Let's get this over with, so these fools can leave and I can tend to my patrons." Callum looked around the room. "Where is my son, Ian?" he asked.

"Da is upstairs restin'." Storm took another swig of whisky. "He's no' feelin' well again. We'll have to continue without him."

"What's wrong with Ian?" asked Gavin in concern. "He's

been ill for a while now, but no one can tell me what ails him."

"We're no' sure," said Storm, looking down at his tankard. "My wife has tried everythin' with herbal concoctions, but he doesna seem to be improvin'."

"Is it a bout with his stomach?" asked Gavin.

"Or is it his head?" Nash wondered. Their chieftain, Ian, didn't seem to be in the right mind lately, in Nash's opinion.

"It's no' the sweatin' sickness is it?" asked North, giving a fake shiver.

"Boys, what I am about to tell ye, must stay here and no' be repeated." Storm looked very upset. "My faither is havin' trouble grippin' a sword, and sometimes even walkin'. At times, his mind doesna even seem to be there."

"Why didna someone wake me?" shouted Ian, hurrying down the stairs from one of the upstairs rooms. "I need to be here. I am the chieftain." When he got to the bottom of the stairs, it was as if he tripped, although there was nothing in his way. Gavin shot forward, being the closest one to him, grabbing him under one arm. "Let go of me," spat Ian. "I dinna need yer help." He pushed Gavin's hand away.

"I'm sorry, my laird, but ye stumbled. I didna want ye to fall onto this . . . dirty floor," he finished, trying to lessen the situation, but only managing to infuriate Callum instead.

"Dirty floor?" spat Callum. "My tavern is one of the cleanest around! If ye think this floor is so dirty, then mayhap I should have ye and yer friends wash it!" Callum's pride was wounded, and it looked like Nash and his friends were going to pay for just trying to help their chieftain.

"He didna mean dirty. He just meant . . . bumpy," said Nash, not able to think of anything else.

"Bumpy?" Callum made a sour face. "Humph! Is that what ye think?"

"Stop tryin' to help," North whispered to Nash. "Next thing ye ken, the madman will be makin' us no' only wash the floor, but rebuild it, too."

"Did I hear somethin' about a madman?" Aidan MacKeefe, one of their clansmembers called madman for his crazy, dangerous antics, joined them with his pet squirrel, Reid, perched on his shoulder. His "madmen" friends, Onyx and Ian, were with him. Ian's deerhound, Kyle, was at his side. The dog reminded Nash of a small horse.

"Aye, if anyone is goin' to be called a madman besides us, I dinna ken how I like that." Ian ran a hand over his hound's head. It was so large that when it stood on its back legs it was the same height as he. Ian was a common name in Scotland, and this madman shared the same name as their chieftain.

"North, were ye callin' me a madman?" asked Callum.

"Nay," both North and Nash said together, looking down at the drink board rather than at the old man.

"What's this I hear that ye four are outcasts of the clan now?" asked the third of the Madmen MacKeefe, Onyx. Onyx was the craziest-looking of the three friends, with one orange eye and the other of black. Some even called him the devil.

"Cam and I are no' outcasts anymore," said Gavin. "We've worked off our sentences."

"We've worked them off as well," grumbled Nash, not happy that each time one of his friends got a punishment, he and North were punished as well, it seemed.

"Aye, my brathair and I probably did more of a sentence by now than both Gavin and Cam put together," scoffed North.

"That's nothin' compared to what I have in store for ye two." Callum actually sneered and rubbed his palms together. It seemed he was really enjoying this, and that worried Nash more than anything else.

"Which of us will have our sentence next?" asked Nash, hoping it was him so he could get it over with quickly and get back to being a clansmember soon. He didn't like being an outcast, and missed spending time with the MacKeefes.

Before Callum could answer, Aidan's squirrel scurried down his arm, jumping atop the drink board. It chattered at the dog, as if it were purposely antagonizing the hound. Then Ian's hound jumped up and put its paws atop the counter, barking like crazy. The squirrel took off at a run over the counter, knocking over an empty cup along the way as the dog tried to catch the squirrel.

"How many times have I told ye no' to bring yer doitit pets in here?" yelled Callum, his arms waving over his head now.

"I'm sorry. Reid got spooked." Aidan tried to grab the squirrel, but it jumped up, climbing the wall to the rafters next.

"Come on, Kyle, let's go before Old Callum gives us a punishment, too." Ian grabbed his hound by the scruff of the neck and headed away.

"I hope yer dang wildcat isna in here as well, Onyx," Callum said with fire blazing in his eyes.

Onyx raised up his palms, and his two-toned eyes traveled from Callum over to the others as he answered. "Nay, I left Tawpie back in England with my wife, honest I did." Onyx turned and hightailed it out of there, making Storm chuckle.

"Da, do ye want to tell the boys who is next for his punishment?" Storm asked Ian.

"Punishment?" Ian looked confused.

"Aye, their sentences," explained Storm, looking over at the others. "So they dinna have to be outcasts anymore."

Ian's face flushed and he seemed embarrassed. "Och, it's Cam's turn," he said.

"Mine? I just finished my sentence," Cam replied.

"I – I meant Gavin."

"Nay. I was the first to finish mine," said Gavin. "It's either North's or Nash's turn next."

"I've got a headache and need to lie down. Carry on without me." Ian turned to go, rubbing his leg as he walked.

"I was just goin' up to check on a room so Avianca can take a nap. I'll come with ye," said Cam, getting a nod of approval from Storm.

"Aye. I think I'll tag along, too." Gavin went with them to ensure Ian made it back upstairs without falling over, or forgetting where he was going.

"That's sad," remarked Nash, shaking his head, watching them go.

"It's goin' to be sadder when my da finds out that he can no longer serve as a chieftain of the clan," Storm told them.

"He's no' goin' to take it lightly." North shook his head, watching his friends help the man up the stairs. Once a powerful, ruthless Highland warrior, now chieftain, Ian MacKeefe was a sad story, to be sure.

"Dinna worry about him," said Callum in his high, crackly voice. "My Mountain Magic will fix him right up, but it'll just take some time to do it."

"I've got Reid," said Aidan, coming back to join them with his squirrel cradled in his arms. Aidan was a strong man with a wide chest and long blond hair. It was almost funny to see him care so much about a little squirrel that he'd saved after the thing fell out of its nest as a baby. "What did I miss?"

"They were about to tell us who's goin' to be punished next," stated North.

"It's Nash's turn," Storm answered.

"Yes!" Nash made a fist of victory while North groaned and rubbed his hands over his face.

"Why couldna it be me? I am tired of waitin'," North complained.

"What do I have to do?" asked Nash anxiously. "I'm in a hurry to get this over with as quickly as possible."

"What did ye do to deserve a punishment?" asked Aidan, curiously.

"He set the roof of the tavern on fire, and almost burned the place down . . . among other things," Callum answered for him.

"I put the fire out," boasted Nash. "I saved the tavern."

"Nay, that was me," said North. And Gavin and Cam."

"That's no' how I remember it." Nash didn't want to be the blame for this. Not when they were all involved.

"It doesna matter," said Storm, standing up. "Nash, yer punishment will be to go to the MacKenzie Clan and help them repair the roofs of their buildin's."

"What?" Nash made a face. This was the most ridiculous thing he'd ever heard in his life. "What do ye mean?" he asked, thinking he'd heard Storm wrong.

"The MacKenzies were attacked by the Sutherlands a few days ago, and their camp was demolished," said Callum.

"No' actually demolished, but there were some deaths as well as a lot of damage done," said Storm. "I told them I'd send ye to help them."

"Especially to fix the roofs," sniffed Callum. "After all, if ye can ruin roofs, ye can learn to fix them, too."

"Ye want me to thatch roofs?" Nash was appalled. "That is the work of peasants. I'm a Highland warrior. Surely, there must be somethin' else I can do."

"Now that ye mention it, there is," said Storm. "We have been enemies with the MacKenzies, but I would like to no' only help them out, but make an alliance with them, too. I feel it is time."

"We're makin' an alliance with the MacKenzies?" gasped North. "They've always been our enemies and deserve to rot in hell after killin' my parents."

"Our parents," Nash added.

"Dinna forget that a couple of their people were killed by ours durin' that event, too," interrupted Aidan. He looked over to his squirrel, petting it as it once again perched on his shoulder.

"How are we goin' to form an alliance?" asked Nash, not understanding this at all. "I hardly think thatchin' a few roofs is goin' to make us friends. Plus, I'll be riskin' my life just bein' there at all."

Callum started cackling, and Nash realized this wasn't going to be good. "That's why I suggested that ye marry one of them. That'll form an alliance." The old man's face lit up, but Nash's jaw dropped.

"Marry?" His head snapped around as he looked at Storm.

"Storm, nay! Please."

"I'm sorry," said Storm.

"But Gavin and Cam didna have to marry anyone to work off their punishments and be accepted back into the clan. This isna fair. Especially no' with the situation with my parents."

North shook his head. "Blethers, I am glad this is yer punishment, Nash, and no' mine. I'd hate to have to marry one of the daughters of Ciaran MacKenzie. My horse is even more comely than those two wenches."

Nash's eyes popped open wide, remembering the stories sung by the bards about the homely daughters of Ciaran MacKenzie. "Nay," he said, feeling as if he were being choked. "God's eyes, Storm, please tell me I dinna have to marry one of them."

"Relax, Nash. Nay, ye dinna," said Storm, causing Nash to let out a deep breath.

"Thank God! That is a relief. It'll be bad enough just havin' to be there in the first place."

Storm continued. "It seems both of the man's daughters as well as his wife were killed in the raid by the Sutherlands."

"Oh," said Nash, hanging his head, feeling like a fool now. Even if the MacKenzies were their enemies, Nash didn't like to hear of innocent women and young girls dying needlessly. "Sorry to hear that."

"Who is he goin' to marry then?" asked North.

"Laird MacKenzie has a niece," Storm explained. "Her name is Kellina. She'll be teachin' ye how to thatch the roofs as well."

"I'm marryin' his niece?" This didn't sit right with Nash either. "What does she look like?" His eyes darted over to his brother who was grinning from ear to ear.

"I dinna ken. I've never met her," said Storm. "I've already confirmed the betrothal with MacKenzie. Ye will be married as soon as ye get there. Then ye will help them to rebuild their camp."

"Well, have fun, Brathair." North scooped up an empty tankard off the drink board and poured himself a cup of whisky. "I'll be thinkin' of ye while I'm here waitin' for my own sentence."

"Nay ye willna. Ye're goin' with him." Callum snatched the bottle away.

"Nay, no' again!" North looked over to Storm, but Storm just nodded his head.

"Sorry, but it'll be better to have someone there to watch Nash's back in case of trouble," said Storm.

Now it was Nash's turn to grin. "I hope ye're no' afraid of heights, North. After all, those roofs willna be mended on their own."

"He's no' goin' to thatch roofs," said Storm.

"I'm no'?" North's expression turned from sour to sweet. "Guid. I'll help the lassies in any way I can."

"Ye will help with replantin' their crops, and tendin' to the livestock that is left," Callum told them. "Aidan will travel with ye since he is on his way to see Chieftain Shaw Gordon at Edinvale Castle to pick up somethin' for me."

"I'm goin' with them?" Aidan looked more surprised than the rest of them to hear this.

"Ye ken the MacKenzies better than the rest of us, Aidan, so it will be guid to travel with them." Storm put his hand on Aidan's shoulder. "It willna be out of yer way, and done as a favor to the clan. I'd like to have a strong warrior such as ye with them in case trouble breaks out."

"Aye. Of course," said Aidan with a nod, his sense of self-worth even greater than Nash's. "I'll just let my wife ken. We'll be leavin' on the morrow then?"

"At first light," said Callum, wiping a rag over the drink board. "Now, everyone out. I have a business to run."

Still in shock, Nash stepped away from the drink board with his brother, shaking his head in disbelief. "I canna marry one of the MacKenzies, North. This is the worst punishment ever."

"Ye dinna have a choice. No' if ye want to be accepted back into the clan," North told him.

"This punishment is goin' to be worse than both Cam's and

Gavin's put together." Nash couldn't help but feel sorry for himself.

"It'll be over soon, and then it'll be my turn," said North.

"Nay. That's where ye're wrong," said Nash. "Since I'm to marry, this is a sentence that'll never be done. It's one that is goin' to last for a lifetime!"

◆•◇◆•◇◆•◇◆•

CHAPTER TWO

KELLINA'S HEART OVERFLOWED with grief for the dead members of her clan. All she wanted was revenge on the Sutherlands who had devastated Clan MacKenzie. Looking around their camp, she felt as if she were living a nightmare. The charred remains of their thatched roofs stared back at her while the ominous sky behind it told her it was about to rain. All of their belongings in their living spaces were about to get soaked.

It had been just days ago when the Sutherlands attacked, stealing most of their livestock, killing their people, and burning the roofs of their homes.

Kellina had insisted on being trained as a warrior after the deaths of her parents, so she had fought in this battle as well. She was good with a sword. Being a girl was an advantage since her attackers didn't feel threatened by her. But they should have. She managed to bring down more than one of the Sutherlands, and even protected one of the young children of the clan from being killed. She had also scarred the face of their chieftain, Iver Sutherland, although she failed to kill him.

It didn't matter that she was a woman. Kellina was good at many things – one of them being able to help protect her clan. For this, she was proud.

The cottages still smoldered, sending acrid smoke in tendrils up into the sky like a signal of distress, even if no one would see it or respond. The roofs of their homes were gone now, the thatch having burned quickly. Since the buildings were made of stone, they were not really harmed, but some of their belongings inside had caught fire as well.

Kellina looked up to the hills where less than a third of their livestock still grazed. The rest of the Heilan Coo – long-haired, Highland cattle and Blackface sheep had been taken by the Sutherlands, leaving them with barely enough to survive. She was sure they'd never have enough food to last throughout the winter. Not when their enemies burned the crops as well.

She let out a deep sigh, wondering how they were ever going to recover from this devastating blow. It would be hard, but they would manage. They had to survive. She needed to stay strong for the clan since too many, including their chieftain, had already seemed to lose hope.

Most of the damage could be fixed. What couldn't be reversed was the fact that she'd lost her aunt and two cousins, as well as some good men from the clan in this deadly battle.

"Uncle," she said, approaching Ciaran, the chieftain of the clan. Broken shards of dishes crunched under her feet as she walked toward him. Women and children wept and moaned as they mourned their dead loved ones that were buried up on the side of the mountain. They slowly picked through the ruins, trying to salvage as much as they could. This once beautiful and virgin land was now desecrated in more ways than one, looking like the bowels of hell.

"Kellina, come here, lass," said Ciaran, who wasn't really her uncle, but she and her siblings called him that. He and his wife had taken them in twelve years ago after the death of her parents.

Ciaran's weary eyes sought her out. She could tell the life from within him was draining quickly, and not just from the state of the camp. Her heart went out to him to have had to endure so much loss all at once. His leg and also his side had been stabbed during the battle. His body was bruised and beaten. Kellina had sewn up his wounds and wrapped them as well, but the man walked with a crutch and a bad limp. She wasn't sure he'd ever be able to recover completely. He would be of little use now, should another battle arise. But even with his physical challenges, the worst was what he'd have to endure mentally. This battle seemed to have broken his spirit and she wasn't sure he'd ever get over the loss of his wife and two daughters.

She hurried over to him, slipping her arm around his waist in a half-hug. He was the closest thing she had to a father although, for some reason, she'd never felt close to him at all. He and his late wife, Lorna, had raised her as their own since the time she was naught but a young child.

"Walk with me, Kellina. To pay respect."

"Nay, Uncle," she protested, her eyes scanning the height of the hill. "Ye canna walk up the mountain to visit their graves," she told him. "No' in yer condition. We should have buried them down here instead, as I suggested."

"Nay, never!" This was the first amount of life she'd seen in him since the battle. "This is where they died. I couldna bury them in the same place." His sad eyes scanned the ground that had been covered in spilled blood. "They will rest in peace now up on the virgin hill, as they should. Now, they will look down on us, and watch over us as well."

For days now, her uncle had done nothing but mourn. She felt his pain, but their clan was suffering and needed him to lead them. They needed to rebuild. They needed to replant the crops. And most of all, they needed to know that there was hope that they would survive this, and never have to endure something so wretched again.

Kellina knew what had to be done. She also realized it was she who had to do it.

"We need to start rebuildin', Uncle," she told him, wondering if he would even hear her since he was so lost in such deep thought. "Before the winter comes," she continued. "It is still early enough. We have time."

"I'm no' sure it will make a difference." He stopped, and sat down on a stump by the cooking fire, resting his face in his hands.

"Nay. It's no use. They'll only come back for more, I'm sure of it. Next time, we willna be able to stop them from takin' what little we have left. We'll die along with the rest of them, Kellina."

"Haud yer wheesht," she shouted, not liking to hear her uncle speak in this way. "Ye are the ruler of this clan, so start actin' like it." She wasn't afraid of much, and didn't fear the consequences that might occur from her speaking to her chieftain this way. "Ye need to stop mournin' the dead and start celebratin' the livin' instead."

"What?" His head snapped up and his gaze seemed feared. "This is no time for celebratin', lass, and I canna believe ye think so."

"I meant no disrespect to our dead, or ye, or even the clan, Uncle. I am sorry." She slowly reached out and rested her hand on his shoulder. He felt hot, and his muscles beneath her fingers almost seemed to tremble. "I only meant that our thoughts now should be on those who survived. I understand how hard this is for ye. I have lost my parents, and ken how much pain ye are feelin' right now. This may never truly pass, but we have the others of the clan to think about, too. We are all in a bad way."

"I ken what ye are sayin'." He gently pushed her hand from his shoulder, shaking his head and looking at the ground. "However, I canna think of anythin' but Lorna and the girls. Those barbarians struck them down to weaken me, takin' their lives before my eyes. It all happened so fast that I couldna get to them in time to save them. God's eyes, lassie. Lorna and the girls couldna defend themselves the way ye can. They were weak and vulnerable. They had no chance at all. What kind of men would kill women and children?"

Kellina didn't answer that. While her cousins had been nearly as old as she, her uncle would always think of them as children. Either way, it was wrong that anyone should attack them. Her uncle was right about that. It made her very angry.

Kellina scanned her surroundings, feeling like she didn't know this place anymore. Everyone seemed to have lost their spirit.

The men that had survived were mostly injured, and the women and children were so frightened that all they did was cry. They truly were weakened, but she refused to be defeated. If only the rest of their clan had been present, instead of away at a trade fair, then mayhap they would have had a fighting chance. Even so, it was important that she convince her uncle not to give up.

"Well, I see their plan worked. Especially on ye." Her words were harsh, but she figured that mayhap a shock was what the man needed to snap him out of this daze he was in.

Ciaran took his hands from his face and stared up at her. His body was bruised and scarred, and one of his eyes was so swollen that it would barely open. "What is yer point, lass? If ye have somethin' to say, then be out with it, or hold yer tongue."

"Ye've let the Sutherlands break ye, Uncle. I have never seen ye so weak as now. Ye need to do somethin' to make things right," she told him, pacing back and forth. "We need to make the Sutherlands pay for what they did. We should strike them down when they least suspect it."

"Kellina, ye ken that most of our clan is away right now at the trade fair, and we are severely weakened without them. That is why the Sutherlands attacked when they did. They kent we were no match for them and greatly outnumbered."

"Then do somethin' about it, before they attack again," she challenged him. "We need to rebuild and regain our strength. Then, when the rest of our clan returns, we need to pay back the Sutherlands in the same manner."

"Yer heart is blackened by revenge, lass. That is no' an admirable thing to see in such a young lass."

"I am no' young. I am nine and ten years of age now. I am no' a child anymore. I ken how to use a blade, and I intend to do it."

He hesitated to answer, causing Kellina to hold her breath. Finally, he spoke. "Ye're right, somethin' needs to be done. But ye're also wrong if ye think I am doin' nothin' to help this clan, because I already have taken measures for our safety."

"Ye did? What do ye mean? What did ye do?"

"I have taken the first step to strengthen this clan, and to secure yer future as well." He struggled to stand, and she ran over to help him.

"That's great! Tell me all about it."

"I have a few men arrivin' at camp today to help us rebuild. Since yer late faither was a thatcher and ye ken buildin' roofs better than anyone in the clan, I want ye to lead them."

"Of course. I will be happy to do so," she said. "I will teach them everythin' I ken about thatchin' roofs." She felt happy that her uncle had done something, until she heard the rest of his solution.

"Ye will also marry one of them as well."

"What?" She stood frozen, not able to believe her ears. "What do ye mean I'll marry one of them? Who are we even talkin' about?"

"I've already made the betrothal. It is for the guid of the clan. It'll make us stronger."

"Uncle, I dinna even ken who ye've summoned, nor who ye decided to betroth me to without even tellin' me about it."

"His name is Nash MacKeefe, and I believe he will make a guid husband for ye. We'll gain their alliance from the marriage. The MacKeefe Clan is strong, and they'll help to protect us."

"MacKeefe?" Her heart almost stopped, hearing this name spring from his lips. It was even worse than marrying a stinking Sutherland. "God's eyes, nay! Never. How could ye? Unless ye've forgotten, it was the MacKeefes who took the lives of my parents."

"I didna forget," he said through gritted teeth. "Bid the devil, I will never forget that." He moaned and bent over to rub his leg. "I purposely chose a clan with whom we arena aligned because we canna risk bein' attacked by anyone else right now. With this alliance, we'll have a strong clan at our backs should we need to fight off the Sutherlands, or anyone else again."

He limped away as if it didn't matter to him what she thought about this arrangement. Kellina stood there for a moment in shock, not able to believe this was happening. Then she ran to catch up and, hopefully, try to talk him out of this absurd plan.

"Uncle, please, reconsider. I dinna think this is a guid idea at all."

"It's too late, Kellina," he told her, looking up at the sound of approaching hoofbeats. "Ah, here they are now. Jamie, sound the horn and call everyone over," he shouted over his shoulder.

Jamie was Kellina's younger brother, who was only twelve years of age. Their sister, Caitlin, was six and ten. They had lost their parents not long after Jamie was born, and had been raised by their aunt and uncle. Jamie was only a baby at the time, and Caitlin was too young to remember much at all about their parents. However, Kellina was seven when it happened. The day her parents died was a memory that she would never forget. Their dead bodies being brought home by the chieftain was something she'd never expected. The MacKeefes were said to have killed them, and that clan name was engraved in her mind and put vengeance in her heart. The last thing she wanted to do was to marry one of the barbaric bastards!

She turned and raised her chin as she watched the MacKeefes ride into their camp. She didn't know which of the three men she was to marry, and neither did it matter. She would never marry or ever accept a MacKeefe into their camp, and especially not into her heart.

The MacKeefes were no better than the Sutherlands in her opinion. Even if they hadn't battled with them for twelve years, they were still the enemy. Kellina's poor parents had paid the price.

Her face remained stonelike as she heard her brother blow the horn, calling everyone to gather. She walked slowly with her fists balled up tightly, feeling the flat end of her sword strapped around her waist hitting her in the leg as they approached.

She would have her revenge after all, but it would not be with the Sutherlands this time. Or at least, just not yet. First, she would have to do away with the MacKeefes. She'd kill all three of them, she decided. And the first to go would be Nash MacKeefe — the man she was to marry.

✦•◦◇◦•✦

CHAPTER THREE

"STOP YER COMPLAININ', Nash," said North over his shoulder as the three MacKeefes approached the MacKenzie camp later that day. "My ears canna take anymore." North faked a shiver from atop his horse.

"But it's no' fair, I tell ye." Nash rode up next to his brother while Aidan watched the rear. "I shouldna have to marry a wench as part of my punishment. Especially no' a bluidy MacKenzie! I dinna want to get married. But if I did, I would want to choose a wife for myself, and no' be told who I have to take as my bride."

"Ye dinna have a choice, Nash. No' if ye want to be welcomed back into the clan. If ye dinna do it, ye'll be an outcast of the MacKeefes forever."

"God's eyes! The MacKenzies are our enemies, North."

"I ken that, Brathair. What do ye want me to do?"

"And as if it's no' bad enough already, Laird MacKenzie's daughters have been avoided by every man in the Highlands. So what does that tell ye? I'm goin' to marry a dog."

"Ye're no' marryin' his daughters. Ye're marryin' his niece," North reminded him.

"No difference, I'm sure," said Nash with a sigh.

"We're makin' an alliance," Aidan shouted from behind them. "Yer marriage is what solidifies the deal. Ye canna turn it down, Nash. Ye are doin' it for the guid of the clan."

"I didna ask for this," Nash ground out, clenching his fists as well as his jaw. "North, ye take this punishment, and I'll take the next one."

"What? Nay." North chuckled. "It doesna work that way, Brathair. "Ye canna choose what ye want to do, or it wouldna be called a punishment."

"We're twins. They willna notice if ye take my place."

"Brathair, I think ye must be dafter than I thought. We're no' identical and ye ken it. It's no' like they willna notice."

"We're close enough in looks, I assure ye. Just do me this one favor, North. Please."

"Nay! And if I hear another word about ye no' wantin' to marry this lass, I swear I'll tie ye up and stick a gag in yer mouth until the weddin' is over."

"Fine," mumbled Nash. "But dinna think I am comin' along with ye when ye get yer sentence, because I willna help ye at all."

"Guid." North gave a quick nod of his head. "I cherish the thought of peace and quiet. Anythin' no' to have to listen to ye complain anymore." North kicked his heels into the sides of his horse and shot up to the lead. Aidan came from behind to join Nash.

"I'm sure it willna be all that bad," said Aidan, which only sounded ridiculous to Nash.

"How would ye ken? Ye are married to a lovely redheaded lass. She's a bonnie one, too. Ye didna have to marry yer enemy's homely daughter."

Aidan laughed heartily. "So that's the real problem. Ye are no' really concerned about marryin' the enemy at all, are ye? Ye are just too damned proud to marry a lass if she isna bonnie."

"Mayhap that is true, but it's only part of the reason, I assure ye. Can ye blame me?" he asked. "If the marriage isna for love, then looks is all I have to go on."

"Alliance. Ye're doin' it for an alliance," Aidan reminded him once more. "To help yer clan."

"To help their clan is more like it," Nash scoffed.

"Everyone canna have the perfect lass to marry," Aidan told

him.

"Why no'? Ye did."

"Is that what ye think?" Aidan grinned. "That bonnie wife of mine no' only betrayed me by stealin' the stone of destiny from right under me, but almost got me killed, if I must remind ye."

"And yet, ye still love her?"

Aidan nodded slowly. "It comes in time, Nash. Give this lass a chance and someday ye might find ye actually love her, too."

"I dinna have a choice, do I?" He directed his horse to catch up to his brother. With his hand resting on the hilt of his sword, Nash scanned the area, watching for trouble as they entered the MacKenzie camp where his life would change forever . . . and most likely not for the better.

"Welcome, MacKeefes," called out a man who came limping over to greet them. He had a wooden crutch under one arm.

"God's eyes, this is bad," North said in a low voice, as the three MacKeefes got their first glimpse at the damage done by the Sutherlands.

"Aye, it has devastated us all. I'm Ciaran MacKenzie, chieftain of the clan," said the man. A crowd of people cautiously approached, mostly women, children, and older men.

"I am Aidan MacKeefe, and these are my friends, Nash and North." Aidan nodded to the others. His red squirrel sat perched atop his shoulder, so steady that Nash wondered if the thing was even real.

"I thank ye for comin'. Please, join us." The chieftain held out his arm. "We dinna have much to offer, but all that we have is yers."

Aidan dismounted and so did North.

Nash sat atop his horse, eyeing up the women of the clan, wondering which of them he was going to have to marry. He had just dismounted when he felt a prick at his back that was the unmistakable tip of a sword.

Without asking questions, he drew his blade, spinning around on his heel, ready to take off the man's head. His sword clashed with another. He was ready for a fight, until he realized it was a beautiful young woman who sparred with him. She wore a tunic and breeches instead of a skirt, looking more like an Englishman than either a woman or man of a Highland clan. He stopped, not wanting to hurt the lass. When he did, she knocked the sword out of his hand and to the ground.

Nash heard Aidan and North behind him drawing their swords, ready to defend him.

"What the hell is this?" growled North.

"I thought we were makin' an alliance," ground out Aidan. "Is this some sort of trick, MacKenzie?"

"Kellina, stop that!" shouted Ciaran. Aidan's squirrel squeaked and ran down Aidan's arm and between the chieftain's legs, almost knocking him down before it darted across camp. The man used his crutch to right himself and keep from falling.

"It's no problem." Nash quickly snatched the blade out of the girl's hand before she even knew what happened. Now he held the tip of the girl's own sword to her chest. "However, if ye're goin' to play that kind of game, lass, be damned sure ye're ready for the consequences."

"Nay. Enough of this. We have enough trouble and dinna need more." Ciaran hobbled over and held out his hand to Nash. "Will ye forgive my niece for her foolishness? I'm afraid she's just still a little spooked after the Sutherland raid. She was never goin' to hurt ye, and didna mean anythin' by it."

Nash's eyes went to his brother and then Aidan. They both nodded slightly and sheathed their swords.

"I think it's the girl who should be beggin' for my forgiveness for her foolishness," said Nash. "Still, I will accept yer sincere apology, Laird MacKenzie." He handed the sword hilt first to the laird, then bent down to scoop up his own. The girl's foot atop his blade stopped him. Nash clenched his teeth and looked up at her. "Still no' done playin' yer doitit games, Wench?"

"Dinna call me Wench! Take yer sword if ye want it. I dinna care." She moved her foot and kicked at the blade, causing dirt to fly up and get in Nash's eyes.

Nash gripped the hilt of his sword and sprang to his feet, wiping his eyes with his free hand. This girl was nothing but trouble and she was trying his patience. He didn't care if she was bonnie, or that she was the niece of the chieftain, she needed to learn her place.

"Brathair, nay," warned North in a low voice, grabbing his arm tightly, not letting him touch the girl even though a good swift kick on the doup is just what she needed. "We are here for an alliance," his brother reminded him. "Dinna mess this up or ye'll never finish yer sentence."

"Ye're right." Nash nodded and sheathed his sword. "I'm supposed to marry a lass from this clan to finalize the deal and make our alliance." He looked from one young girl to the next, since a huge crowd surrounded them now. "So, Laird MacKenzie, which one is it who will be my bride?" All the girls of the clan dropped their gazes to the ground or looked the other way. "Which of these fine young lassies is goin' to have the pleasure of marryin' me?"

"It's me," said the girl who'd tried to hurt him. "However, I sincerely doubt it will be a pleasure. As a matter of fact, I'm sure bein' married to ye will be naught but hell." She glared at him and crossed her arms over her chest.

"Aye. Ye are to marry my niece," the chieftain explained.

"Damn," Nash swore under his breath, willing to accept anyone right now other than her. This was going to be a lifelong sentence! The worst part was his guard in this temporary prison was this hellion who'd tried to stab him. Now, sadly, this same wench would be with him for the rest of his life.

KELLINA PERUSED THE man she was to marry, not liking the fact at all that he was a MacKeefe. Still, she realized that to break the betrothal would ruin the alliance with a strong clan like them. It might only bring about another battle, and that was something she couldn't risk. Her clan was weakened, and missing many of their strong warriors right now. They never would survive. Not now, at least. Mayhap when the rest of their men returned from the trade fair they'd have half a chance but, by then, it would be too late.

She probably shouldn't have pricked the man's back with her sword, but she couldn't help herself. It was only sheer will that kept her from running it right through his heart. Her anger was growing stronger, and she hated to admit to herself that mayhap she was losing control. After a good meal and a full night's rest, perhaps she'd see things differently. She hoped.

The man was handsome enough, but that still didn't make up for the fact that he was a MacKeefe. He had long, brown hair and hazel eyes that seemed as if they could look right through her. His appearance was very similar to one of the other men that was with him. This one was just a little shorter.

"Which one are ye? North or South?" she asked him, having heard Aidan say their names, but not being sure which was which. She knew damned well that South wasn't one of the names, but only did it to irk him.

"I'm North," the taller one spoke up. "The one ye're marryin' is my twin . . . South." Both he and Aidan chuckled.

"Haud yer wheesht, ye fool," said her betrothed, glaring at his brother. "I'm Nash," he told her. "And ye'd be best to remember my name since ye're soon to be my wife."

"Hmph," she said raising her chin in the air. "Why bother? I'm sure ye dinna even ken my name, so what's the difference?"

"All right, then . . . Kellina. If that's the way ye want it."

"H-how did ye ken my name?" she asked him, surprised to hear it springing from his lips.

"I suppose I'm just a little more aware of what is goin' on around me at all times," he boasted.

"Really." She saw Aidan's squirrel sneaking up behind Nash

and she was sure he didn't know it was there.

"That's right," he told her. "I'm guid at a lot of things, which ye'll find out in time."

The squirrel jumped up, scurrying up the back of Nash's plaid, making him cry out in surprise. He spun around on his heel as he drew his sword. Everyone laughed as the squirrel settled on his shoulder, chattering in his ear.

"Come here, Reid, before South lops off yer head." Aidan reached out and took the squirrel back. He put it on his own shoulder where it seemed to like to perch.

"That wasna funny," said Nash through gritted teeth, sheathing his sword.

"It's a guid thing that ye are so aware of everythin' that goes on around ye, my betrothed." Kellina smirked and headed away.

"I kent the damned rodent was there," she heard Nash calling out from behind her. "I was just tryin' to scare it so it would stay off of me."

"Give it a rest, Brathair," she heard North saying to Nash. "Yer boastin' is only makin' ye look more like a fool than ye really are."

Kellina couldn't have agreed with North more. She didn't like men who were full of themselves, and this one named Nash needed to be put in his place. She might not have managed to get rid of him yet, but once they were up thatching the roof, she wouldn't be surprised if, by some chance, he slipped and fell to his death.

◆◦◇◦◆

CHAPTER FOUR

"I AM SURPRISED to see three of ye here," Ciaran told them as he showed them all the damage that had been done by the Sutherlands. "I was only expectin' one MacKeefe to show up here today."

"Just two, actually," said Aidan. "I'm just passin' through on my way to see the Gordon Clan," so I thought I'd escort them to yer camp. However, North will be stayin' to help ye rebuild. And of course, ye'll have Nash who is here to work off his sentence so he'll no longer be an outcast, and be welcomed back into the clan."

"I heard some of ye are outcasts," said Ciaran, watching them carefully. "I hope ye didna do anythin' that would make ye dangerous here."

"Hah!" laughed North. "I'm in trouble mainly because a silver goblet went missin'. But Nash almost burned down Old Callum MacKeefe's tavern, so I canna vouch that he isna dangerous."

"I put the fire out," snapped Nash. "Laird MacKenzie, we have no real crimes and I assure ye that we are of no threat to ye. We are only here to offer our help."

"Well, that is guid to ken. Aidan, ye said ye're on yer way to the Gordon Clan?" The chieftain seemed very interested.

"Aye," he answered.

"The Legendary Bastards of the Crown have a sister that married their chieftain, Shaw Gordon if I'm no' mistaken. Is that right?" asked Ciaran.

"That's right," said Aidan. "Lady Spring is a true warrior, and tougher than any lass I've ever met."

"Ye should see her with a bow," added North.

"Why do ye ask? Are ye friends with them?" Nash wondered.

"Well, we're no' enemies, but have never truly formed an alliance either," answered the chieftain. "Although I'm no' sure why no'. I wonder if ye could do me a favor, Aidan."

"Of course. What is it?" Aidan took his squirrel off his shoulder, cradling him in one arm, giving him a nut to eat.

"My niece, Kellina, has turned bitter ever since the death of her parents." The chieftain looked back at Kellina who was across camp, talking to others of the clan. "My late wife and I took her in, as well as her siblin's and raised them as our own."

"Yer late wife? Och, that's right. Our chieftain said she was killed along with yer daughters. I'm sorry," said Nash.

"Thank ye." The man's eyes teared up. "I was wonderin' if ye could convince Lady Spring – Shaw's wife, to come for a visit and mayhap talk some sense into my niece. Lady Spring is a strong woman, and verra independent, so I hear. I thought perhaps she could give Kellina some advice."

"I suppose I could," said Aidan. "I must admit though, that I dinna see anythin' wrong with a lass wieldin' a sword. Why do ye want to discourage yer niece?"

"Blethers, it's no' the swordplay I want to discourage. I am glad the lass can defend herself as well as others."

"I'm confused." North rubbed the back of his neck. "What is it ye want Spring to do?"

"I ken she used to be an enemy of the Gordons when she was with the Gunn Clan. I would like Spring – Lady Spring, to talk some sense into Kellina."

"I'm confused, too," said Nash. "Ye mention enemies, but yer clan and ours are no' enemies any longer. That's why I'm here. To marry the lass – to form an alliance."

"If ye even make it to the weddin'," mumbled the man.

Nash and his friends all looked at one another. "What do ye mean by that?" asked Nash.

"I mean, Kellina blames the MacKeefes for the deaths of her parents. She wants revenge I'm afraid."

"The MacKeefes killed her parents?" asked Nash. "When?"

"It was about twelve years ago. There was a battle between us, and her parents died. It's a long story but, in the end, Kellina's parents died, when they never should have."

"Our parents died twelve years ago, too," said North. "I believe it was in this same battle ye speak of."

"Aye. I'm sorry," said Ciaran, his gaze dropping. He reached down and rubbed his leg.

"Och, no wonder Kellina is so bitter," said Nash. "Now it makes sense why she put her sword to my back."

"That's no' the half of it," said Ciaran, letting out a deep sigh. "Och, I never should have said anythin'." He waved his hand through the air. "Just forget all about it."

"Nay. What do ye mean?" asked Nash. "If I'm goin' to agree to marry the girl, I want to ken everythin' about her."

"Ye dinna want to ken what's goin' through that head of hers," Ciaran said in a mere whisper.

"Like what? Tell us," Nash persisted.

"Do ye promise to still marry her? Even if I tell ye?" asked the chieftain.

"I dinna like this," mumbled Nash. "I dinna like this at all."

"The betrothal is already set," Aidan assured the chieftain. "If either of our clans back out now, it could be the cause of a battle, and neither of us wants that, I'm sure."

"Tell me," said Nash, feeling anxious and uncomfortable. He was liking this less and less every minute.

"I'm sorry to put ye boys in this position. When I made the alliance, I didna ken how spiteful Kellina felt toward the MacKeefes. After all, she was just a child when her parents died, and she really kens nothin' about it."

"And . . ." Nash waited, and would not let up until he had an answer.

"I'm ashamed to tell ye, but I feel I need to warn all three of ye. Watch yer backs."

"From her?" North chuckled. "I dinna see the trouble."

"She's a lass, and we're grown men," said Aidan.

"A lassie is no threat to us," agreed Nash.

"Dinna bet on it," mumbled the chieftain. "Kellina helped fight the Sutherlands and even brought a few of them down. She has no qualms about killin' a man if she feels he deserves it."

"I see." Nash ran a nervous hand over his head, smoothing back his hair. "So . . . ye're sayin' that I might be next on her list?"

"Och, I'm sure it's nothin'. I mean, she never said it aloud, so mayhap I'm worryin' for no reason. On the other hand, mayhap I'm no'. Ye see, I wouldna doubt that thoughts are runnin' through her head about killin' every MacKeefe for bein' responsible for losin' her parents."

"Och, that's just great." Nash threw his hands in the air. "So, now, I no' only have to marry the madwoman, but I've got to go up and repair roofs with her, too? How convenient."

"I sure am glad I was told to help with the crops instead," said North, looking up to the roof of one of the burned-out buildings. "It's a long way down, Brathair. All I can say is, it's a damned guid thing that ye are always so aware of what's goin' on around ye at all times."

Aidan kissed his squirrel, and held it tightly when it tried to jump on Nash again. Nash jolted back and waved it away. Damn, if his brother and Aidan weren't laughing at him under their breaths once again. "Keep that pesky squirrel away from me, Aidan, or I swear I'm goin' to kill the damned thing."

Aidan's smile disappeared and his free hand went to the hilt of his sword. "No one threatens my squirrel, especially no' a MacKeefe."

"Calm down, Aidan," North tried to ease the situation. "We both ken that yer squirrel is too fast to ever get caught by Nash anyway, so dinna worry."

Nash looked over at Kellina. She happened to look up at him at the same time and an evil grin spread across her face. A shiver ran through him. He didn't like this lass, and the last thing he wanted was to make her his wife. His life was getting worse at every passing minute. This was going to be the worst punishment of all . . . if he even lived to tell about it later.

"Is that the MacKeefe ye have to marry?" asked Kellina's sister, Caitlin, smiling at Nash as she brushed a lock of dark hair behind her ear. She and her brother had dark hair, but Kellina's locks were as golden as the sun.

"Quit lookin' at him like that!" spat Kellina. "He's a bluidy MacKeefe, a murderer. Dinna forget the MacKeefes are the ones who killed our parents."

"Are ye sure?" asked her brother, Jamie, overhearing them and running over to join them. "I like the MacKeefes. Aidan has a squirrel, and I hear his friend, Onyx, has a wildcat as a pet. I want one, too."

"Dinna admire people like them." She glanced over at the three MacKeefes and narrowed her eyes. "I'm goin' to kill them all, startin' with the one I have to marry. Then I willna have to marry him anymore."

"Kill them?" gasped Caitlin. "Nay, Kellina. What are ye sayin'? That would only turn our clans against each other and start a battle. Sister, please, dinna ever talk that way." Caitlin's eyes filled with tears. "We will all die next time, and I dinna want to die."

"I'm tellin' Uncle Ciaran." Jamie started to leave, but Kellina's hand clasped around his arm tightly and she spoke lowly into his ear.

"Ye do that, and I'll make sure Uncle kens it was ye who left the gate open, losin' many of our sheep before the Sutherlands ever arrived."

"That was an accident," said Jamie.

"Was it? Or were ye too lazy to check it in the first place, too eager to go swimmin' in the loch with yer friends?"

"I willna say anythin'." He shook out of her hold and ran off in the other direction.

"Kellina, ye're no' really goin' to kill yer betrothed are ye?" asked Caitlin. "Ye are so lucky to have a handsome man like Nash MacKeefe to marry ye and be a faither to yer children."

"Blethers! Dinna say such things. I dinna want to marry, and I never want to have children."

"How can ye be serious?" asked Caitlin. "Family is important. I want many children someday."

"I have all the family I want or need. I have ye and Jamie, and Uncle, too."

"Just dinna harm him," said Caitlin, her eyes still fastened to Nash. "If ye really dinna want him, I might ask Uncle if I can marry him instead to keep the alliance." She turned and left Kellina standing there alone. Kellina didn't want either of them marrying a MacKeefe. Then again, she realized she couldn't really kill them in cold blood either. That would make her no better than the MacKeefes who killed her parents. She let out a deep sigh, not knowing what to do.

Mayhap, the sooner they got up on the roof, the faster Nash might have an accident and die on his own, without her help.

CHAPTER FIVE

"**N**ASH, WAKE UP," said North the next morning, kicking Nash's foot.

"What is it? I'm up!" Nash bolted to his feet, drawing his blade, almost hitting North as he did so. The three MacKeefes had slept by the fire last night. Nash had spent most of the night wide awake, watching for Kellina to sneak up trying to kill them. It was only from sheer exhaustion that he'd finally closed his eyes at all.

"Watch it! Ye almost took my head off with that thing," complained North.

"Put the sword away, Nash." Aidan walked over with the chieftain hobbling alongside him. Between them was, to Nash's dismay, a priest. "The priest is here to marry ye."

"Oh," said Nash, scoping the area and then slowly sheathing his sword. "Are ye sure this is necessary? I mean . . . right now?" He had hoped to have time to think of a way out of this betrothal. He figured he'd have a day or two, not knowing that the priest was arriving so soon.

"Of course, it is necessary, ye dolt," said his brother. "It's to form an alliance with the MacKenzies. Now, stop stallin'."

Nash leaned over and spoke to North quietly so the others wouldn't hear. "Are ye sure ye dinna want to marry the lass instead of me? I'll let ye have her. I'm sure Storm and Ian willna mind if we switch up our sentences a little."

"Nay, Brathair. This is yer sentence, no' mine. Now stop bein' so afraid of the wench and marry her and put her in her place."

"Uncle, what is the meanin' of this?" Kellina hurried out of one of the burned huts with her brother and sister at her heels. She was half-dressed, wearing only a blanket over her shift. She walked outside with bare feet. "Jamie said the priest is here to marry me. What is goin' on?"

"Jamie is right," said Ciaran. "The marriage will take place now, so the alliance is in full agreement before the MacKeefes even lift a finger to help us."

Nash felt extremely uncomfortable by this situation. He could tell that Kellina didn't like it at all either. All he could hope for now was that she would be able to talk her uncle into postponing this ceremony. He wasn't ready for this. He needed time to think. This couldn't really be happening. It was all too fast.

"May I talk to ye privately, please?" Kellina grabbed her uncle's arm, walking a short distance away to talk to him without the others hearing. Nash couldn't make out their words, but could tell it was a heated conversation between them. Kellina's arms flew in all directions and she looked madder than all hell. Nash felt the same way, although he remained silent. He secretly hoped this betrothal would either last for a while before they had to take their vows, or possibly not even happen at all.

Finally, they returned, and Kellina was quiet. She gripped the blanket around her, almost as tightly as her jaw was clenched.

"If we're goin' to do this, let's get it done and over with. I have things to do," she blurted out. "There are roofs to be thatched and plenty of repairs to be made." She turned and stared at Nash next. "Are ye ready to go up on the roof, Highlander? I hope ye arena afraid of heights, since ye are so afraid of tiny little squirrels."

She was trying to belittle him in front of everyone, or perhaps it was a warning that she planned on throwing him off the roof. He wasn't sure. No matter what she meant, he didn't care. Nash wouldn't let her speak this way to him. Especially since he was stuck with her for a wife. The sooner she learned he wasn't going to tolerate her nasty attitude, the better.

"Haud yer wheesht, and get over here and marry me," he commanded in a gruff voice, getting an odd look from his brother and Aidan.

Her eyes and mouth opened wide. She looked speechless as she stood there clutching that damned blanket around her.

"Uncle, tell him he canna talk to me that way," said Kellina, seeming shocked and appalled by what he'd just said. Nash obviously caught her off guard and he liked her startled reaction. Two could play this game. Nash liked games, and he was used to winning.

"Kellina, please. I dinna want trouble," begged Ciaran. "Now, just come stand next to Nash, and we'll get on with the weddin'. Jamie, tell the others the ceremony is about to begin."

"Aye, Uncle." Jamie ran off to round up the rest of the clan.

It was early, the sun just having lifted past the horizon. The night had been cool, but the day would be hot, just like all the others. A slight mist hung over the mountains with the early morning dew. The air smelled fresh, and the birds sang happily. If he hadn't been getting married right now, this would almost prove to be a perfect day.

"Just let me get my book here, and then I'll be ready." The priest strolled back to his horse, talking with the chieftain. Aidan was busy chasing down his squirrel, and North took up to flirting with Kellina's sister. That left Nash standing alone with Kellina. He didn't know what to say.

"I dinna want to marry ye, ye murderer," hissed Kellina, looking straight ahead rather than at him.

"I am no' the one who murdered yer parents, and I willna have ye takin' out yer revenge on me," Nash answered. "I'm no' thrilled about havin' to be saddled with ye for a wife!"

"What does that mean?" Her head snapped around and she glared at him now.

"Well, look at ye, lass. Ye are no prize for any man. Ye're walkin' around barefoot and half-dressed. Plus, it looks like ye never comb yer hair since it is so tangled. What are ye? Some kind of witch who spent the night makin' a poisonous brew for me around her boilin' kettle?"

Nash reached out and picked up the ends of her long, blond mess of hair to prove his point. Then he wished he hadn't. Her hair was as soft as silk. The loose, long curls fell gently around her shoulders, and a lock of hair disappeared into the top of her bodice. It lifted slightly in the breeze. When he pulled his hand back and scratched his cheek, the strong scent of heather drifted from his fingers, smelling tantalizing and alluring. It had come from the witch's hair.

"If ye're insinuatin' that ye think I might kill ye, then I'll take that as a compliment," she told him, one side of her mouth curving up in a satisfied smile. "But on the other hand, if ye're thinkin' I'm goin' to cook for ye once we're married, then ye've got another guess comin', because I surely am no'."

"Really, Witch? Do ye think that frightens me?" He challenged her, pushing, wanting her to back down. But she didn't.

"I think everythin' frightens ye, especially me," she had the nerve to say. Who did she think she was talking to? Nash was one of the best warriors the MacKeefe Clan had. He wasn't afraid of anything. Especially not her!

"Believe me, the only thing that scares me about ye, is how ye look right now," he said, continuing his game of cat and mouse with the wench.

She turned and smiled at him – or was it a sneer? "Ye can call me Witch all ye like and it willna rattle me, because I'm a warrior, just like ye. The only difference is, I am much braver."

He shouldn't have let that bother him, but he did. Nash didn't like her saying such things to him, because none of them were true.

"Ye're no' a warrior, and ye are nothin' like me," he ground out. "And I wouldna call ye brave. I'd call ye stupid, walkin' around like that." His eyes ran down her body. "Unless, ye're tryin' to get ravished by every man here, ye shouldna be wanderin' around in yer nightshift."

"If I want to walk around naked, I dinna see what concern it is to ye." In an obvious act of defiance, she dropped the blanket from around her, leaving her standing there barefoot and only in a thin, nearly transparent shift. The sun's rays became stronger, and Nash realized he could see her naked body right through her shift. Perky little breasts poked out with her nubs of hardened nipples trying to burst through the fabric. She wore no braies. He could even see a blond thatch of hair at the juncture of her thighs every time the wind blew her shift tightly against her.

Nash swallowed hard, not able to look away. Her body enticed him, already making him hard. How he wished she had not done that. Then he realized if he could see this, so could everyone else.

"Kellina!" shouted her uncle, hurrying over to her. He leaned on his crutch to pick up the blanket, trying his best to secure the cloth around her shoulders and hide her nearly naked form. "Go back to the hut and find yer clothes and put them on immediately. Caitlin, take her to my cottage and help her don one of my late wife's gowns."

"I have my own clothes, thank ye," she told her uncle, feeling odd about wearing the clothes of the dead.

"Nay!" the chieftain shouted. "Ye'll no' get married wearin' breeches. Ye'll put on a skirt and tunic and don the colors of Clan MacKenzie with a shawl. I'll no' hear another word about it. Now hurry and dress. The priest canna stay long, and the weddin' needs to proceed as planned."

As soon as they walked away, North came over to Nash, grinning from ear to ear. "Well, Brathair, it looks like ye decided ye like the lass after all."

"Nay, I dinna. Why would ye even say such a thing about such a horrible wench as her?"

"Ooooh, I dinna ken." His eyes shot downward and he chuckled before turning and walking away.

Nash looked down to see his randiness showing as his hardened manhood tented out his plaid. Damn, this was the last thing he wanted right now. How could his body be reacting this way to a woman he truly despised? What the hell was the matter with him? He hoped Kellina hadn't noticed, because he was trying his best not to like her. Then again, his body was giving out another message completely, and it was one that he wanted more than anything to avoid.

⯮⯮⯮✳⯬⯬⯬

"WHAT ARE YE gigglin' about, Sister?" asked Kellina as she entered the stone hut where their uncle lived, closing the door behind them. The roof of this house was only partially damaged, but rays of sun shone in from the ceiling.

"Didna ye see the way Nash's plaid poked out at his waist?" asked Caitlin. "I am sure he canna wait to bed ye, Sister."

"Nay. That's no' true. He doesna even like me." If this was true, she wondered how she had missed it. Perhaps dropping the blanket hadn't been a good idea after all. And if it made Nash randy, how many other men out there were lusting after her right now as well?

"Mayhap it's all an act, Sister, but I dinna see how. After all, ye did tempt him, standin' there like . . . that."

Kellina looked down to see the sun shining on her shift, showing her naked body clearly though the material. She only meant to defy him by dropping the blanket, but now she realized that her little trick might have only made things worse. She had no idea how transparent this nightdress really was in the bright sun.

"Losh me!" she exclaimed. "Caitlin, I didna ken he could see through my shift."

"Everyone could, Sister. Here, put this on." She held up a long-sleeved tunic, pulling it over Kellina's head. Then she took a blue and green plaid skirt, and helped Kellina don that as well. "I am sure mathair wouldna mind if ye wore this. I only wish she could be here to see ye on yer weddin' day." Caitlin brushed away a tear.

"Lorna was no' our mathair," she told her sister, walking over to the trunk to look for the shawl. "She was our aunt, and ye ken it. Dinna call her that, please.'"

"Lorna is the only mathair that Jamie and I remember." Caitlin picked up a boar-bristle hairbrush and ran it over Kellina's head. "We would call Ciaran, Faither, but we ken it would make ye so upset, therefore we dinna do it."

"I remember mathair as well as faither," said Kellina. "And they were nothin' at all like Ciaran and Lorna." Her heart felt suddenly heavy. "I miss Mathair and Da, Caitlin. I was young, but still have the vision of them lying dead in a puddle of blood on the back of a wagon. It is stuck in my head, and I canna forget it." Anger as well as sadness flashed through her. "I saw what the MacKeefes did to them. If ye had seen it, too, ye would be offerin' to help me kill the MacKeefes in retaliation."

"Nay." Caitlin didn't agree with her. "I'm no' sayin' it was right of them to do it, but it was a long time ago, Kellina. It's no' right to want to kill anyone, unless it is in self-defense. I'm sure Nash and his brathair and even his friend were no' responsible for the deaths of our parents. They were young at the time, too. Ye need to forgive the MacKeefes, Sister. Ye are about to be married to one of them."

"Caitlin! What is the matter with ye?" asked Kellina. "Sometimes I canna believe ye are my sister. We think in such different ways."

The door opened and Jamie stuck his head inside the room. "Everyone is waitin' and the priest has to leave soon. Hurry up, Sister. Ye are holdin' up the weddin'."

"Fine!" Kellina threw her hands in the air, marching out to marry a man she didn't know or love. It seemed silly to her to try to make an alliance with the MacKeefes. She didn't want to do it. However, she had no choice, so she would hold her head high and bravely go through with this horrible, life-changing plan.

NASH SHIFTED FROM one foot to the next, waiting for the wedding to begin. Everyone was gathered around, and all they needed now was the bride. Part of him wished she wouldn't show up. If not, mayhap he wouldn't have to go through with this horrible plan after all. He cursed Old Callum for making this part of his punishment. It wasn't right. It wasn't fair. No one but him should be able to make these life-changing decisions for him.

"All right, I'm here. Let's get this over with. I told ye I have things to do!" Kellina stormed across the camp, stopping right next to Nash. She didn't even look at him, and neither did he care. He only glanced at her long enough to see she'd donned a skirt instead of breeches today. Well, he supposed anything was better than her standing there in her nightclothes. He decided he wouldn't look at her anymore. After all, he didn't like the wench and it would be better if his body didn't betray him again.

The priest opened his book and said the required words. Then, it was time for them to take their vows.

"Do ye, Kellina MacKenzie, take Nash MacKeefe as yer husband?" There was more to it, but Kellina was in a hurry and didn't wait to hear it.

"Aye, I do. Now move on," she said curtly.

Nash looked up to see the chieftain nodding to the priest to continue.

"Do ye, Nash MacKeefe, take Kellina MacKenzie as yer –"

"Aye, I do. Let's go," he said, returning the favor to his hurried bride.

The priest, looking forlorn, shook his head and closed the book. "Well, then I guess all there is to say, is I pronounce ye married. Ye may kiss the bride."

"That's no' necessary." Kellina's words were clipped and she ended them with a sniff. "And neither is me wearin' a skirt. I'm goin' to change back into breeches."

"But Kellina, it's no' proper," protested Caitlin. "Ye should wear a skirt like the rest of the lassies of the clan."

"Why?" asked Kellina. "My husband wears a skirt, so why do I need to? I like wearin' breeches." She turned on her heel to leave, but Nash wasn't about to let her go.

He grabbed her by the arm to stop her. She looked up with wide, blue eyes as he spoke lowly through his teeth.

"I dinna care how much we hate each other. We're goin' to do things the proper way, whether ye like it or not. Wife."

With that, he pulled her into his arms, kissing her deeply. He did it as a warning not to defy him, and perhaps as a punishment to her as well. However, his plan seemed to backfire, as all it did was punish him instead. Her lips were soft and unyielding, and surprisingly sensuous as well. He honestly thought she'd try to bite him, or do something to ward him off, but she didn't. She let him kiss her, and that was the biggest surprise of all. Nash liked the kiss, and was in no hurry to rush it. Surprisingly, for how busy she claimed to be, she didn't hurry it either.

Everyone clapped and cheered for them. Nash released her lips, but not her body. Instead, he slipped his arm around her waist, holding her tightly up against him.

He decided it was time to make some sort of speech. "We would like to thank everyone for joinin' us, even though this was short notice. We're glad that the MacKeefe Clan and the MacKenzie Clan are now aligned. Are no' we, Wife?"

She looked up and scowled. He pulled her even closer, bending to whisper in her ear.

"Answer, or I willna ever let ye go," he threatened, as she started to struggle in his hold. Finally, she realized it was of no use to thwart him.

"Aye. Thank ye," she said, while trying to pry his fingers off her waist.

"No longer are the MacKeefe and the MacKenzie Clans enemies," Nash continued. "It is a verra welcome day. Right, Wife?" He looked back over to her once again.

"Quit callin' me Wife," she whispered back. "I dinna like it."

"Answer and smile," he told her, looking out at the others with a fake smile of his own.

"Aye, we're aligned," she ground out, purposely stepping on his foot. Nash now wished she was still barefooted.

"Ow!" he yelped, releasing her, which gave her the opportunity to walk away.

"Meet me by the stables in fifteen minutes," she ordered.

"The stables? Whatever for?" asked Nash.

"That is where we'll start."

"Start?" Of course, Nash wasn't thinking along the same lines as her right now. After all, he just got married and was wondering about the consummation, and also the celebration. Sadly, she had naught on her mind today but work.

"We need to start thatchin' the roofs before it rains," she instructed, giving him a look that said she thought he was daft.

"Aye. Of course. I kent that."

She let out a sigh, starting to walk away. Then she turned back to talk to him. "I hope ye're no' afraid of heights, MacKeefe."

"Me? Nay, no' at all." Nash chuckled and waved his hand through the air. "As a matter of fact, I've been told I'm a lot like a goat."

"A goat?" She raised a brow. "Because ye eat everythin' in sight or that ye're stubborn or perhaps just destructive in general?"

"Nay. Because I can climb. I'm sure-footed. Like a goat." He smiled proudly.

"We'll see about that. Ye'd better hope so, Husband, because ye will be tested. And after all . . . we wouldna want ye to fall and break yer neck now, would we?" As if the idea of him dying pleased her, that evil little sneer crossed her face again. Then she turned and almost strutted away, humming to herself.

"What was all that about?" asked North, coming to his side.

"I'm no' sure." Nash's eyes stayed fastened to the girl as he rubbed his throat, thinking about what she'd just said. "However, I'm no' sure I like it."

"Do ye think she's anxious for the weddin' night?" asked North.

"If ye mean the weddin' bed, then nay. And I can say I'm no' eager for it either."

"Ye ken ye'll have to consummate the marriage, or the alliance willna be finalized. Do ye think that bothers her? After all, she doesna seem to like ye much."

"Is it that obvious?" asked Nash with an edge to his voice. "North, somehow I get the feelin' I willna have to worry about the weddin' bed at all."

"Why no'?"

"I might no' live that long. I think Kellina is plannin' on throwin' me off the roof and to my death."

"Let's hope no'," said North, not seeming at all upset to hear this. "After all, if ye're dead, Old Callum might decide to make me marry her for the alliance instead. I wouldna want the wench for my wife, that's for sure."

"Ye're no' the only one," Nash muttered, heading over to the stables, wondering if he could somehow tie a rope around him for safety while he was up on the roof with the murderous witch.

$$\blacktriangleright\!\cdot\!\circ\!\Diamond\!\circ\!\cdot\!\blacktriangleleft$$

CHAPTER SIX

KELLINA MADE HER way back to the cottage she shared with her siblings, to quickly change back into her tunic, breeches and boots. Her lips still tingled from Nash's kiss, and she held her hand to her mouth, cursing herself for enjoying it so much. She should have pushed him away and not let him do it. It was what she'd intended to do, but then she had liked it too much to stop him.

"Sister!" Caitlin came into the cottage and closed the door. "Why are yer cheeks so flushed? Are ye ill?"

"Nay, they're no' flushed. I am fine." Kellina turned around and continued dressing.

"Wait. Yer lips look swollen." Caitlin peeked around her, perusing her lips. "Ye liked the kiss, didna ye?"

She hesitated before she answered. "Nay. Of course, I didna. He's a MacKeefe. I hate the MacKeefes." She walked over to a trunk and pulled out a pair of boots and sat down on the bed to pull them on.

"Was he a guid kisser?" Her sister giggled, sitting down next to her on the pallet.

"Caitlin, I dinna want to talk about it."

"Are ye scared to share the weddin' bed with him tonight? Ye ken that is next."

"What?" Her head snapped upward and a sinking feeling came to her stomach. She'd been so caught up in the whole wedding, she'd almost forgotten about that part. It was something that scared her out of her mind. "I'm no' consummatin' the marriage, no matter what," she snapped.

"Losh me! Ye have to. It's no' a true alliance with the MacKeefe Clan if ye refuse to let him bed ye. The consummation is what seals the alliance. Even I ken that."

"I've had enough of this kind of talk." Kellina stood up, tying back her hair with a leather cord. The last thing she wanted to think about right now was making love with Nash MacKeefe. "There are roofs to be thatched and ye and Jamie need to help. Find Nash and meet me in the stables to collect the thatch. We'll start with the roof on Uncle's cottage. There isna much damage and it can be fixed quickly."

"Dinna ye want to start with the infirmary?" asked Caitlin. "After all, that is where the box bed is that ye'll be sharin' with Nash tonight." She said it in a sing-song voice, which only infuriated Kellina even more.

The bed in the corner of the infirmary was a special one. It was a box bed that had walls built around three sides of it for privacy. A long curtain attached by iron rings to a bar pulled across the front of the bed to stop curious eyes from watching a couple get intimate. The bed wasn't used all that much. It was only for consummating marriages, birthing babies, or to lay out the dead before burial.

"Aye, mayhap ye are right. We should start with the infirmary," Kellina agreed.

Caitlin giggled. "So, ye'll have more privacy on yer weddin' night now."

"Nay," Kellina answered. "I am doin' it so we'll have a private place to lay out Nash's dead body, since I'm no' expectin' him to live that long."

"What are ye sayin', Sister?" Caitlin's smile turned to a frown. "Ye truly sound as if ye mean to kill Nash. He's yer husband now. Please tell me this isna true."

"I wish I could," said Kellina, her hand going to her tingling lips once again. "The truth is, I would have no qualms about him dyin', because it is what he as well as the other MacKeefes deserve."

"Nay! Dinna say that. No one deserves to lose their life. Besides, all the MacKeefes that have come here seem so nice. Please, change yer mind," begged Caitlin. "I could tell ye liked his kiss, so ye canna really hate him as much as ye let on."

Kellina's tongue shot out and touched her upper lip, savoring the essence of Nash MacKeefe. Damn, why did he have to kiss her so passionately? And why did her little sister have to be so observant? Kellina didn't want to admit it to herself, but she did enjoy the kiss, although she didn't think she would. Her plan at first was to kill off the three MacKeefes one by one. She wanted it in vengeance, to make them pay for killing her parents. She hated them. She didn't want them around.

Or did she?

"We'll start with the infirmary's roof, just as ye've suggested, Caitlin."

"Then ye've changed yer mind, and want to bed Nash after all?" asked her sister.

"Nay, that is no' the reason at all. Now, no more chatter. We need to get to work."

She headed for the door, touching her lips once more as she started to wonder if being married to Nash MacKeefe would really be so awful after all.

"I'M SUPPOSED TO help in the fields with the crops, no' thatch roofs," complained North as he and Nash approached the stables. "I dinna ken why ye even want me here."

"Just keep yer eyes open, and dinna trust the lass at all." Nash nervously walked into the stables and stopped just inside the door. "Hello?" he called out, trying to see into the darkened area.

"Is anyone here?"

"Watch out," snapped Kellina, slamming into him with the bundle of long straw she carried over one shoulder. It had to be as tall as her, if she were to set it on end. "Both of ye, go get some thatch and bring it over to the infirmary right away. We'll need plenty of it."

Jamie and Caitlin walked out after their sister. Jamie held his bundle in two arms, but Caitlin dragged hers, since it was too awkward for her to carry alone.

"Let me get that for ye," offered North, being a lady's man. He took the bundle from her, throwing it over his shoulder with ease.

"Och, ye're so strong," cooed Caitlin, admiration lighting up her eyes. It was no doubt she liked the attention from a man. She was at that age now, Nash supposed, where she was a woman with needs, just like a man had.

Nash looked over to see North beaming with pride. He heard a grunt from Kellina as she left the stable. Nash felt like grunting, too, since his brother was flirting with a girl too young for him.

"Thank ye," North said. "I tend to think I'm strong, as well."

Nash picked up a bundle of straw, throwing it over his shoulder. Then he grabbed a second bundle under his other arm. They were about as long as his body, mayhap longer. He pushed past his brother, not wanting to watch his twin shamelessly flirt, making a fool of himself anymore.

"Watch it, North, or the spiders will lure us into their webs."

"Spiders? What is he talkin' about?" asked Caitlin. "I dinna see any spiders. I dinna like spiders."

"Nothin'. Nothin' at all," said North. "Dinna worry. If there are any spiders, I'll kill them for ye. Now, just let me grab another bundle or two and I'll walk ye over to the infirmary."

By the time Nash got to the infirmary, Kellina had already leaned a wooden ladder against the building and was climbing to the roof with the bundle of straw thrown over her shoulder. Egads, was there nothing this girl couldn't do?

Not wanting her to outshine him, Nash decided to climb the ladder with both bundles, which he realized was a mistake as soon as he started. Still, he didn't want to look weak by turning around so he continued although he couldn't see where he was going at all. It was awkward trying to climb this way. The bundles were too large, and hard to hold. He had no real way of gripping onto the ladder, so had to just balance himself as he started up the rungs. The roof was missing, and only some wooden beams were in place, leaving the top of the building open to the elements. If he wasn't careful, he could end up on the ground inside.

"Where did ye want this?" asked Nash, feeling himself swaying back and forth as the wind lifted the end of the bundles in his hands.

He saw Kellina up near the top of the wooden beams surveying the situation. She stood upright, looking down into the cottage through the open roof. He couldn't see much more. Nash tried to balance himself, bringing both of the bundles with him, teetering as he walked carefully across one of the slanted roof beams, trying to get to her. She had climbed all the way up to the apex.

"Nay, no' up here, ye fool," she chastised him. "Everyone kens that we need to start at the bottom with the thatch."

"What?" he asked, not being able to hear her well since the straw was poking him in the ear.

"The bottom, I said. Put them down there." She pointed back to the start of the roof.

"Och, all right," groaned Nash, wishing she had told him this before he'd climbed all the way up here. When Nash turned around, the long bundle of straw that was flung over his shoulder must have hit Kellina because she screamed.

His heart raced. What had he done? "What's the matter?" He turned too quickly, causing himself to lose his balance. The bundles slipped from his grip, falling through the open roof and into the infirmary. When Nash tried to catch them, he fell into the building from the roof right after them. Thankfully, his fall was softened when he landed atop the straw that had fallen on some kind of box bed. While the straw and the mattress broke his fall, it unfortunately broke the bed as well.

"Ooomph!" The air was knocked from him as Nash's body lay sprawled out face down over the bed. His arms and legs hung off the ends of the bed in every direction.

"Nash!" North cried out from outside the cottage. The door to the infirmary banged open and North and Caitlin rushed in.

"Are ye all right?" asked Caitlin. "We saw ye fall."

"Mmmmph," he groaned, lifting his head. His long, brown hair covered his eyes. "Aye, I'm fine." When Nash rolled over onto his back, he saw Kellina up on the roof, looking down at him like a Viking warrior woman. Her hands were on her hips and her feet were firmly planted. She looked fierce. He swore he saw a smile on her face but he couldn't be sure since his vision was a little blurry at the moment.

"Hurry up, Goat," she called out, and then walked down a beam, out of sight.

"Let me help ye, Brathair." North lent Nash a hand as he got up off the broken bed.

"I told ye she was out to kill me," Nash whispered. "Where the hell were ye? I needed ye to watch my back."

"I thought ye said ye were sure-footed. Like a goat," said North, grinning. "How in the devil's name did ye happen to fall?"

"I didna fall. No' on my own. I tell ye, I was pushed. She pushed me, I'm sure of it. Right after she lured me high onto the top of the roof while I was carryin' two bundles of straw. She purposely didna tell me to leave them at the bottom until I got all the way up to the top. Then, she screamed, causing me to lose my balance."

"I think ye're imaginin' all this, Nash. I'm sure she wasna really tryin' to kill ye at all."

Although they spoke in hushed tones, their conversation stopped when they heard Caitlin giggle.

"What is it, Wench? Does it amuse ye that I almost died?" snapped Nash, angry at everyone right now.

"Nay, I'm sorry ye fell," she answered. "I just thought it was funny that ye were just married to my sister and ye landed right in the weddin' bed."

"The weddin' bed?" both Nash and North asked together, turning to look back at the broken bed. The top was open, but his fall had caused the mattress ropes to snap. The pallet was now lying on the ground, with the high wooden sides of the bed all around it. One of the sides was cracked. The curtain that could be pulled across for privacy had ripped partially at the iron fasteners, and was also lying on the ground.

"Is that where we'll . . . where I'll . . . I mean . . . where the marriage will be consummated?" asked Nash in shock. If so, this couldn't be a good omen at all. Not that he thought this marriage had a chance from the beginning but, still, it didn't look good to him.

"Aye," said Caitlin, turning and heading for the door. "It's also where we lay out the dead."

She exited the infirmary, leaving North and Nash staring at each other, not saying a word.

"Now do ye believe me?" asked Nash. "She all but pushed me to my death bed."

"I think I'd better get over to the crop fields where I belong," said North, almost running out the door.

"Thanks for nothin', Brathair," Nash called out after him, disgusted to be in such a position.

"What's all the shoutin' about? We need to get to work." Kellina appeared in the doorway. To Nash's horror, she stood there holding a wooden mallet, a long blade attached to a good-sized handle, a curved knife like a small scythe, and some kind of wooden block mounted on a long wooden pole. Egads, this girl was determined to kill him in one manner or another!

"W-what's all that?" he asked, with a slight chuckle.

"They are knives and things I need to do my job."

"What job might that be?" he asked, starting to think of all the ways she would try to kill him with that many weapons. Surely, one weapon was more than enough.

"They are the tools we need for thatchin' the roof."

"Och, is that all?" Relief washed through him and he chuckled under his breath, glad to hear it.

"Aye. Why? What did ye think I was goin' to use them for?" She made a face, and looked at him from the corners of her eyes.

"Well I thought . . . I mean . . . for thatchin', of course. Here, allow me to carry them for ye." It was in his best interest to keep these sharp tools far away from his mad bride.

Kellina shrugged. "Have it yer way." She let him take the tools and then led the way back to the ladder. By now, Nash realized that more of the clansmembers had arrived to help, including her brother. They had carried over a lot more bundles of straw for them to use as thatch.

"Ah, so I am guessin' the Sutherlands didna burn everythin' after all," he remarked, laying the tools on the ground.

"Apparently no', or we wouldna have anythin' to use to thatch the roofs," was her wry answer.

"Do ye always use straw? To thatch a roof, I mean?"

"Nay, no' always. Sometimes we use reeds or rushes. It can include flax, wheat, heather or broom. We were savin' the straw for the animals, but since the Sutherlands took most of our livestock, there doesna seem to be much need for it anymore. We will use straw for this roof, but will have to collect reeds from the loch to add to the thatch we have left, as it willna be enough."

"All right. I am ready to learn." Nash rubbed his hands together, eager to get this unpleasant chore over with.

"We start at the bottom and work our way up," she instructed. "The straw is placed down, with the tassel ends goin' upward. It is spread out slightly. Like this." She grabbed a bundle, ascended the ladder, and showed him what she meant. "The long ash or willow sways that are split will be used to hold down the straw to the roof beams." She came down the ladder, pointing to a pile of sticks that her brother threw down at her feet.

"What holds the sways in place?" he asked, honestly not knowing how a roof was thatched since he had never done it before. Back at the MacKeefe Clan, he was always busy fighting and protecting the others, or hunting. He also spent a lot of time tending to the livestock. The roofs were managed by others of his clan, and he'd never had the interest to learn the skill.

"That's where these come in." Kellina bent down and picked up another stick that was flatter and about the length of his arm. "The straw will be fastened down by twisted hazel spars. She yanked a sharp dagger from her belt, causing him to jump back. Was she really going to stab him right here in front of everyone? The woman was even crazier than he thought.

"What's the matter?" she asked, her knife gleaming in the sun. "Ye're a little jumpy, Husband, arena ye?"

"What's the knife for?" he asked, hoping he didn't already know the answer to that.

"It's for sharpenin' the ends of the spar after I twist it." She twisted the wood, bending it in half, then used her knife to make the ends pointy. "See how sharp they are now?" She flicked her finger over the points.

"I see. Deadly sharp," he mumbled under his breath.

"It needs to be sharp in order to pierce the straw and hold the bundles together."

"Of course, it does. So, what comes next?"

"Let me show ye." She climbed back up the ladder and he followed.

After a row of thatch was laid out, she started stabbing the sharp spars over the sway and through the straw to make it secure. He swore she had a maniacal look on her face, as if she liked stabbing things . . . or perhaps people. God's eyes, how did he get himself married to such a crazy wench?

"Now ye try," she told him. "But first, let me show ye the finishin' steps." She climbed around him and back down the ladder to the ground. When he joined her, she was holding a large wooden mallet in one hand and a block of wood secured to a wooden handle in the other.

Bid the devil, was she going to hit him with this now? He looked out to all the others who were still bringing bundles of straw and sticks to the sight. None of them even seemed slightly concerned. Mayhap he was overreacting. Nay, he decided. She wouldn't be so stupid to try to whack him right there in front of everyone. Would she?

"What are ye goin' to hit with that?" he asked, backing up a step, just to make distance between them.

"Just ye wait and see." That evil grin was back on her face again, doing nothing to calm him.

She headed over to the ladder, climbing up just enough to reach the bottom of the thatch. Then she put the wooden block against it and gave it a good whack with the mallet. The thatch moved upward on an angle, causing the pitch of the roof to become smoother.

"Ah, I see," he said, understanding now just what she was doing. "Ye are smoothin' out the roof."

"That's right. And when it is finished I'll use those knives to cut off the overhang where I don't want it. There is more to show ye when we get to the top of the roof, but it will take a while and I'm sure we'll no' even get to it today."

"Well then, I suppose we should get movin'," he said, heading back for another bundle of straw. Building a thatched roof proved to be interesting. Nash liked to be good at everything he did, and was anxious to get his hand into this to show the girl that he was useful and could learn the skill quickly.

Now that he realized what she meant to use these tools for, he felt a little more relaxed. Perhaps she wouldn't attempt to kill him again. Or at least, not until the roof was almost finished. After all, she did need his help. Or at least he hoped.

CHAPTER SEVEN

NASH SAT AROUND the cook fire with North and the others, just finishing off their meal of pottage that the women of the clan had made and shared with them. Pottage was a staple food for the poor. This one consisted of boiled vegetables and grain, and no meat. Usually, it was served as a thick stew, but this was more like a thin soup. The chieftain had apologized, saying they were short on supplies since the raid.

It was dark now, and Nash was tired from thatching the roof all day. The infirmary was a long building, and the work seemed endless. His body ached. He was so tired that all he wanted was to get a good night's sleep. Morning would come fast, and then he'd have to do it all over again.

"Where is Aidan?" Nash asked, just noticing that he was missing.

"He left earlier for Edinvale Castle," said the chieftain. "He and his squirrel should be back tomorrow. He is goin' to bring back Lady Spring for a little visit."

"Spring Gordon is comin' here?" Kellina overheard, and looked up in surprise. "Why is that, Uncle? She is a fierce warrior woman, and we arena aligned with them. It could be dangerous. I think ye've made a mistake. Why would ye do such a thing?"

"Daughter, calm down," said Ciaran. "I figured ye might want another woman to talk to, that's all."

"Another woman?" Kellina looked around at the rest of the

clansmembers eating and going about their business. "There are enough lassies right here for me to talk with. I dinna need to converse with one who is our enemy. What is yer real reason for askin' her here, Uncle? And by the way, please dinna call me yer daughter. I am yer niece."

"I ken that." Ciaran stirred uncomfortably on the stump he was using as a stool. "Yer siblin's called Lorna, Mathair, and I just thought –"

"Nay! Ye thought wrong." She stood up abruptly, seeming suddenly upset. "I will never call ye Faither. I remember my parents and I willna pretend to forget them. Now, I am goin' to bed."

She turned to go, but her uncle stopped her. "Ye and yer husband will use the weddin' bed tonight," he told her. "I'll make sure ye have the entire buildin' to yerselves since it is important that ye consummate the marriage."

Nash saw her stop and her body stiffen.

"That's no' necessary," she ground out, never turning around to talk.

"I'm afraid it is, Kellina." Ciaran struggled to stand with his bad leg. Nash ran over and helped him. "Thank ye, Nash."

That got her to turn around.

"I suppose ye two have been plottin' about this all day long," she snapped.

"Plottin'?" asked her uncle. "Kellina, ye two must consummate yer marriage, or the alliance does no' hold true." The chieftain seemed very concerned about this, but Kellina didn't care at all. She wanted nothing to do with it.

"Ye are right, my laird," Nash answered, helping him to walk. "I'll do as is expected to seal the deal between our clans."

"What about ye, Kellina?" asked the chieftain.

Kellina looked out at the rest of the clan, all staring at her, waiting for her answer. She didn't want to couple with Nash MacKeefe, even if they were married.

"I never agreed to this marriage, and shouldna be forced to

make love with a MacKeefe!"

"Sister, ye must," said Caitlin.

"It is part of the alliance," added North. "Without the consummation, the alliance will be broken."

"If it is broken, the MacKeefes willna be our allies," called out a man of the clan.

"I dinna want them attackin' us next," cried a woman, cradling her young child to her bosom. "I've already lost my husband and son to the Sutherlands, and willna lose my daughter, too."

"Me neither," called out someone else.

"If ye dinna honor the alliance, it'll be yer fault when we're attacked by the MacKeefes," called out someone else.

"We're all goin' to die," screamed a young girl, causing all the children to start crying.

"Nay! We're no' goin' to die." Kellina held up her hand. "Please, stop it. This isna doin' anythin' to calm the others."

"Kellina, ye're the one makin' the children cry," shouted her brother. "Ye should be helpin' our clan, but ye're hurtin' it instead."

"He's right, Sister," said Caitlin. "Ye need to honor the agreement and do what is expected. If no', we will all pay for it when the MacKeefes find out ye went back on yer word."

"But it wasna my word!" cried Kellina. "I didna ken anythin' about this, and neither did I agree to it."

"Neither did I," interrupted Nash, stepping forward and holding out his hand. "We dinna have a choice, lass. Yer clan needs ye, and I need to honor the agreement as well, or I will always be an outcast. Let's do what we need to do and stop frettin' about it."

Kellina's heart beat wildly as she looked out at the rest of the clan watching her with hope in their eyes. She couldn't let them down. Not after everything they'd been through. Then she looked at Nash's hand. Here was the hand of a MacKeefe – a man from the clan who was responsible for the deaths of her parents. She didn't want him for a husband, and she really didn't want to get intimate with him either. Mayhap she should have killed him today on the roof when she'd had the chance. She didn't know what to do.

"Please, lass," said Nash, smiling at her. "I'm no' so bad once ye get to ken me."

"He is a pushover with the lassies," called out North, taking a swig of ale. "Plus, he's nothin' like a goat in bed. Or at least, I dinna think so. He does snore like a beastie though, just to warn ye."

North's jesting broke the tension. Kellina realized that she had to do this in order to help her clan. She didn't want to couple with a MacKeefe, but neither did she want the clan to lose hope and blame her for anything bad that might happen in the future.

"All right," she said with a sigh, pushing away his hand. "But I can walk on my own." She turned and headed to the infirmary, not wanting to touch him on the way to their wedding bed.

The clan talked happily amongst themselves. In a way, she felt like this sacrifice on her part would be worth it. She had to help rebuild the hope as well as the physical parts of her clan. She hated this, and was sure she'd hate every minute of the MacKeefe touching her, but hopefully it would end quickly. She'd seen his erection poking out from under his plaid earlier. If he was like every other man, he'd be sated before she even knew it began. Mayhap she could endure this . . . but only for one night and not more.

She walked into the infirmary, followed by Nash.

"Shall I light a lantern?" he asked, but she decided doing this in the dark would be better.

"Dinna bother," she told him, seeing the light of the moon shining in the open roof right above the bed. They'd managed to put part of the roof up, but it was still open to the sky since it wasn't finished yet.

"All right," she heard him say as he closed the door behind them. Kellina's arms closed around her in a protective manner as she took a few steps toward the bed.

"I suppose I could fix this quickly." Nash bent down to inspect the ropes that had held up the mattress, but had snapped when he fell on the bed through the roof earlier.

"Nay. Dinna bother. We can use it the way it is." Her body trembled, thinking of what she had to do next. She didn't want him to fuss with the bed ropes because she just wanted this over with as quickly as possible. Every minute she had to wait made her more and more nervous.

"All right then," said Nash, clearing his throat. "I suppose we should . . . get undressed?"

Kellina let out a deep sigh, closing her eyes and whimpering slightly.

"Let me help ye, lassie." His gentle hands were on her arms and he pulled them apart so he could untie her tunic at the neck. She kept her eyes closed as he pulled it up and over her head. Then his hands went to her waist, but she pushed them away and opened her eyes.

"I'll get the breeches. Just get undressed so we can get this over with as fast as possible."

"Now, that's no' somethin' a lassie has ever said to me before." He frowned and turned around to undress as she pulled off the rest of her clothes and stood there naked in the light of the moon. She heard the rustle of his clothes as they hit the floor. When he turned around and headed toward her, she crossed her arms over her chest again and squeezed her eyes shut.

"Just make it quick." She heard the quaver of her voice, and wondered if he could hear the rapid drumming of her racing heart.

"Lass. Kellina," he said softly. "Please, open yer eyes."

She slowly opened one eye and then the other, almost gasping when she saw his manly beauty bathed in the soft bluish-white light of the moon that spilled inside the building from the open roof.

Nash's long, brown hair was loose and fell over his broad shoulders. It led to a very sturdy chest with just a smattering of dark curly hairs. Curiosity overcame her, and she let her gaze drop lower. She drank in his tight abs, feeling her resistance lowering with her eyes as she saw the curly hair lower, below his waist. Then she noticed his manhood straight and hard, lit up by the luminous moon.

"Oh!" she cried, wondering if it would hurt when he penetrated her with that large object of lust.

"It's all right, lass. Dinna be afraid. I promise I willna hurt ye. Now give me yer hand."

Slowly, she uncrossed her arms, giving him her hand, allowing him to see her nakedness as well.

He wasn't shy about looking. "God's eyes, ye are bonnie," he whispered as he perused her nakedness from head to foot. Then his eyes traveled back up to her face again.

"Can I kiss ye, lass?" He asked her permission, which she thought odd since they were married now.

"If it's necessary," she said, keeping her jaw firm. She still didn't want to do this.

"I think it'll help ye relax."

"Then do it already, and stop standing there gawkin' at me."

He hesitated, and then shook his head. "Nay," he said, dropping her hand.

"Nay?" She didn't understand. Was he really going to walk away now? He couldn't. She didn't get naked in front of him for no reason. They had to consummate the marriage. What was he doing?

"Let's just go lie down." He led the way over to the mattress that was on the floor.

"Oh, ye want to make love without all the foreplay. I understand. Why bother, right?"

He held out his hand again to help her step over the side of the bed and onto the pallet. Then he followed her, and they both laid down on their backs, staring up at the stars and moon above.

"I rather like lookin' at the outdoors while I'm inside in bed," he told her.

"Aye. It's bonnie," she said, staring out the open roof.

"Kellina, ye ken, we need to consummate the marriage," he told her, after they both remained silent for a few minutes.

"I suppose so. What are ye waitin' for? Do it already."

"Lass," he said, pushing up on one elbow, his long hair making a tent around him as he spoke to her in a soft, sultry voice. "I ken that, right now, the entire clan is most likely standin' right outside the hut."

"Ye think so? What for?"

"They are waitin' and listenin' for the sounds of consummation. With the roof open the way it is, it'll be easy for them to hear us."

"Lovely," she replied, not happy about this at all. "What's yer point?"

"I ken ye dinna want to make love to me, and I willna force ye to do it."

"How can ye say that? We were told we have to do it. Everyone is expectin' it to happen. They are countin' on us. The alliance between our clans will be broken if we dinna obey."

He let out a frustrated sigh. "I was thinkin' . . . as long as they believe we did it, they'll be satisfied. That should be enough. No one ever needs to ken the truth."

"Wait. What are ye sayin'?" Curious and intrigued as to what he meant, she slowly unfolded her arms from over her breasts and looked up into his beautiful, hazel eyes. There was just enough light from the moon to see small specks of green and brown and even ochre within his orbs. They had a soft, caring quality to them, and she believed him when he told her that he didn't want to hurt her.

"Shhh," he said, putting his finger to her lips, making her body quiver as he slowly pulled his finger away. Her tongue shot out to taste his essence on her bottom lip. "We dinna want everyone to hear our plan."

"Our plan?" she asked, taking a deep breath. His scent was of woodsmoke and fresh air, and of course, straw.

"We will fake our . . . consummation with our cries of passion. They will hear it and think the marriage was finalized, and then they will leave us alone."

"B-but it will no' be finalized. The alliance willna be real."

"They dinna need to ken that. The only ones who will ken the truth are me and ye."

"Why would ye do this? I dinna understand."

His eyes looked down at her body and he wet his lips with his tongue. "I have never forced myself on a lass in my life, and I dinna plan on startin' now, even if ye are my wife."

"But it's yer duty as a husband to take yer wife. It's what ye are supposed to do. Why wouldna ye do it?"

"I see the way yer body trembles, and I hear the malice ye hold for me in yer voice. Nay, I willna bed ye, Kellina, since I ken ye despise me and dinna want me to touch ye. Therefore, I willna lay a hand on ye tonight."

"Y-ye willna?"

He shook his head. Part of her felt better to know this, but there was an aching in her heart at the same time. Was she so undesirable that he really didn't want to make love to her after all? Even when they were married, and he was looking at her naked body? She probably should have been grateful, but somehow this only infuriated her more.

"Fine, then let's do it. How shall we proceed?"

"Well, they'll want to hear our moans of passion, and also our cry of elation as we find our release."

"I've never made love before, Nash. I dinna think I can fake passion or release."

"Then let me help ye." He reached out for her and her body stiffened.

He stopped.

"Dinna be afraid. I told ye I willna touch ye . . . no' in that manner. I promise to keep my word. Now give me yer hands."

"Whatever for?"

"Just do it."

"Here," she said, giving him her hands. He took them in his. Then, being ever so careful not to touch her naked body, he put one of her hands on her breast, and directed her other hand between her thighs.

"What are ye doin'?" she asked.

"Shhh," he said again, warning her to stay quiet for now. "If ye have never felt passion in lovemakin' before, then ye willna be convincin'. Therefore, ye are goin' to have to get excited. For real."

"I hardly think that's goin' to – oh!" she said through a ragged breath as he directed her fingers to caress one nipple, bringing it to a peak. "What's happenin'?" She watched with wide eyes as her nipples got taut, and she felt suddenly warmer.

"It's workin'," he said with pride. "Now use yer other hand to fondle yerself between yer thighs."

"Nay. I dinna think I can do that. It is wrong."

"How old are ye, lass, that ye have never done this to yerself before?"

"I am nine and ten years of age, and I never had the desire."

"Then I think it is long past due. Just relax, and I will guide yer hand."

She let out a deep sigh. "If ye say so."

With his hand, he didn't touch her, but used her own hand to stroke herself gently, urging her to open her legs wider.

"Do ye feel anythin' yet?" he asked.

"I'm no' sure."

"I think ye need to use yer finger. Inside ye."

"Inside?" she gasped.

"Ye heard me. It willna hurt. And play with yer womanly folds. Use yer finger inside, and yer thumb on top on the nub. And keep stroking yer breast as well. Close yer eyes. It will help."

With his guidance, she did as he instructed. It surprisingly didn't take long for her to relax. Then she felt a tingling vibration, and her inner core seemed to be brought to life.

"That's right," he whispered, his hot breath in her ear only making her feel more excited. "Rock yer pelvis back and forth as ye move yer finger in and out now."

Her eyes popped open. "This feels so wrong."

"It's no', I assure ye. Just remember . . . it is for the guid of the clan."

"Aye," she said, closing her eyes once again.

"Just breathe deeply, and when ye feel ye need to moan or cry out, just do it."

Her eyes popped open once again. "Are ye sure about this, Nash?"

"It's either this, or ye agree to let me enter ye right now."

"Nay. I'll do it this way." She continued with the stroking, and he whispered into her ear once again.

"Now, pinch yer nipple slightly. That's right. Keep rockin' yer hips."

"Oh . . . I feel somethin', Nash. It . . . it feels guid."

"Do ye feel wetness between yer thighs?"

"I – I do."

"Then ye're just about ready. Now just pretend yer finger is my . . . well, just pretend ye are makin' love with a man that ye lust for. Ye want this badly. Can ye feel it, love?"

"I do," she said, letting out a small moan. "Oh, this feels so guid, I dinna believe it."

"Moan louder," he told her, only making her more excited.

"Oooh. Oooooh," she moaned loudly. At first she almost laughed. But then she heard him moan, too, and realized he'd taken his one hand off hers at her breast, but he still helped her to finger herself.

"Aaaaaah, aaaah," he moaned louder and louder. She felt his hips moving back and forth and when she opened her eyes she saw his eyes were closed. "God's eyes, I canna hold back any longer," he said loud enough for everyone outside to hear him.

"Nash?" she asked, her eyes following his hand that was clasped around his erection. "Oh," she said, realizing he was satisfying himself right next to her. His hand moved up and down his shaft and the look on his face was one of pure elation.

He moaned louder and louder and his hand moved faster and faster. All the while, he guided her hand on herself. Her body grew hotter and hotter and she felt herself climbing to a height of ecstasy that she'd never felt before.

And when she looked back over to him, he'd released her hand and she saw something squirting up into the air as he shouted loudly. "Kellina! Yes, yes . . . yes! Ye are now my wife."

When she saw and heard that, she could no longer hold back. She felt her body vibrating, and she shouted out just as loudly as him as she reached her peak and fell over the edge.

"Aaaaaaah, Nash! Oh, God, Nash, this feels so guid." And then she squealed in delight, not pretending, but feeling herself being sated for real for the very first time.

They both fell back, breathing heavily, listening to the sound of everyone outside clapping and cheering for them.

"We did it," he said, turning his head and smiling at her. "They think we've consummated the marriage. I kept my promise no' to touch ye in a lustful manner."

"Ah, we did," she said, watching the rise and fall of her own breasts as she tried to calm herself down. "We sure fooled them, didna we?"

She looked over to him, wanting more than anything to throw herself into his arms and kiss him wildly right now. She almost decided to do just that, but when she heard him snoring, she realized that he had fallen asleep, just that fast.

"What a wonderful weddin' night," she said, feeling sad, and also mad at herself now for telling him she didn't want to consummate the marriage. Nash's kind actions tonight touched her heart, and made her see him in a whole different light.

She was left lying there, feeling sated but not happy about how it had happened and how she had fooled her clan. Nay, she didn't like this after all. It was wrong. Now, she wished she had just coupled with the man the way everyone was expecting them to do.

Watching him lying there so peaceful, so calm, and looking so happy, she felt as if he didn't even need her after all. That didn't feel good either. She felt like a traitor now, and a liar. But most of all, she felt so undesirable to her new husband. If he had really lusted for her and been attracted to her the way a husband should be toward a wife, he would have taken her even against her will. Wouldn't he?

She turned on her side and pulled a blanket up over her, feeling naughty, and all alone when she didn't have to be.

"Damn ye, MacKeefe," she spat through her teeth, going back to hating the man once more.

Chapter Eight

N ASH WAS DREAMING about making love with Kellina all night long. Then he felt something hit his face and, with his eyes closed, he brushed it away. He felt it again, as well as a warm feeling encompassing him.

His eyes flickered open to find sun streaming in through the roof. Straw fluttered down atop him. That's when he saw Kellina up on the roof staring down at him through the hole.

"Get up, ye lazy oaf. We have a roof to finish before it starts to rain."

"What?" His head snapped around to look next to him, but he realized Kellina was no longer lying with him. For a moment, he thought she was really there and they'd been making love. Then reality hit him. He'd never consummated their marriage – only in his dreams.

"Ye heard me. It's goin' to rain. Now get yer lazy arse out of bed. There is work to be done."

"Rain?" He rubbed one sleepy eye, looking up at the sky through the open roof again. All he could see was a blue sky, and not a single cloud in it.

"I think ye're wrong," he called back to her. "It's no' goin' to rain."

Her angry eyes stared down at him. "Dinna think ye are so smart because ye ken nothin' about nothin' at all."

"What is that supposed to mean?" he asked, pushing up in

bed. "Kellina, are ye angry with me about somethin'? I mean . . . other than the weather?"

"Put yer clothes on before my sister walks in and sees ye like that!"

"Oh." He looked down, realizing he was still naked. After their pretend consummation last night, he was so tired that he must have fallen asleep and slept through to morning. "All right, I'll be right there. Dinna start without me."

"Hmph," she said with a sniff. "How about I just finish without ye? After all, ye've made it quite clear last night that it's no' hard to do."

"What are ye complainin' about?" he asked, hopping out of bed and hurriedly dressing. "Kellina, ye are makin' no sense at all."

She disappeared from sight. He heard her pounding on the roof, and she no longer glared down at him. At least that was a relief. Being married was already proving to be very confusing and complicated. Nash wasn't sure at all what his new wife was angry about, or if she just always acted this way.

He needed to hurry, because he wanted to know how to finish the seam at the apex of the roof if he was going to master this skill. He liked knowing how to do many things, and he wanted to be good at all of them. Nash didn't doubt for a minute that Kellina would somehow try to finish the roof without him, just to spite him. Well, he wasn't about to let that happen.

He sat down on the edge of the bed to don his boots. He couldn't imagine for a minute what was upsetting her so much. He thought that by faking the consummation and not touching her in a lustful manner, she'd be relieved. After all, she'd made it quite clear that she didn't want him as her husband. She didn't even like him in the least. Now that he'd taught her how to pleasure herself without even needing him, he thought it would have made her happy. Sadly, that didn't seem to be the case. For some odd reason, he got the distinct feeling that it only made her mad.

Kellina was proving to be a very complicated woman – not to mention wife. Nash didn't know what he was going to do about their situation. He couldn't stay married to a lass who hated him. Nor could he be married to a girl who he was never allowed to make love to. If this was to continue, they would never have babies or raise a family. It was more than clear to him that these things were never going to happen with Kellina.

The trouble was, he couldn't divorce her either. Not without bringing strife to one or probably both of their clans. Damn, why did he have to be in this situation? Why couldn't he just have to make shoes or candles to work off his punishment like Gavin and Cam did? His friends had it easy compared to him. Nash's punishment now was one that would last the rest of his life. Unfortunately, there was nothing he could do to change that.

He looked up and saw the top of the bedcurtain hanging loose from the rings, and this bothered him. The broken bed ropes made him unsettled as well. He liked things to be as perfect as they could be. He didn't have time to re-string the bed ropes now, but figured he could at least somehow attach the top of the bedcurtain quickly before he went to work.

The ceiling was almost touching the top of the box bed since the structure was so tall, and the ceiling low. Nash climbed up the side of the bed, reaching up high to refasten the curtain. He heard a loud thump from above and, all of a sudden, something spiky pushed through the roof. It hit him, scratching his hand and drawing blood.

"Bid the devil!" he cried out, pulling his hand away, seeing one of those damned sharp, twisted spikes sticking through the ceiling. "Who the hell did this to me?"

"Is somethin' wrong?" Kellina peered down from the opening in the roof again. "I thought I heard ye scream. Did ye see a mouse, perhaps?" She was playing her little games again, trying to make him feel worthless. Well, he'd had enough of this, and it was going to stop.

"Ye did this to me," he accused her, holding up his bleeding hand to show her.

"I did no'. I'm up on the roof. How could I have even touched ye way down there?"

"It was that damned sharp spike. Ye pushed it through the roof, because ye kent I was up near the ceilin'. Ye were tryin' to kill me by stabbin' me. Just admit it."

"Are ye talkin' about the twisted hazel spar that is used to hold down the thatch?" she asked, sounding innocent, although Nash knew that was far from the truth.

"Whatever ye want to call it," he grumbled. "The fact is, that thing is downright dangerous. It could have stabbed me to death. It's only by pure luck that it ended up just bein' a deep scratch."

"Well, mayhap if ye were up here instead of down there, it wouldna have happened at all. Ye brought it on yerself, and ye ken it." So much for thinking she'd feel guilty or sorry for him at all.

Nash pulled at the bedsheet, ripping off a strip and winding it around his wound to stop the flow of blood. It wasn't a bad wound, and would heal quickly, but that still didn't make what she had done to him acceptable. Furious with his new wife, he stormed out of the infirmary, only to bump into North who was carrying a big bag of seeds over his shoulder. The bag fell to the ground and broke open. Seeds scattered everywhere.

"Nice work, Nash." North bent down and tried to scoop the seeds back into the bag. "However, they're supposed to be planted in the field, no' here."

"Sorry about that." Nash hunkered down and helped his brother pick up the spilled seeds.

"What's wrong with yer hand?" asked North, eyeing his bandage.

"Oh, it's nothin'. My lovely wife just tried to kill me again, that's all. This time, it was with a twisted hazel spar."

"Losh me, is that what ye call it? After all, everyone heard how she was tryin' to kill ye last night . . . in the weddin' bed." North waggled his eyebrows. "It sounds like she's a real vixen in the sack."

"Stop it, North. It's no' like that at all. Ye dinna ken what ye are sayin'."

"Are ye sure it isna?" he asked sarcastically. "It sounded pretty satisfyin' to me."

"We didna even do anythin', I swear," said Nash in a low voice. He looked around as he said it to make sure no one heard him.

"What are ye sayin'?" North stopped picking up the seeds.

"Kellina didna want me to touch her, so I just showed her how to pleasure herself instead."

"What? Please tell me this is just a sick jest." North's mouth fell open in surprise.

"Shhhh." Nash finished scooping the seeds back into the bag and tied it closed. "Dinna let anyone ken. We want them to think we consummated the marriage."

"Nash, what is the matter with ye? Ye ken that consummation is important to seal the alliance between our clans. What have ye done?"

"I refuse to bed a lass who doesna want me, no matter who she is. I have never forced myself on a wench before, and willna start now." Nash stood and brushed off his hands.

"That wench is yer wife, ye fool!" North grabbed the bag and stood up. "If ye let her get away with that on yer weddin' night, she is goin' to rule ye the rest of yer life. Ye will have to look to whores for yer release, and yer marriage will never be consummated now. I'm sorry to say ye've made a big mistake, Brathair."

"Mayhap ye're right." Nash rubbed his injured hand and glanced up to Kellina who was on the roof, thatching furiously. "I only did it, hopin' she would like me. But I can see by the madness in her eyes this mornin' that she hates me more than ever. I dinna ken why."

"Ye're just imaginin' it, I am sure. She is yer wife. She's scared, but doesna hate ye."

"Now ye're the fool, Brathair." Nash held up his hand. "Yesterday she threw me off the roof. Today she tried to impale me. What's next? Slitting my throat as I sleep? And how many times will I be able to escape death? Even a cat only has nine lives, so they say, and I've already used up two."

"Nash, listen to yerself. Ye're overreactin'."

"Am I? Ye heard her uncle. He warned us to watch our backs because she is goin' to try to kill any MacKeefe. She is vengeful and will stop at nothin' to make the MacKeefes pay for the death of her parents."

"Well, nothin's happened to me yet, so I dinna believe it."

"Watch out," came a cry from the roof. Nash and North looked up to see a wooden mallet flying right at them. Nash pushed North out of the way, both of them falling to the ground. The mallet landed just next to their heads. "Sorry about that. It slipped," Kellina called out with a shrug. She did not sound sorry at all to Nash. He had no doubt she did it on purpose.

"That's three lives used up now," said Nash. "North, now do ye believe me?" He helped his brother to his feet.

"Aye. Mayhap ye're right." Concern washed over North's face as his eyes lifted to Kellina on the roof. "Ye'd better do somethin', and fast. Ye need to keep that wife of yers under control, before we're all killed off one by one," spat North, grabbing the bag of seeds and quickly heading toward the fields.

"What is takin' so long? I need yer help. It's goin' to rain." Kellina hurried down the ladder and stood next to him with her hands on her hips again.

"Aye, well, next time ask nicely instead of tryin' to kill me with yer mallet, and mayhap I'll move faster." He scooped up the wooden mallet and shoved it back into her hands, hurrying over to the ladder.

"Sister, is somethin' the matter?" asked Caitlin, joining Kellina. "Yer husband looks angry with ye."

"He's no' my husband," she grumbled. "Well, no' really." She looked down and played with the mallet.

"What are ye talkin' about?" Caitlin giggled. "Ye were married yesterday, or did ye forget?"

"Never mind."

"Did I hear Nash say ye tried to kill him? Och, Sister, I hope this isna true. He's yer husband now, so please dinna kill him, I beg ye."

"I am no' tryin' to kill him, although I canna say he doesna deserve it."

"But ye said ye were goin' to do it. Did ye have a change of mind? I hope so."

Kellina thought about it for a moment, realizing now that her anger had possibly been misdirected. She still didn't like the MacKeefes and would never forgive them for the deaths of her parents. But after last night, she was confused. Nash refused to couple with her even though they were married. He said he didn't want to force himself on her, even though she was his wife. What man would be so kind? This made her wonder if he could ever purposely hurt someone. Or kill them. It didn't seem so.

"I ken I said I wanted to kill the MacKeefes, but I am no' a murderer, Caitlin. However, I am gettin' the feelin' that, for some reason, Nash thinks I want him dead." She looked down to the wooden mallet again, turning it over and over in her hands.

"Then ye didna really try to kill him?" Caitlin's eyes opened wide in disbelief.

"Nay! I swear, I didna. He is sayin' I pushed him off the roof and tried to impale him, but it isna true. I didna try to kill him with a fallin' mallet either. Those were all accidents. They werena done on purpose."

"Did ye tell him that?"

"It doesna matter what I say." She looked at the ground and kicked at the dirt. "He hates me, Caitlin. I didna think I would care, but I do. He doesna want me as his wife and is no' attracted to me in the least. It hurts."

"Nay. Ye're wrong, Sister." Caitlin's face lit up. "After all, everyone heard ye two last night, and it sounded as if he liked ye a lot."

"Right," she said sadly, not wanting to tell her sister that they'd faked the consummation just so the clan wouldn't think they broke the alliance with the MacKeefes. She didn't believe her sister could keep a secret. Caitlin would more than likely run right to their uncle and tell him everything. Kellina didn't want to be blamed for it, and be the cause of a battle between the clans.

Honestly, she didn't want Nash to be blamed either. Even if he didn't want her in his bed, she couldn't blame him. She hadn't been very nice to him, she supposed. God's eyes, she hated being in this position. Especially since she was now married to a man who didn't want to touch her, and would rather pleasure himself. Was she really that undesirable that Nash wouldn't have tried harder to bed her on their wedding night?

"Kellina, get up here before it rains," Nash called out, throwing her words back at her. "Or do ye want to take a nap and let me do all the work instead?"

"Calm down," she told him, gripping the mallet tightly and heading back to the ladder. "Ye canna finish the roof yerself since I have yet to teach ye how." Her words only made her think of last night again, and how Nash had taught her to finish something else on her own. "Bid the devil," she spat, talking to herself. "Rain is the least of my worries right now, MacKeefe."

CHAPTER NINE

"HOW DOES THIS look?" asked Nash a while later, hoping to hell he was constructing the ridge at the top of the apex correctly.

Kellina had shown him how to bend the layer of straw over the tip of the roof. Then she taught him how to use hazel ligging to hold it in place, and also to add lots of twisted spars to secure it. The spars were tightened by hitting them with the wooden mallet.

"It needs more liggin,' as well as more spars. If it isna secured tightly, the wind is goin' to take it," she told him. "We need to move faster if we're goin' to finish before it rains. The sky is already gettin' dark and the winds are pickin' up. It willna be safe to stay up here much longer."

"Och, I am goin' as fast as I can," complained Nash, stabbing a spar into the straw to hold it. Each time he did, all he could think about was how Kellina had tried to stab him with one of these earlier. He had a deep scratch on his hand to prove her hatred for him. It was hard to keep an eye on her and also an eye on the roof at all times. Still, he had to, or risk losing his life at the hands of his disgruntled wife.

"That's guid, but it could be better," she told him. "If ye make a crisscross pattern with the liggin', it will help to make the roof more secure. Here, let me show ye."

To Nash's surprise, she took his hand, guiding him in placing the wooden strips. She gently and carefully instructed him how to secure the strip over the bundles of straw. Unfortunately, it only reminded him of how he'd guided her hand last night, teaching her something else! Damn, it was hard to focus his mind on what he was doing.

Thunder rumbled in the distance, and a light mist began to fall.

"We've got enough covered that it'll keep out the rain for now," she told him, looking over at him, still holding on to his hand. "We'll have to put on the finishing touches later."

Her bright blue eyes stared deeply into his, making him feel as if she could see straight into his very soul. Nash wondered if the girl could see his desire for her right now. He hoped not. Then, he thought, if she did, it would only scare her and make her want to try to kill him again. Nay, it would better if he just kept his desires a secret for now. He reached out and tenderly pushed her hand away from his.

"Thank ye," he said. "I think I've got it now."

Was that a shadow of disappointment to cross her face since he pulled away from her? Or mayhap it was only the lack of sun now that the storm was approaching. He was sure it was naught more than his imagination. Or mayhap it was his hope tricking him, since part of him wanted to relive his wedding night but, this time, doing it the proper way.

"Once the rain stops, we'll have to come back and use the leggett on the straw to hit the ends and smooth out the angle of the roof." Kellina was all business. There was naught on her mind but working right now. "Afterwards, we'll trim the ends of the thatch with the knives." She collected up the tools as she spoke.

Rain started to fall more heavily now. Lightning lit up the sky, and thunder boomed directly overhead. A storm was brewing and, this time, it didn't have to do with Kellina, but rather the weather.

"Fast, let's get the tools out of the rain and get under cover." Kellina turned too quickly. With the rain coming down so hard, her footing was off and she slipped. "Och!" she cried out, dropping the tools, sending them clattering down the roof.

"Kellina!" shouted Nash, instinctively reaching out and grabbing her arm, keeping her from sliding down the roof to the ground. "I've got ye. Dinna worry, lass. Ye're safe with me."

Nash guided her back to the ladder, and they both hurried down the rungs. When Nash got to the bottom, he saw North standing there, rubbing his head, but not running for cover.

"Nash, she tried to kill me again," North said in a low voice, his eyes going to the knives and tools stuck into the ground all around him. "Ye were right about the wench. No MacKeefe is safe here."

"Hurry, pick up the tools before they rust," shouted Kellina, heading toward a hut as the downpour of rain soaked them now.

"Come on, North," said Nash, ignoring what his brother had said, collecting the tools and running to a covered cottage. This is where everyone gathered to eat. There were long trestle tables and benches set up inside. It was filling up with clansmembers quickly.

"It's crowded in here," complained North as they pushed into the room. The clansmembers touched them on all sides.

"That's because it is one of the only buildin's that still has a full roof," explained Kellina. "Nobody wants to get wet if they dinna have to."

"Too late for that, since our clothes are already soaked from the rain," Nash answered, sloshing his way across the dirt floor.

"Daughter, did ye finish the roof of the infirmary?" Laird Ciaran pushed through the crowd to join them, using his crutch to clear a path for him to walk. Mothers sat their children atop the trestle tables, and a few of the women brought out platters of food to share with everyone.

"PLEASE DINNA CALL me Daughter," Kellina answered with a scowl, hating when her uncle did this. "Ye ken I dinna like it, Uncle."

"All right, Kellina. I'm sorry. Did ye finish the roof?" he asked her once again.

"I almost did."

"She means we. We almost did," Nash interrupted. "Kellina has taught me a lot, and I'm gettin' pretty skilled in the art of thatchin'. I'm just a fast learner." The fool's face beamed with pride, as if he really thought he was any good at it. "It willna be long now before I pass her up, since I am gettin' so fast at the skill. I must say, I'm surprised I'm so guid at thatchin' roofs."

"And braggin'," she mumbled under her breath, wondering if the man would ever stop talking about himself.

The door to the cottage burst open. Aidan MacKeefe rushed in. A few seconds later he was followed by a group of people who were all running for cover. Kellina realized it was the rest of their clan who had been away at the trade fair.

"They've returned!" she exclaimed excitedly, running over to meet them. "The rest of our clan has returned from the trade fair, everyone."

Screams of joy went up from those whose loved ones were still alive and rejoining the clan. Those who returned, ran to hug their families. When Kellina heard crying, she realized it was from those who had lost their loved ones in the battle with the Sutherlands.

"What's happened to our camp?" asked Tomas, one of the men from the clan as he hugged his wife and children.

"We were attacked by the Sutherlands," the chieftain told them. "My wife and daughters were killed."

Silence fell over the room and the mood saddened.

"We are all so sorry, my laird," said Tomas, speaking for all of them. "I only wish we had been here to help. If so, mayhap we could have saved the lives of those who are now lost."

"Thank ye," said Kellina's uncle. "It is an unfortunate situation, and could have been any one of us."

"Aye," added Kellina. "We dinna realize how precious the lives of our friends and loved ones really are until they are gone forever."

One of the women who had just returned pushed her way through the group. "Where is my husband?" she screamed. "Where is he?"

"Alice, I'm sorry." Kellina ran over and hugged the woman, trying to comfort her. "Yer husband died protectin' the clan."

Alice wailed loudly. The mood turned even more solemn as others found that their loved ones were missing and had been killed as well.

"The bluidy bastards burned the roofs and took most of our livestock," shouted Kellina's brother, Jamie, letting everyone know what happened while they were away.

"Kill the Sutherlands," yelled a man, causing those who had just arrived to go into a fit of frenzy.

"Let's slaughter them while they sleep, and then take back our livestock," yelled someone else.

"We'll impale their heads on spikes," shouted another angry man.

"Nay! Stop it. Haud yer wheesht!" shouted Ciaran. "We will discuss this later. No one goes anywhere, and no' a one of ye will attack the Sutherlands unless I command ye to do so."

"But we canna let the Sutherlands get away with this," spat Tomas. "I will take a group of men and approach their camp in the dark. We'll take them by surprise."

"Nay, Tomas, please dinna go," begged the man's wife. His young son clung to his leg.

"I said nay," Ciaran ground out, becoming more and more agitated by his men's reactions. "Havena enough lives of those we love already been lost? It will do no guid to lose the rest of ye as well."

"He is right. Besides, ye're highly outnumbered now," Nash pointed out. "Reactin' like this without first devisin' a plan could be disastrous in the end."

"Why are ye tellin' us what to do? Who the hell are ye?" growled Tomas.

"I am Nash MacKeefe," he answered, making Kellina cringe since she hadn't wanted him to reveal his surname to her angry clansmen right now. It wasn't a good idea since as far as Tomas and the others still knew, the MacKeefes were their enemies. "I am here with my brathair, North, helpin' to rebuild the camp."

Kellina saw North step closer to his brother, shaking his head. Aidan walked closer to the twins, his hand on the hilt of his sword. His squirrel disappeared inside a pouch hanging at Aidan's waist.

"Did he say MacKeefe?" someone called out from the group who had just entered.

"We dinna want MacKeefes here!" shouted a man in the crowd, once again causing a ruckus.

"I agree. The MacKeefes are our enemies, so that means ye are, too!" Tomas drew his sword, followed by many of the other MacKenzies doing the same. It looked like another battle was about to begin. Kellina had no idea how to stop it.

"Whoa!" Nash held up his hands as North and Aidan drew their swords as well. Even so, Nash did not reach for his weapon. That surprised Kellina since she thought he'd be the first one to do so. Especially when they were being threatened.

"Are ye ready to take them down, Brathair?" asked North in a low voice.

"I am proud to be a MacKeefe and I'm with ye," mumbled Aidan, his eyes flicking back and forth, watching the MacKenzies like a hawk. "Let me warn ye all, they dinna call me Madman MacKeefe for nothin'."

"Please, calm down," Nash begged them all. "This is naught but a misunderstandin'. Everyone, put away yer swords. The MacKeefes and the MacKenzies will no' battle today or ever again, because we are now allies."

"Allies?" growled Tomas. "That's a bold-faced lie. The MacKeefes have been our enemies for many years now."

"Ever since they killed Robena and Avery," added someone else.

"Nay, listen to Nash. It's true," Ciaran spoke up. "I have made an alliance with the MacKeefes through the marriage of Nash MacKeefe and my daughter . . . my niece . . . Kellina."

"Kellina's married a MacKeefe?" asked Alice, pulling out of Kellina's arms to look at her in disgust. "Why would ye do such a thing, lass? Ye hate the MacKeefes more than any of us since they were the responsible for the deaths of yer parents. They are nothin' but murderers, yet ye took one of them to yer bed? How could ye? That is no' right, lass. No' right at all."

Kellina's stomach twisted in a knot as she listened to Alice's words. Her own clan looked at her as if she were a traitor, or perhaps some kind of monster. All this talk of the MacKeefes killing her parents was doing nothing but bringing her hatred for the MacKeefes back to the surface once again.

"I had no choice in the matter," she told them, her eyes darting over to Nash. Nash slowly shook his head in a silent warning for her to stay quiet.

"When did this happen?" asked Tomas. "Lass, if the marriage hasna yet been consummated, then it is no' too late. Just tell us it isna so, and we can still kill these three MacKeefes right now without objection."

"Have ye consummated the marriage, lass?" asked Alice. "We need to ken."

"I – I . . ." Kellina wanted to tell them the truth, but when she looked over to Nash, he was begging her with his eyes not to say a word about what they'd really done to trick the clan. If word got out, Nash and North, as well as Aidan, would be dead by her clansmen in minutes. Her uncle would be powerless to stop it. Revenge was a strong emotion, and one that couldn't be reasoned with at all. She knew this from experience. If these warriors knew the truth, they would kill the MacKeefes, and not think anything was wrong with their actions.

"Tell them, Wife," said Nash, making it clear what he wanted from her when he called her Wife.

"I . . . I mean, I . . ." Her eyes darted back to Nash – her husband. Even if she wasn't in love with him, and didn't really want to be his wife, could she let him die? His life, as well as the lives of his brother and friend, now rested in her hands. One word was all her clansmen needed from her, and Nash and the other MacKeefes' fates would be sealed.

"I think my bride is just shy about this," said Nash with a chuckle, walking over and slipping his hand around her waist. "Everyone here can vouch that the marriage yesterday has been consummated. They all heard loud and clear last night what transpired in our marriage bed. Isna that right, North?" he asked his brother.

"Huh?" North looked like a deer in the torchlight, being put on the spot. His eyes darted back and forth. It was obvious that he wasn't sure how to answer. Mayhap he just needed more of Nash's guidance.

"Didna ye say ye heard our cries of passion in the marriage bed last night?" he asked North. "After all, the roof of the infirmary was no' in place yet, and sound travels."

"Well, aye. I did hear yer cries of passion in the marriage bed. We all did." North nodded furiously, not saying anything more.

"I heard them, too," agreed Caitlin. She was followed by others who had been there, saying one at a time that they had heard the consummation that had occurred.

"Well, I didna hear them," growled one of the older men of the clan.

"Forbes, ye are nearly deaf," said the chieftain. "Ye wouldna hear me bangin' on yer head either."

"What's that?" asked Forbes, cocking his head and cupping his ear, trying to hear over the noise of the crowd.

"My point exactly," said Ciaran, holding out his arm. "Now, all of ye, put away yer swords. I willna hear another word about harmin' a single MacKeefe."

"For those of ye who are still in doubt, I'll display proof that we are man and wife and that the marriage is real," said Nash, dipping Kellina down and kissing her. The passionate kiss in front of everyone lingered so long that she actually felt herself becoming excited by it.

Then Alice's words rang out in Kellina's mind, and everything changed. She decided she didn't like Nash making a display of her. She didn't appreciate him speaking for her either. It infuriated her that Nash even thought to put her in this position.

Men shouted out a few things that weren't respectable, and some of them whistled and clapped, apparently enjoying the show.

When Nash pulled her back up and broke the kiss, Kellina decided to slap him. But when she raised her hand up, Nash quickly grabbed it, kissing it, trailing more kisses all the way down her arm.

"All right, that's enough," said Ciaran, waving a hand through the air. "Save some of it for the marriage bed later."

"Marriage bed?" asked Kellina, her heart jumping into her throat. "Uncle, we already did that, so why would we be in the marriage bed again tonight?"

"Since the roofs of most of our huts are still open to the elements, I'm afraid half the clan will be sleepin' in the infirmary until ye finish repairin' all the thatch," stated her uncle.

"Well, what does that have to do with the marriage bed? And me?" she asked, not understanding. That box bed in the infirmary was only used once by newly married couples. After that, they slept on pallets on the ground, surrounded by all the others of the clan.

"Ye two have just become wed," her uncle reminded her. "Ye'll sleep in the marriage bed until the rest of the roofs are repaired. After that, ye and Nash can decide what kind of cottage to build for yerselves and the family ye'll have soon."

"Thank ye for the offer of the new cottage, but that's no' necessary, Chieftain," said Nash. "Ye see, we'll be livin' with the MacKeefes as soon as I finish my punishment." Nash spoke up, never having talked this over with Kellina. Then again, since they weren't really married, the conversation had never come up between them in the first place.

"Nay! I canna sleep in the marriage bed again," Kellina protested, not wanting to sleep with Nash. It would only remind her of the deception that went on in that bed last night. It was an act that she now regretted wholeheartedly.

"Why no'?" asked her uncle. "If ye have a reason, I'd like to ken it."

"She means, she canna sleep there, because the marriage bed is broken, my laird," Nash said before she could even answer. "However, I promise to fix it at once since it was all my fault. It will be repaired by bedtime, I assure ye."

"Guid," said the chieftain. "Ye two will want to start makin' bairns right away, I suppose."

"Aye, of course," said Nash, pulling Kellina closer. "Isna that right, Wife?"

She grimaced, but looked up at him, knowing she had to answer. "Aye," she said softly, using all her will just to push the word from her mouth.

"Say it so everyone can hear ye, my dear." Nash was goading her and she didn't like it. "Tell them all how eager ye are to make bairns and raise a family with me."

If he kept up this nonsense, she swore she was going to belt him in front of everyone and not regret it for one second.

"I could never express what I really feel in my heart, Husband," she said, flashing him a smile to tell him she'd won this round.

"Reid, it's safe. Ye can come out now." Aidan MacKeefe sheathed his sword and opened the large leather pouch hanging at his side. His squirrel poked his head out, looking around and sniffing the air as if he were searching for trouble before he left the safety of Aidan's pouch.

"Put away yer swords, men," ordered Tomas, since he was second in charge after the chieftain. Everyone grumbled, but did as they were told. Then they started talking amongst themselves, and heading to the table to get food and ale.

"Aidan, did ye bring Lady Spring back with ye like I asked?" The chieftain scanned the room.

"I am here," said a woman at the back of the crowd. She'd been so quiet that Kellina hadn't even seen her standing there.

"Come. Meet Kellina, Lady Spring." The chieftain smiled and held out his arm, inviting the wife of Shaw Gordon over. Kellina knew of the woman, but had never met her personally.

"Please, just call me Spring," said the tall, blond woman, making her way forward as the crowd passed and let her through. Her blond hair was in a long braid, trailing down her back. She wore a long tunic with tight breeches that looked like long stockings underneath. Thrown over her shoulder, she carried a bow and a quiver of arrows. Kellina immediately liked her. "Hello," said Spring. "Ye must be Kellina."

"I am," Kellina said with a nod. "Why are ye here?" she asked directly, thinking it odd the woman should show up without her husband, and especially now, of all times. While they weren't enemies with the Gordons, they had never formed an alliance either.

"Yer faither asked me to come talk with ye," said Spring.

"My uncle," she corrected the woman. "And I dinna understand. Uncle, why did ye ask her here? I told ye, I have plenty of lassies to talk to right here in our own clan."

"I kent ye are havin' a hard time with the quick marriage," said the chieftain. "Kellina, I ken ye still hold revenge for the MacKeefes in yer heart. I thought Spring could talk with ye since she was once an enemy of her husband, too."

"Ye were?" asked Kellina.

"Aye," said Spring. "It is a long story, but I once wanted to kill my husband, Shaw. The last thing I wanted was to marry him."

"I see. Well then, I guess we do have somethin' in common after all." Kellina looked over to Nash, who quickly excused himself.

"I think I'll head over to the infirmary to fix the marriage bed," said Nash, looking very uncomfortable.

"I'll help him," said North, seeming more than anxious to get away from there.

"I'll start a fire to warm the infirmary since some of the clan will be sleepin' there tonight," offered Aidan, placing his squirrel on his shoulder as all three of the MacKeefes left.

"I'll let ye two talk then," said Ciaran, hobbling away, leaving Spring and Kellina alone.

"It sounds like the rain stopped." Spring looked up at the roof. "Do ye want to take a little walk and talk?"

"I'd like that," said Kellina, leading the way. Mayhap now that Lady Spring was here, someone would understand exactly what Kellina was going through. After all, she looked like a warrior the way she dressed and carried a bow and arrows on her back. This was the first time in forever that Kellina felt someone would really understand all the chaotic thoughts crowding her head. Especially where Nash MacKeefe was concerned.

CHAPTER TEN

"I DINNA UNDERSTAND why ye are even botherin' to fix this marriage bed when we both ken that ye dinna need it," said North, pulling one of the ropes tightly and tying a knot, preparing it to hold up the mattress.

"Shhh," said Nash, glancing over to Aidan who was fixing a fire in the infirmary, right near the hole in the eaves where the smoke would be able to escape. "I dinna want Aidan to ken that Kellina and I never consummated the marriage. He'll go back and tell the rest of the clan."

Nash used a hammer and nails to straighten the spindle of the box bed that held up the curtain.

"Brathair, ye need to bed the wench, and ye need to do it quickly," North warned him. "If word gets out, it might cause a battle between our clans. If I must remind ye, the reason ye were betrothed to Kellina in the first place was to form an alliance to keep that from happenin'."

"I ken all that!" Nash spotted Aidan's squirrel atop the box bed, and waved his hand in the air. "Shoo. Get out of here, ye dirty rodent."

"Call my pet a rodent again, and ye'll have to answer to me," came Aidan's warning from across the room. He kept his head down, making the fire. Nash hoped that Aidan hadn't heard his conversation with his brother.

"Sorry about that, Reid," said Nash loudly, calling the squirrel by name so Aidan was sure to hear him. Aidan was very protective over his pet. "Notice how he never complained that I called the squirrel dirty?" Nash said in not much more than a whisper to his brother.

"He may be dirty, but it's because he doesna like the rain," Aidan called back, once again, not looking up at all.

"Damn, he's got guid ears," mumbled North, his hands stilling as he eyed Aidan across the room. "Do ye think . . . he heard us?"

"It doesna matter." Nash lifted up the mattress and North helped him to put it atop the bed ropes. "I have decided to take yer advice, Brathair."

"What advice would that be?" North brushed the dirt off his hands.

"Kellina is my wife now. Even if she doesna agree with it, she is goin' to have to start doin' her . . . wifely duties."

"Now ye're talkin'," said North with a smile. "How do ye intend to get her to do it? After all, now she has no need for ye, if ye ken what I mean. Mayhap ye were too guid of a teacher, Nash."

"I suppose I should have thought of that sooner," said Nash, regretting showing Kellina how to pleasure herself. "I'll get her to change her mind about me. Dinna ye worry."

"The wench is tryin' to kill us, or have ye forgotten? And now she has the sister of the Legendary Bastards givin' her advice. This canna end well for us. I think ye're forgettin' that Spring was raised by the Gunn Clan and has been trained to be a killer since she was a child. No' at all the person to be givin' Kellina advice, if ye ask me." North took it upon himself to tell Nash what to do, and Nash didn't like that.

"I didna ask ye."

"I canna believe she's been called here," said North. "I think the chieftain has lost his mind."

"Laird MacKenzie kens how Spring changed," Nash heard from a voice across the room. "I believe he is hopin' that Spring will convince Kellina to like ye, Nash." Aidan came over to join them. He reached up, and his squirrel jumped from the top of the box bed, running down his arm. His pet hid inside his sash. "Mayhap, she'll even convince Kellina to consummate the marriage before yer foolish actions bring about consequences that will keep ye an outcast forever."

"Losh me! Ye heard." Nash felt a sinking sensation in his gut.

"I did. However, I didna have to hear yer conversation to ken the truth," said Aidan.

"What do ye mean? Are ye sayin' ye kent they never consummated the marriage?" asked North. "How could ye ken that?"

"I think ye are both forgettin' that before I married my angel, Effie MacDuff, she betrayed me. Any woman who has somethin' to hide, has a certain look about her. Kellina has it."

"Did ye notice that look on Effie before or after she stole the Stone of Destiny out from under yer arse?" asked Nash in spite, wanting to make his point.

"All right. So I didna ken it at the time, but hindsight is a guid teacher. Lookin' back, all the signs were there. I just was too infatuated with the lass to notice."

"Then ye agree that Kellina is tryin' to kill us?" asked North.

"I wouldna say that, but I can tell she is confused. If she wanted to kill ye, Nash, I'm sure ye'd already be dead."

"If ye're sayin' I'm a bad warrior, then how about I show ye my skill with my blade right now?" Nash reached for his dagger, holding it up for Aidan to see.

"Put it away," scoffed Aidan. "I'm tryin' to help ye understand lassies, no' challenge ye to a fight to prove yer worth. We're on the same team, remember?"

"Sorry. Ye're right," said Nash, running a hand through his long hair and sheathing his blade. "I guess I'm just fed up with Old Callum makin' us be a part of all these punishments to begin with. I still canna believe he ordered me to marry a lass who I didna even ken. Especially, our enemy."

"Ye might think Callum is a crazed fool, but he is probably

the wisest man in the clan," said Aidan with respect.

"How so?" asked North.

"Well, he brings our clan wealth with all the sales of his Mountain Magic."

"Anyone can brew whisky," spat Nash, swiping his hand through the air. "How does that make him wise?"

"He keeps himself alive, and valuable to the clan by not revealing his secret recipe," Aidan continued. "He also is smart enough to be the proprietor of a tavern where Highlanders, Lowlanders, and even the English go to drink."

"So, he's a guid businessman," said Nash. "Who cares? I dinna see what any of this has to do with me."

"Really?" Aidan chuckled. "Ye boys ken that his son, Ian, has been ill lately, right?"

"Aye. What's wrong with him?" asked Nash.

"No one really kens. Or at least that's the way Callum wants it to be." Aidan's squirrel peeked out from under his sash and Aidan ran a finger over its head.

"Why would he want to keep it a secret?" asked Nash.

Aidan shrugged. "I canna answer that, since Callum is a complicated old coot. However, he was wise enough to trap ye boys and yer friends into doin' his biddin'."

"Nay, that's no' true. We broke his silly rules," said North. "The only thing Callum is doin' is makin' us earn our ways back into the clan."

"That's right," said Nash. "We dinna want to be outcasts any longer."

Aidan snorted. "And ye dinna think the whole thing is a little absurd?"

"Well, aye," said Nash. "But we dinna have a choice. We have to do what Callum wants or we'll be outcasts forever."

"Mayhap." Aidan held the squirrel in the crook of his arm. "Then again, I must admit that Old Callum has wanted Ian to make an alliance with the MacKenzies since the battle happened twelve years ago. He's also been sayin' that we need our own cordwainer in the clan."

"Gavin and Davita," mumbled North. "But how could he ken they'd get married?"

"Who really has that answer?" asked Aidan. "All I'm sayin' is that Callum is gettin' everythin' he wants one way or another."

"If so, what about Cam and his punishment?" asked North. "Did Callum want a chandler in the clan, too? I hardly think he planned that. After all, Yvaine showed up at the last minute with news of her husband dyin'."

"Nay. There is no way the old man could have kent that Yvaine was goin' to show up right as he was about to hand out Cam's punishment," said Nash.

"Perhaps I'm wrong then," said Aidan with a shrug. "It is just my humble opinion."

"What caused that battle between our parents and Kellina's parents in the first place?" asked North. "We were only twelve at the time, and I dinna remember much about it."

"Neither do I," said Nash. "I asked our chieftains about it several times while growing up, but they never seemed to give me an answer."

"Or mayhap they really didna ken, either," added North.

"Whatever it was that started that battle, the real reason was kept a secret from the clans for a guid reason," explained Aidan. "I think someone kens the real reason for their deaths, and has a purpose for never divulgin' it."

"Supposedly, no one who was there lived," said North.

"We were told that Lord Ciaran stumbled upon them and hauled all their dead bodies home."

"Well, then mayhap he is the one to ask about it," said Aidan.

"Whatever the reason, I hope Kellina will figure out soon that the MacKeefes are no' her enemies." Nash really meant this, even though he felt sorry for the girl. "Mayhap then, she can stop blamin' the rest of us for what happened to her parents twelve years ago."

KELLINA WALKED UP the hill to the MacKenzies' graveyard, just as the sun was starting to set on the horizon.

"This is where we buried the dead from the battle," Kellina told Spring, blessing herself as she looked out at the grave markers. "The chieftain's wife and daughters are buried here, too."

"I see," Spring answered. "Deaths in a battle are never easy to accept. Especially if the ones to die were lassies who were probably unarmed and unable to even protect themselves."

"I miss my aunt and cousins." Kellina felt tears form in her eyes as she stared down at the ground. "I still miss my parents, as well, even though I was verra young and dinna remember them much at all."

"It's never easy," remarked Spring.

"Have ye seen yer share of death?" asked Kellina, admiring Spring for her strength.

"I have." Spring kept her face stonelike and nodded slightly. "This bow and arrows I use came from a dead Scot on the battlefield durin' Burnt Candlemas. I was only a wee lass at the time, and I will never forget it."

"I learned to wield the sword as a child," said Kellina. "It was right after the MacKeefes killed my parents. I swore at seven years old I would someday make them pay for what they did. I still stand by it, too. They need to be responsible for their actions."

"Do ye really feel that way?" Spring's brows dipped. "Even though ye're married to a MacKeefe now and have an alliance with them?"

"Aye. Especially since I had to marry one of them."

"Oh, I understand it all now." Spring nodded and looked out over at the setting sun.

"What do ye understand?" asked Kellina. "My hatred for the

MacKeefes?"

"Nay. I'm talkin' about the fact that ye never consummated yer marriage."

"What?" Kellina's heart jumped into her throat. "Of course, I consummated the marriage. I mean . . . Nash is my husband, and then there's the alliance and all. Why would ye even think I havena?"

Spring turned and looked directly at her. "Ye may be able to fool yer uncle and the rest of the men, but no' me, Kellina. I'm a woman and can see right through ye."

"Losh me! How did ye ken?" Kellina felt scared but impressed at the same time. This woman almost seemed to be able to read her mind. "I havena told a soul. Did ye hear it from Nash? I swear, I'll kill him for sayin' somethin'."

"Stop it." Spring took Kellina's arm, still staring into her eyes. "I kent ye never coupled with Nash, because if ye did, I dinna think ye'd still want to kill him."

"Why no'?" she asked. "Just because I'm married to a MacKeefe, it doesna change the way I feel about him."

"Even the hardest and strongest of warriors often have a change of heart once love is shared between two people."

"What are ye sayin'? I dinna love Nash!" She shook out of Spring's hold.

"Are ye sayin' ye have no feelin's for him at all? Be honest with yerself. After all, he seems like a guid man."

"I was forced to marry him against my will!" Kellina felt her anger growing. "Just because my uncle wants the alliance, doesna mean I do."

"Perhaps yer uncle sees things differently than ye do about the MacKeefes. After all, if he really thought they were bad or untrustworthy, I dinna think he'd even suggest the alliance in the first place. Would he?"

"Ye were married off to yer husband for an alliance. Did either one of yer clans really trust each other?"

"Nay. I canna say we did," she admitted. "But it didna take

me long being with Shaw to see that the Gunn Clan was wrong about the Gordons. Mayhap this is the same situation, in a way, between the MacKenzies and the MacKeefes."

"My uncle is injured and weak," Kellina told her. "He's lost his wife and daughters and he isna thinkin' with a right mind. He has lost all hope, and canna lead the clan any longer. That's what this is all about."

"Do ye really believe that? Because those are harsh and disrespectful words about yer clan's chieftain."

"What I believe is that the MacKeefes need to be punished for what they did. No alliance with them – forced or otherwise – is ever goin' to make me think differently."

"I'm no' so sure yer uncle is wrong, Kellina. Have ye spoken to him about his reasons for makin' the alliance in the first place?"

"I ken his reason. He's scared! He's lost his wife and daughters to the Sutherlands, and couldna protect them. He kens he is a weak laird and will lose the entire clan next."

"I think yer hatred has blinded ye, Kellina. Even to those around ye who love ye."

"What do ye mean?"

"I'm sure yer uncle has his reasons for the decisions he makes. Ye need to trust and support him. No' just because he's yer chieftain, but because ye share the same bluid. He is yer family."

"Nay, that's no' true. He is no' my real uncle. We just call him that since he raised us. We dinna share the same bluid. Besides, the whole clan is a family no matter if they share bluid or no'."

"True. And that is why support by all the clansmembers is really what makes a clan strong. Once they are divided, they will fall fast. Trust me, I ken."

"My uncle has no guid reasons, believe me. Ye dinna see him makin' an alliance with the Sutherlands, do ye? And he willna. No' ever. No' when they killed his wife and daughters. That is how I feel about the MacKeefes killin' my parents."

"All I am askin' is for ye to give Nash a chance," said Spring.

"Get to ken him first, before ye judge him. Sometimes when ye push aside yer criticism, or expectations, things look different in a whole new light."

"Is that the way it was for ye and Shaw? Did ye end up seein' yer enemy in a new light?"

"It was exactly that way," said Spring. "I despised him and wanted nothin' to do with him, until I saw what lay beneath his tough façade. I got to ken him as well as the three children he has from his late wife. Before long, I started thinkin' of them as my family instead of the Gunn Clan where I was raised. That is, even though the Gunns, I found out, werena my real family at all. I hated Shaw at first, as much as ye hate Nash."

"I dinna hate Nash. No' really," said Kellina, biting her lip and looking at the ground. She couldn't help thinking of how he'd never pushed himself on her even though they were married. His kisses were gentle, and he was trying so hard to learn the skill of thatching that her heart went out to him every time he used the wrong name for a tool. Sometimes, he even seemed . . . adorable, in a way.

"Guid. That's a start," said Spring.

"Did couplin' with Shaw make ye fall in love with him?" Kellina asked curiously.

"Nay. No' couplin', but makin' love. There is a difference between the two, ye ken."

"There is? I didna ken that. What is the difference? I dinna understand."

Spring put her hand to her mouth in thought, as if she were trying to think of how to explain this to Kellina. "I suppose the way to explain it is that one is a physical action only. The other is no' only physical, but emotional, mental, and, at times, a little spiritual, too."

This all seemed too much for Kellina. She didn't think she could ever couple with Nash and have it feel all of the ways that Spring had just mentioned. Nay, she decided. Neither did she really want it to.

"I dinna care why my uncle really brought ye here, it was all for naught," she said stubbornly. "I will never be in love with Nash MacKeefe and feel all those ways ye've just described. It just willna happen."

"Since ye seem to feel my visit was a waste of time, then I suppose there is no reason for me to stay." Spring turned and started to walk down the hill.

"Wait. Ye're leavin'?" Kellina ran after her, not wanting Spring to go. She liked having another woman to talk to about what she was going through. Spring was in the same position as her, and although Kellina didn't welcome it, she truly did need her advice. "Please, dinna go yet. I like talkin' with ye. I have no other women to speak to about these things I'm feelin' inside. Especially where Nash is concerned."

Spring stopped and turned back to Kellina. "What about yer sister?" she asked. "She is a woman. Talk to her."

"Caitlin?" Kellina blew air from her mouth. "Nay. She's just a child. I could never talk to her about these things the way I do with ye."

"A child?" Spring raised one brow. "How old is she?"

"She's six and ten. Actually, she'll be seven and ten tomorrow, as it is her birthday."

Now it was Spring's turn to blow a puff of air from her mouth. "Blethers, she is an adult, no' a child, Kellina. She is also yer sister. Ye need to confide in her – no' me."

"I dinna think I can do that."

"I have three sisters that I never realized even existed for many years," Spring told her. "But now that I do, I only wish I would have grown up with them and been able to share things like this with them, too. Ye have been given a gift, Kellina. Do no' overlook the things or people who are the true treasures in yer life. If ye do, ye'll regret it for as long as ye live."

"I – I'll try," Kellina answered, taking Spring's advice to heart even though she wasn't sure she agreed with it wholeheartedly. "However, it might take a while before I can talk to my sister about the things we just discussed. Ye see, I need someone to do that with now. I canna wait."

"Then confide in yer husband," were Spring's words of wisdom. They also were not what Kellina wanted to hear.

"I'm no' sure I can do that either."

"Do ye even ken how Nash feels about ye?" asked Spring. "Did ye ask him?"

"I dinna need to," Kellina answered. "I think the fact that he wouldna touch me on our weddin' night answers that!"

"Tell me, what was his reasonin' for no' touchin' ye?"

"What do ye mean? It was because he didna find me attractive or desirable."

"I canna believe that. Is that what he said?"

"Well . . . nay. No' exactly," said Kellina, thinking back on what had really transpired in the wedding bed. "He said he had never forced himself on a lassie who didna want him, and that he wouldna do it to me, even if I was his wife."

"And that doesna sound honorable and respectful to ye?" she asked.

"I suppose it does."

"It sounds to me that he cares for ye and yer wishes too much to make ye do somethin' ye didna want to do."

"I didna want to marry him, and yet I had to do it."

"That was yer uncle's choice, but was it Nash's as well?"

"I . . . guess no'," Kellina answered, starting to think about this more. "I dinna believe he wanted to marry me either."

"Ye are bein' selfish, Kellina. Think about how Nash feels, too. Before ye dismiss him as yer husband, get to ken him a little. Find out exactly what is in his heart."

"I – I suppose I could do that," she said, starting to almost feel bad for Nash now. She'd been so angry with him that she didn't take the time to think that he was in this situation, too, and feeling the same way.

"Ye have the people around ye that ye need, as much as they need ye. Ye are too blind to see it, and I'm afraid I canna do anythin' to change that. I'll stay until the mornin', but only to help yer clan hunt for food. I'll be headin' back to Clan Gordon at first light."

"But it's too late to hunt now," Kellina told her, hoping to find an excuse to talk with Spring some more, and to keep her from leaving. "It's already gettin' dark. We'll never be able to catch a thing until first light. Mayhap we should try then instead."

"Have faith," said Spring with a smile. She pulled an arrow from the quiver on her back and nocked it. Then she spun on her heel and let the arrow fly. "Let's go see what we caught, shall we?" She headed away and Kellina followed.

"Ye couldna have possibly caught anythin'. It is nearly dark and –"

"Here, take this," said Spring, picking up a dead rabbit, retrieving her arrow, and handing the animal by the ears to Kellina.

"That's amazin'," said Kellina in awe, holding the rabbit, inspecting Spring's clean kill. "How did ye –" She stopped in midsentence when Spring released another arrow, and a bird fell from the sky to the ground at their feet.

"Is that a . . . grouse?" Kellina asked in amazement, bending down to see it clearly. "Ye just shot a grouse out of the darkening sky that I didna even ken was there."

"Shhh," said Spring, cocking her ear and listening. She turned her head and looked over the hill to a small cluster of brush. "There is a red deer over there that must have gotten separated from the others. I will hunt that next. It willna be hard to take it down. Deliver the kills back to camp and in five minutes, send a few of the men over to help me carry the deer carcass."

"Ye are amazin'," said Kellina, smiling from ear to ear. "Our clan will eat well tonight because of ye."

"I used to be the hunter of the Gunn Clan," explained Spring. "Since I married Shaw, he likes to do most of the huntin' so I enjoy havin' this chance once again."

"Thank ye," said Kellina, picking up the grouse in her free hand, watching Spring dash away. The woman was so brave, so skilled, and so strong. If she could marry her enemy and end up being in love with the man, then mayhap Kellina could do the same.

Kellina turned and headed down the hill, wondering what it would be like to actually make love with Nash. Or, at this point, even just to couple.

CHAPTER ELEVEN

"WE OWE THIS sumptuous feast to Lady Spring Gordon and her bow and arrows," announced Ciaran, raising his hands in the air to get everyone's attention before the meal began. It was already night, but it had taken a while to clean the food and cook it. Still, it didn't matter. Everyone was just happy to have a good meal, no matter how late it was.

"I'm so hungry, I could eat it all myself," said North, being greedy and reaching out for some food before it was offered. Nash slapped his brother's hand away.

"Och, what did ye do that for?" complained North.

"The chieftain and the lassies are first." Nash held out the platter to the chieftain across the table, who took some food and gave it back.

"Lady Spring?" Nash held the food out to her. Spring sat next to him on one side and North on the other. Kellina was across the table, next to her uncle.

"Give yer wife first choice," said Spring, turning to talk to someone else at the table.

"Of course." Nash held the platter for Kellina. "What would ye like, Wife? There is plenty of catch here for ye to choose from."

"I'd like ye to stop callin' me Wife and start usin' my name is what I'd like." Kellina scooped a little food onto her plate.

Nash looked down to the tiny bit of food and shook his head.

"Lady Spring has graced us with enough food that ye dinna need to be modest. There is more than enough for everyone. Have some more," he said, but Kellina shook her head and looked the other way.

"Tomorrow, I will hunt for the clan and bring just as much food to the table as our guest," she said softly.

"I see. Ye are jealous," replied Nash, still holding out the platter. "Does Lady Spring's skill with huntin' upset ye that much, lass?"

"I am no' jealous, and I dinna want more food!"

North kept trying to reach around Nash to get his share, but each time his hand came near, Nash moved the platter away from him.

"Everyone has their skill and place in the clan," Nash explained. "Lady Spring's place is no' only as wife of Laird Gordon and mathair to his children, but also as a hunter of the clan. It's what she's guid at. Ye, however, Kellina are a thatcher. Ye dinna have to feel inferior because of it. The skill is an admirable one."

Her head snapped up and she scowled at him. "I dinna feel inferior."

"I'm feelin' a little inferior right now," said North over Nash's shoulder. "I'll take some of that if ye dinna mind." Once more, North reached out for the food. Nash turned his back to his brother and continued to talk to his wife.

"Kellina, now that we're married, I'll hunt for food. Ye dinna need to do it, or feel like ye have to. It's no' yer job."

"Well, then what is my job besides thatchin' roofs?" she demanded to know. "Is it just sittin' around and waitin' for my husband to take care of me? Because if so, I dinna like that."

"How about cookin'?" mumbled North from behind Nash. "Can ye cook at all? I hope so. If ye can do that, then at least the rest of us might get a chance to have some food at a meal."

"Sorry, Brathair." Nash took some meat for himself and then handed the platter to his brother.

"I dinna need a man to do anythin' for me." Kellina took a

bite of food and smiled wickedly at him.

"Aye, I suppose no'," he mumbled, thinking of what other skills he'd taught her lately. Skills in the bedchamber that didn't include him.

Nash turned to North and spoke in a soft voice, keeping his back to Kellina. "I think I must have done somethin' to make her angry, but I'm no' sure what. Tell me, what should I say or do?"

"Why dinna ye show her how much she really needs ye after all," said Spring softly, standing right behind him. Nash hadn't even known the woman had left her seat and come up behind him. "Do what ye ken needs to be done. Give her a reason to want ye near her. Dinna give up so easily, Nash." Spring stabbed her knife into a hunk of venison on the platter and plopped it onto the plate in her hand.

"It sounds to me as if my wife has been possibly spillin' some family secrets." Nash took a bite of the meat and chewed, glaring at Kellina from across the table. There was no doubt in his mind now that Kellina had told Spring they'd never consummated the marriage.

"Sometimes, a newly married couple just needs to relax and spend a little time away from the rest of the clan," Spring continued.

"Hah!" Nash stabbed his eating knife into a hunk of venison and sawed. "That's never goin' to happen. I'm forced to stay here at the MacKenzie camp until my punishment is over. I canna be accepted back into the clan before then."

"Try bein' accepted back into the bedchamber first." Spring grinned and sat back down next to him. "Laird MacKenzie, I'll be leavin' in the mornin'," Spring told the chieftain.

"Thank ye for all ye've done, Lady Spring," answered the chieftain.

"Please. Just call me Spring."

"But arena ye a lady?" asked North. "I thought ye are a sister of the Legendary Bastards of the Crown. After all, their faither is the king."

"I am a lady, but I prefer no' to use my title," Spring answered. "Actually, I am really a cousin of the Legendary Bastards, but we grew up like siblin's."

"Och, I see," answered North, reaching for more food.

"I noticed that ye need more thatch or ye'll never finish all the roofs that need to be repaired," Spring told the chieftain.

"We'll have to fetch water reeds, since most of our extra thatch was burned by the Sutherlands," Kellina told her. "But we'll have what we need eventually, so dinna worry."

"Kellina, willna water reeds need time to dry before we can use them on the roofs?" asked Nash.

"He's right," said Spring. "That will take too long. However, I have a solution."

"What would that be? Please, tell us," replied Ciaran.

"Back at Edinvale Castle, we have a whole barn filled with dried thatch that we arena usin'. I am sure my husband willna mind lettin' ye have it."

"We canna pay for it, I'm afraid." The chieftain seemed disheartened.

"Ye dinna have to. It is a gift," said Spring.

"We dinna need yer gifts," said Kellina, her pride showing in her words. "Thank ye, but we can rebuild our camp on our own."

"There's no need for pride durin' a time of need," Spring answered.

"Nay, Kellina is right," agreed the chieftain. "It is a fine offer, but I wouldna feel right by acceptin' it."

"Then we'll do a trade instead," suggested Spring. "Surely, ye should have no qualms about that."

"Trade?" asked the chieftain. "We've had almost everythin' stolen from us by those bluidy Sutherlands. What they didna steal, they burned. I'm afraid we have nothin' to offer."

"That's no' true," said Spring. "Ye have skills that my clan could use right now."

"Skills?" asked Kellina. "What skills could we possibly have that ye dinna already possess on yer own?"

"I hear Kellina is the best thatcher there ever was," Spring told the chieftain. "I have been tryin' to convince my husband to rethatch the roofs on the mews and kennels, but he doesna seem to think they need it. If Kellina can provide that service for us, then ye can have the thatch in trade to finish yer cottages. How does that sound?"

"Ye want me to come to yer castle?" asked Kellina in surprise. "But we arena even allies."

"Neither are we enemies," said Spring. "Actually, when I return I had already planned on talking to Shaw about alignin' with yer clan."

"Losh me, that is a kind offer," said the chieftain.

"But we canna accept it," intervened Kellina.

"On the contrary, I think we can," answered Kellina's uncle. "Lady Spring, I will put together a travelin' party to send back with ye and Kellina for protection. They'll be ready to go at first light."

"Uncle!" gasped Kellina. "Ye'd really send me away right now? How could ye?"

"I think it is a great idea," said Nash, trying to support Kellina. "After all, Kellina kens more than anyone about thatchin' a roof. I think it sounds like a fair trade indeed."

"Ye canna wait to get rid of me, can ye?" Kellina asked Nash.

"Well . . . no," said Nash, looking over to his brother for help. "I just meant . . ."

"I ken what ye meant." Kellina held her chin high. "Well, I would be happy to go, Spring. After all, I could use a change of my surroundin's."

"I'll summon Tomas to put together a few men for the journey." The laird raised his hand to call over Tomas, but Spring stopped him.

"There's no need to bother Tomas since he's just returned," she told him. "Why dinna ye send Nash instead? He can help on the roofs as well, since I hear he kens how to thatch a roof now."

"Nay, we dinna need him," said Kellina, but her uncle didn't agree.

"I think that's a grand idea. However, I would feel better if ye took at least one more man with ye."

"North will come with us," Nash said quickly before the laird thought to send Tomas again. Nash wasn't a favorite with the clansmen and he wouldn't enjoy having Tomas along. He also wasn't happy about the idea of leaving his brother behind.

"All right then. It's settled. North will go as well," said Laird Ciaran with a satisfied smile.

"Me? What?" North stopped chewing and looked up with a defeated look on his face.

"Dinna act like it's a bad thing, Brathair," Nash told him. "After all, with the way Spring can hunt, I'm sure the Gordon Clan has more food than even ye can eat."

A smiled spread across North's face. "I'd be happy to go along to visit the Gordon Clan. After all, I canna leave my brathair in his time of need."

When Nash looked back up at Kellina, she was no longer sitting at the table. He never thought having a wife was going to be so much trouble. He would have to use this trip as a way to get Kellina to like him, and to accept him as her husband. Hopefully, he could convince her to consummate the marriage as well. The alliance between two clans depended on it now, and it couldn't wait any longer.

CHAPTER TWELVE

"I DINNA KEN about this idea," said Ciaran the next morning as Kellina and the others were preparing to leave.

Kellina had insisted on her sister going with them. After spending the night in the same bed with Nash again, and both of them facing opposite directions, not touching and not talking, things only seemed to be getting worse between them. That was why Kellina decided she needed her sister along for a welcome distraction.

"I don't see the problem, Uncle," said Kellina.

"Well, I think Caitlin needs to stay here," he told her.

"Either my sister comes with me, or I dinna go," said Kellina, demanding her terms. She didn't want to feel alone at Edinvale Castle and needed someone she could talk to. Spring had been acting more like a mother to her than a friend, and what she really needed was someone who could understand how she felt. Perhaps, as Spring had suggested, she'd start confiding in Caitlin and trusting more in her sister. "After all, today is Caitlin's birthday, and this will be a guid present for her. Dinna ye agree, Sister?"

"Aye, I want to go to the Gordons' castle with ye," said Caitlin with excitement. "I would love to meet Lady Spring's family and see where she lives. Can I go, Faither, please?" she begged the chieftain.

"Uncle, no' Faither," Kellina mumbled to herself.

"I want to go, too," chimed in Kellina's little brother, Jamie. "Please let me go with them, Da."

Hearing what her siblings called Ciaran sickened Kellina. She didn't like it one bit. "He's our uncle, no' our da," Kellina tried to remind them, but to no avail. They usually called him uncle, but when they got excited, they slipped back into calling him Da again. Ciaran was the only father her siblings ever really knew. It was obvious Kellina was never going to change things where this was concerned.

"Jamie, ye will stay here, but Caitlin can go," said the laird.

"Oh, thank ye," cried Caitlin, giving the laird a big hug. Jamie pouted, then turned and ran off.

"The wagon is ready," said North, bringing around the horse-drawn cart, as well as his horse with him. In the back of the wagon were some travel bags with their things. They also brought with them the tools that would be needed for thatching. Hay lined the wagon, to keep everything from banging about.

"Caitlin, ye'd better get yer things together, so ye willna slow them down," suggested the chieftain.

"Too late," said Caitlin with a giggle. "I already have my things loaded. I was hopin' ye were goin' to decide to let me go." Caitlin ran over and climbed up to the seat of the wagon.

Spring and North mounted their horses as the party prepared to leave.

"I'll drive the wagon," offered Nash. The wagon would be used to bring back a load of thatch that they'd use on the roofs later. It would be a full load, and possibly not easy to handle.

"I'll ride with my sister, and ye can use a horse instead." Kellina pushed past him and climbed atop the bench seat, settling herself next to Caitlin.

"Reid, get back here." Aidan MacKeefe ran up to the back of the wagon, collecting his squirrel that had scurried into it. "I'm sorry I'm headin' back to the MacKeefe camp today. I'd like to see what happens when ye unload all these . . . interestin' things."

"What do ye mean?" asked Kellina. "We are hardly bringin'

anythin' with us."

"It might be more than ye ken." Aidan chuckled, holding his squirrel in two hands, backing away. Kellina didn't know why he was acting so odd, and neither did she care. All she wanted was to get on the road so she could arrive at the Gordon Clan and get her chore taken care of quickly.

"Are ye sure ye can handle that wagon?" asked Nash.

"Better than ye can, I'm sure. Hold on, Caitlin. We're goin' to lead the way." Kellina slapped the reins and the horse took off, pulling the wagon at a good clip.

"WAIT, KELLINA," YELLED Nash, quickly mounting his horse. "The fool wench is goin' to get herself killed. North, ye take the lead and watch the road as well as the tree line. I dinna want to meet up with any trouble."

"Nay. I'll take the lead," said Spring from atop her horse. "I ken the area leadin' to the Gordons better than anyone. It will only take a few hours to get there. I will show ye which trails are the safest."

"All right. I'll take the back door then," said Nash.

"Why dinna ye ride next to the wagon and try to mend things with yer wife?" Spring suggested. "After all, I didna convince the laird to let ye two come on this journey for nothin'. Ye ken what ye have to do, Nash." With that, Spring took off atop her horse, leading the way to her castle.

"She kens, doesna she?" asked North as he and Nash rode their horses, trying to catch up with the women.

"I'm startin' to get the feelin' that everyone kens we didna consummate the marriage, North."

"So, that's what Spring was talkin' about when she said ye ken what ye have to do?"

"I guess so. And she's right," agreed Nash, looking up at the wagon that was bumping one way and then the other as Kellina continued to drive the cart too fast over the rugged terrain. "I will no' have another night like the last. I canna sleep next to her without touchin' her again."

Nash rode up to the side of the wagon, wondering what he could say to smooth things over between them. He finally decided that mayhap he'd better give Kellina some time, therefore, he said nothing at all.

After riding for an hour with barely any conversation at all, Nash decided he'd talk to Caitlin first, easing into a conversation with his wife.

"Happy birthday, Caitlin," he said, riding up closer to the side of the wagon.

"Thank ye, Nash. That is kind of ye to say that. Did ye ken that I am seven and ten years of age now, and a fully fledged woman?" Caitlin's face beamed with pride.

"Well, nay, that's no' all true," he told her. "Ye're no' a fully fledged woman until ye . . . until ye . . ."

"Until I what?" she asked in a naïve manner. Nash had no doubt that Kellina's sister was a virgin just like Kellina was.

"Until ye get married," said Nash, not wanting to come out and say what he meant. If so, he was sure there would be trouble.

Kellina looked over and scowled at him like he knew she would. By now, Nash realized that whatever he said, she'd frown at him and never smile. Mayhap it was no use even trying anymore.

"Nash is talkin' about couplin', no' bein' married," she told her sister. "Most men dinna think a woman is worth a thing unless they've coupled with a man first."

"Nay, that is no' what I said, and that is no' true," protested Nash. "I didna mean it like that at all."

"Ye dinna sound verra convincin', Nash." Kellina was up to her cat and mouse game again, and he was tiring of it.

"Kellina, I dinna want to fight with ye. Please. We need to get along. God's eyes, ye are my wife!"

"Am I?" Her words were crude, cold, and careless.

"Of course, ye are, Sister," said Caitlin, coming to Nash's rescue. "Ye two are married now. It is so excitin'. I canna wait until I get married, too."

"She means she canna wait until she can get naked with a man." Jamie popped his head up from under the hay in the wagon, laughing.

"Aaaaah!" Caitlin screamed, not expecting anyone to be in the back of the wagon. Kellina's head snapped around so fast that she nearly lost her balance and fell off the seat.

"Jamie! Ye shouldna be here," scolded Kellina.

"Why no'?" he asked. "If ye and Caitlin can go to the Gordon Clan, then why canna I?"

"Ye'd better stop the wagon," suggested Nash. He put his fingers to his mouth and whistled, getting both Spring's and North's attention.

"What's the matter?" North came quickly, and so did Spring. "Did ye see someone waitin' to ambush us?"

"Nay. It seems Kellina's little brathair has snuck into the wagon," Nash explained. "We need to turn around and take him back, anon."

"Nay! I dinna want to go back," whined the boy.

Kellina spoke to him over her shoulder. "Jamie, Uncle Ciaran will be worried about ye. Ye canna leave without tellin' anyone. Ye have to return right now."

"Someone kens where I am," the boy told her. "Aidan MacKeefe saw me in the wagon when he came to collect his squirrel that followed me there. I put my finger to my lips to tell him to stay quiet."

"Aidan kens?" asked Nash with a chuckle. "He'll tell the chieftain then, I am sure of it."

"Aye," agreed North. "Aidan can never keep a secret."

"Uncle will be furious with ye, Jamie." Kellina gripped the reins in one hand. "I think lettin' ye come with us to the Gordon Clan is a bad idea. We should all just go back to our clan right now."

The sky darkened overhead and thunder rumbled in the distance.

"Nay. We need to move on," said Spring, looking at the sky. "There is a storm approachin'. We have just enough time to make it to the castle before the rain falls. If we go back now, we willna be able to make the journey today at all."

"Then let the boy stay," said North. "He's no' causin' any trouble."

"I agree," said Spring. "Shaw has a son about yer age that I think ye'll like to meet," Spring told Jamie.

"Yay!" cried Jamie, jumping up and down in the wagon.

"Brathair, if ye are comin' with us, then ye'll stay still and silent," warned Kellina. "If no', I swear I'll leave ye on the roadside all alone to be eaten by the wild beasties that come out at night."

"I'll be quiet, Kellina. I promise I will." Jamie quickly sat back down, holding on to the side of the wagon as Kellina sped away. Spring quickly followed on horseback.

"Wild beasties?" North said to his brother with a chuckle. "Such an imagination."

"Aye, that's what she said." Nash shook his head.

"I'm no' sure Kellina is goin' to make a guid mathair with talk like that," said North.

"Dinna worry about that," Nash answered. "If I canna convince her to make love to me soon, then there is no chance in hell that we're ever even havin' children."

IT WASN'T LONG before they rode over the drawbridge and into the courtyard of Edinvale Castle. Light rain had just started to fall. Kellina looked up to the battlements, seeing clansmen manning the walls. It was a large place, and very impressive. She was only used to living in a small camp in thatched cottages. Seeing a castle so close up was exciting and overwhelming and also just what she needed.

Shaw Gordon must have money, she decided, looking up to his clan's pennons fluttering from the top of the turrets. Long banners hung from the stone walls, depicting the chieftain's coat of arms on the clan's plaid of blue and green. A stag's head with ten tines stared back at her.

Their arrival drew the interest of the clan, as they started appearing from everywhere to see who approached. The clip-clop of the horses' hooves on the cobbled stones echoed as they made their way forward, finally stopping in the middle of the inner bailey.

"Spring! Ye're back," a man shouted. Kellina turned around to see a Highlander hurrying toward them with a bundle cradled in the crook of his arm. Spring jumped off the horse and ran to him, burying herself in his embrace. They hugged and kissed each other, making it obvious that this man was Spring's husband. It was sweet, but it rather hurt Kellina's heart to see such interaction between them. She longed for a relationship this strong, but she and Nash would never have what these two did.

"Come on, Caitlin," Kellina told her sister, dismounting the wagon and hurrying over to Spring. Spring was kissing the man now, and it seemed so passionate that she almost felt embarrassed just to watch them. The two of them were obviously in love. Kellina was about to make her presence known when the man handed Spring the bundle. Spring held it in two arms, using a rocking motion. This caused Kellina's mouth to drop open in surprise.

"Y-ye have a baby," she said in amazement, not expecting this at all.

"Aye," Spring answered. "Kellina MacKenzie, this is my husband, Shaw, and our baby boy, Blair."

The baby couldn't have been more than a few months old. It surprised Kellina. Her heart went out to Spring. The woman had left her new baby to come to the MacKenzie camp, just to talk to her. It had been a true sacrifice on Spring's part, and a dangerous trip for her as well.

"Spring, who are all these people and why are they here?" asked Shaw, seeming very cautious.

"I am Nash MacKeefe, and this is my brathair, North," said Nash, walking up and extending his arm. They shook hands and greeted each other.

"Ah, MacKeefes. Welcome," said Shaw. "I am friends with yer chieftain, Storm. I also love Old Callum's Mountain Magic."

"Did someone say Mountain Magic?" Another man came running over. "Where? And who are these lovely lassies?" He smiled at Kellina and her sister. "I am the laird's brathair, Leod."

"Stop the flirtin', Leod," warned Shaw. "They're too young for ye."

"I'm seven and ten today," said Caitlin, her face glowing, as she looked at the handsome man that was nearly ten years older than her. Leod was a big man with blond hair and striking blue eyes. His brother, Shaw, was equally as good-looking, but he had dark hair and hazel eyes instead.

"Her name is Caitlin, and I'm Kellina. We're sisters," Kellina explained.

"And I'm their brathair, Jamie." The young boy ran up excitedly, making sure to be introduced. "Can I see yer castle? I've never been inside a castle before."

"Jamie, stop it," scolded Kellina. "It's no' proper to act that way."

Shaw laughed. "I'm sure he's just excited. Yes, Jamie, I'll make sure ye get to no' only see the castle, but walk the battlements as well."

"Really? All the way up there? That seems so high." Jamie's eyes turned upward. He had a look of excitement, caution, and anxiety all mixed into one.

"If ye think it looks high from here, just wait until ye're up there lookin' downward," said Leod with a chuckle.

"Jamie, ye canna be wild up there, and ye must be careful," Kellina warned him.

"I will, Sister," he promised.

"They're here to collect some thatch for their roofs that were burned by the Sutherlands," Spring informed her husband, rocking her baby. "I hope ye dinna mind, Shaw. I told them we have plenty that we're no' usin'."

"Of course, I dinna mind," he said, not even seeming bothered that his wife had made the decision without even consulting him first. This told Kellina that Shaw valued his wife's opinion and that he trusted her as well. She liked that, and hoped that she and Nash could have that someday, too. "If they are in need of thatch, I am more than happy to help them by givin' them ours."

"Give us? Oh, nay," said Kellina. "I think ye're mistaken, Laird Gordon. We canna accept such a gift. We're workin' in exchange for it," she explained, as they all stood there in the light rain talking as if the weather didn't matter.

"Workin'? Doin' what?" asked Shaw with a chuckle. "And please, just call me Shaw."

"I'm goin' to thatch yer roofs," explained Kellina.

"We are. Both of us." Nash slipped his arm around Kellina's waist. "I'm her husband."

"Nash, please," Kellina whispered to Nash, wondering if he was only doing this because Leod had paid her a little attention.

"Well, thank ye, but our roofs dinna need thatchin'," said Shaw. "However, ye're welcome to have as much thatch as ye need, for free."

"But Spring said I could work for it." Kellina was starting to see some of Spring's cunning antics in play here. It was becoming quite apparent that she only brought them here because she was trying to help the marriage work out between Kellina and Nash. Now, Kellina wished she had never come at all, because this made her feel very uncomfortable.

"I'm sure the roofs of the mews and kennels could use a little repair," Spring told her husband. "Right, Shaw?"

Shaw finally caught on and agreed. "Aye, of course, it couldna hurt. But for right now, let's all get out of the rain. Willna ye join us for a bite to eat? My brathair will take care of yer horses."

"Food? Aye, that sounds guid," North said.

"Where is Leith?" grumbled Leod, taking a hold of the reins. "He should be doin' this, no' me."

"Who's Leith?" asked Jamie.

"Leith is Shaw's son who is about the same age as ye," said Spring. "He has a thirteen-year-old daughter, Colina, and an older son who just married as well."

"I'll help ye with the horses, Leod," North offered.

"Jamie, would ye like to come along, and that way ye can see the stables and the blacksmith's shop first?" Leod asked the boy.

"Would I!" Jamie ran over and took the reins from Leod, eager to be a part of this.

"I'd like to see that, too," said Caitlin, joining Leod, North, and her brother. Kellina was sure it was only because Caitlin liked the attention from Leod, no matter if he was too old for her or not. Lately, she was becoming very interested in boys. If she had kept herself busy, the way Kellina always had, she wouldn't have time to think of such things. Kellina put her thoughts on her thatching, and her sword practice, among other chores that her clan needed completed. Kellina didn't have time for eyeing up a man.

The group headed away, leaving Nash and Kellina alone.

"Ye can remove yer arm from my waist now," said Kellina, feeling warm from Nash's body heat. Her breathing became deeper. She liked it, but didn't want him to know.

"Why should I remove it?" asked Nash. "I rather like it there. After all, I am yer husband."

"And that gives ye the right?"

"I didna say that. However, I had hoped it would at least entitle me to a kiss."

Kellina could see that Nash wasn't going to leave her alone until she kissed him, so she just decided to do it and get it over with quickly. At least, then, she could get inside and out of the rain. She leaned closer to him, intending to give him a quick peck on the lips and then walk away. But when he pulled her into his arms and kissed her with passion, she found herself dropping her guard. Nash let the moment linger. Kellina didn't want to like it but, for some reason, she did. Nash was starting to make her feel things for him that she'd never felt before. She'd fought it tooth and nail, but when he kissed her like this, she couldn't help but lose her resolve.

Being enclosed in Nash's warm embrace, tasting his sweet lips, almost made her forget that he was a MacKeefe and how much she hated his clan. Her eyes closed and her head tilted back as he kissed her again. This time, the kiss was accompanied by him rubbing his hand up and down her back in an alluring manner.

Damn, if she didn't feel her body coming to life from his actions. It almost seemed magical kissing him in the light rain. Her thoughts went back to the day they'd gotten married. She had felt her life crashing down around her at the time. She'd been forced to do something she didn't want to by taking her vows. But then when her husband should have forced her to consummate the marriage, he didn't. Instead, he gave her the choice. That made her confused as to why he did it. Still, at the same time, it also made it hard not to actually like him since he had given her the choice.

"Thank ye, Nash. That was no' so bad after all, I suppose." She said it aloud, surprising herself that she had made her thoughts and feelings vocal. She stepped back, looking up into his hazel eyes.

"Is that a tear I see, lass?" Nash reached out and wiped her cheek with his thumb.

Kellina felt embarrassed to admit she was tearing up over him. She didn't want to seem weak around him. So she held back any tears, and lifted her chin, answering him in a different way entirely. "I think it's just a raindrop," she told him. "I suppose it would be wise to get out of the rain, like the others."

"I dinna ken. I rather like it out here," Nash answered. "Besides, it's just a mist really, and no' a downpour or anythin' like that." He cupped the side of her face with his large palm. "If I did somethin' to anger ye, Kellina, I am sorry. I never meant to do anythin' but to make ye happy, I swear."

She leaned into his caress, liking the feeling of his warm skin touching hers. It was starting to feel right when he touched her, instead of wrong. Or mayhap it was just that she wanted what she had seen between Shaw and Spring. Kellina's marriage to Nash wasn't going smoothly, and she didn't know if she could ever have what she'd witnessed between their hosts.

"Och, Nash, how did we get into such a horrible situation?"

"It was done for an alliance," he reminded her, pulling her up against his chest and kissing her atop the head. "And I dinna think bein' married to ye is really that horrible at all. That is a harsh word to use, lass."

"Nay, that's no' what I meant. I wasna talkin' about our bein' married. I am talkin' about our deception."

"Oh." He bit his lip and nodded. "Ye mean the marriage bed."

"Aye, that is what I mean. I'm sorry, Nash, but I was frightened to couple with ye. Everythin' was happenin' so fast, and I dinna ken what to do."

"I understand, Kellina. But ye need to understand somethin' as well. That is the whole reason why I taught ye to pleasure yerself. I didna want to scare ye or push ye into somethin' ye werena ready for."

"I want to believe that, but I'm no' so sure. Sometimes, I think it was because of somethin' else." She sniffled and pulled out of his arms.

"What do ye mean? I was tryin' to show ye respect, lass. I am sorry if it didna come across that way."

"Mayhap, ye're right," she answered, flashing a quick smile and wiping away another tear. "But was it really showin' respect no' to touch yer own wife in that way, of all times, on our weddin' night? Or was it a form of disrespect instead? After all, it made me feel undesirable and as if ye didna want me in that way."

"Blethers, nay! That wasna my intention at all, I promise."

KELLINA SIGHED DEEPLY and turned and walked away. Nash stood alone in the rain, feeling more confused than ever now. It almost seemed like he was damned if he did, and damned if he didn't. Whatever he did concerning Kellina, it was only proving to be wrong. Would this marriage ever take its footing, or would it never even get off the ground?

—◆·◦◇◦·◆—

CHAPTER THIRTEEN

FTER A QUICK bite to eat, Kellina went back to the wagon to
get her thatching tools, accompanied by her sister. The skies
had cleared up, and it was proving to be a beautiful day. Her
sister walked with her as they took in the sights of the castle. It
was far different than their little, broken camp. This was a place
bustling with Scots, every one of them knowing their job and
doing it without complaining.

In the bailey of the castle, the Gordons had small thatched-
roof buildings that consisted of the mews, the kennels, the
blacksmith's shop, the stables, and more. They even had their
own orchards, and fields of crops. Life here seemed so safe and
happy. She was sure when they raised the drawbridge at night
and lowered the portcullis, they had no fears of being attacked.
Back at the MacKenzie camp, Kellina never got a good night's
rest. She felt as if they were always vulnerable, and that was a
feeling she would never get used to.

"I like it here," said Caitlin. "Everyone is so friendly. The
castle is elegant, and they have no need for anythin'."

"Aye, it's nice, I agree. I could get used to livin' like this."
Kellina looked at the outbuildings dotting her surroundings. They
were all tidy, and everything was clean. There was no soot and
ash or anything broken littering the area like back home.

Women of the clan kept busy cooking in the kitchen, or
weaving or washing and mending clothes. She watched the

falconer of the clan leave the mews with a beautiful red-tailed hawk on his arm. The clinking and clanking of the blacksmith's hammer and anvil filled the air, making everything sound so busy. The kennel groom walked by with six dogs on leads, all barking because they saw a squirrel.

Shaw and Spring's daughter, Colina, and her younger brother, Leith, were showing the other children how to not only shoot, but construct bows and arrows made from hickory and ash saplings. They'd told her earlier that Spring and their father had shown them how to do it not long ago. Shaw's father had been a fletcher. Shaw had made bows and arrows as a child, learning the skill from the man.

Children ran around chasing a stray goat, while the older men of the clan gathered at the loch, fishing. Everyone seemed to love Shaw and Spring. Even Shaw's lazy brother, Leod, had a lovable quality about him that made the children as well as the lassies follow him wherever he went.

"Jamie is makin' his own bow and arrows, and he's so excited about it," said Caitlin. "I'm actually glad he sneaked into the wagon now. He's smilin' again, and that is somethin' he hasna done in a long time. It's nice to hear him laugh."

"Now if only we could get Uncle and the rest of our clan to be happy like everyone is here," commented Kellina.

"What about ye and Nash?" asked her sister. "Ye two dinna seem happy together at all. Are ye?"

"Caitlin, the reason I wanted ye to come with me to see the Gordons' castle was because I wanted to confide in ye about somethin'."

"Really?" Her eyes opened wide with excitement. "Sister, ye never confide in me."

"I ken, and that's wrong of me, and I am sorry. Ye are of marryin' age now, Caitlin. Since we dinna have a mathair, I want to be here for ye. In case ye have any questions that need answerin'."

They stopped just outside the stable, next to the wagon with their things.

"Oh, I'd like that. There is somethin' I want to ken, and I hope ye can answer for me."

"Of course. Anythin'. What is it, Sister?" asked Kellina.

Caitlin giggled, looked around and then leaned in and spoke in a hushed voice. "Can ye tell me how it feels to make love to a man?"

Kellina felt a knot forming in her stomach. "What?" she said, stalling, not knowing how to answer since she had never coupled. Right now, she would have gladly answered anything but this.

"Ye ken." Caitlin looked around and giggled again. "I heard ye and Nash on yer weddin' night, moaning and squealin' and all. Was it as guid as it sounded? I'm sure with the handsome Nash MacKeefe, it was even better than I can imagine. Tell me, tell me, Sister. I have to ken everythin' about it. How did ye do it, and how did ye feel? Was it really that guid?"

"Ye'd be surprised," she said, not able to tell her sister now what she'd planned on confessing. She didn't want to lie to her, but neither did she want to disappoint Caitlin by telling her that she was married and, yet, still chaste. Her sister would be horrified to know how naughty Kellina had been. Just thinking about the excitement she'd felt and the height of her peak as she'd found her release had her feeling lusty all over again. Not coupling with Nash was worse than if she'd coupled with a man before she'd married. Oh, what was she to do?

"I hope someday I'm as lucky as ye, Kellina, to find someone as handsome and as guid in bed as Nash MacKeefe."

"Caitlin," yelled Jamie, sounding excited. "Come see what I'm doin'. Ye can make yer own bow and arrows, too." He held up an arrow made from a stick, waving it over his head.

"Oh, I'd love to learn that." She looked over to Kellina, but didn't move. "I'm sorry, Sister. What was it ye wanted to confide in me about?"

"Oh, it's nothin'," said Kellina, trying to make light of the situation. "Why dinna ye join Jamie and have some fun?"

"Ye come with me. Please. We can do it together," her sister begged.

"Nay, I canna, I'm sorry. I'm goin' to be busy repairin' roofs that dinna really need it."

"What?" Caitlin made a face. "Then why are ye doin' it? That makes no sense at all."

"I'm doin' it in exchange for the thatch that the Gordons will give us."

"They said they'd give it to ye for free. Take them up on the offer and then ye'll have time to make bows and arrows."

"Nay, Caitlin, I canna do that. It wouldna be right. I, like Uncle, dinna want charity. I want to earn everythin' I receive."

"All right, then. I'll make an extra arrow for ye." Caitlin ran off to be with her brother and the rest of the children.

"I'm here," said Nash, from right behind her, making her jump. She didn't realize he was so close.

"How long have ye been standin' there?" she asked, glad now she hadn't been talking about him after all.

"Long enough to hear ye say the roofs dinna really need mendin'." He turned and looked up to the roofs of the mews and kennels. "I agree. They look fine. So, why dinna we go for a walk instead?"

"I dinna think so, Nash." She leaned into the wagon and started to pick up the thatching tools.

His hand on her wrist stilled her action.

NASH WAS TAKING a big chance at setting her off again, but he had decided to try making amends with his new wife. He held her wrist, while her big, blue eyes stared up at him. They were clear and glassy, reflecting the puffy, white clouds from the sky above them. A strand of her long, blond hair blew across her face in the breeze, and he gently brushed it away, tucking it behind her ear.

"Wouldna ye like to walk with me, lass?"

"Mayhap. But no' now." She picked up the tools and started toward the mews. "Bring the ladder," she called out over her shoulder.

"Fine, he grumbled, grabbing the ladder and following her. Once they both ascended, they stopped at the top of the roof of the mews, looking out at the vast, beautiful sky.

"It's such a bonnie sight," she said in a breathy voice. The blue, vast sky lit up with a rainbow, now that it had stopped raining. The rainbow arched around from one side of the castle to the other, looking like it stopped right at the loch not far outside the castle's walls. "I feel like I spend lots of time up on roofs, but never really get to look at the beauty of the sky."

"Then, let's sit down for a moment and enjoy it," he suggested. "After all, rainbows don't last long."

"It's some kind of message," she said, sitting down near the apex, laying on her back to look up at the rainbow in the sky.

"I think it means we're lucky," said Nash, sitting down with her, lying back as well.

"Lucky? How so? My clan was attacked, my parents are dead, our houses were burned, and our livestock stolen. No' to mention, our crops were ruined. How is that lucky?"

"Ye're lucky to be alive. And I'm lucky to have ye . . . for my wife." He took the opportunity to move closer, leaning over to kiss her gently. She let him do it. Already, he felt lucky.

"I think I'd rather live here with the Gordons than to go back home," she said, surprising him.

"What? Why?" he asked, looking up at the clouds.

"Didna ye see how happy Spring and Shaw are together? Plus, they have this beautiful, fortified castle where they can feel safe."

"They have a new baby," Nash said. "Their family is growin'. Of course, they're happy."

"What about us, Nash? Will we ever have babies together?"

His mouth fell open, and he didn't know what to say. "Is this . . . a trick question?" he asked, not wanting to say anything that might upset her.

She giggled, and he liked the sound of her laugh. "Nay, Nash MacKeefe, it is no' a trick question. I just wondered if ye thought we'd ever be like Shaw and Spring. With a baby of our own someday."

"Well, I'd have to say nay, I dinna see how that will ever happen. No' if we're never goin' to make love for real, lass."

"Ye're right." She sat up, looking like she'd just discovered some sort of secret. "I've decided that we're married, and we're just goin' to have to live with it."

"Huh?" he asked, not sure what the hell she meant by that.

"I mean . . . I think . . . we should make love. For real."

"Did ye just say what I think ye said?" He sat up now, looking at her as if she'd gone mad. "Up here? Now? On the roof of the mews and right out in the open?"

"Nay, silly," she answered, laughing heartily. "I meant later. Besides, if we did it up here in the straw, it's bound to be uncomfortable."

"Especially if we end up fallin' through the roof." He rubbed his shoulder. "I ken from experience how much that smarts."

"Then it's settled," she said, standing up. "Ready to get to work?"

Once again, he wasn't sure if she was talking about thatching or coupling. "Is this the trick question now?"

"Here," she said, shoving the leggett into his hand. "The roof doesna need more thatch. It doesna really need a thing at all."

"Then why are ye givin' me this?" He held up the block of wood that looked like a paddle, secured to a short pole.

"If we dinna do a thing, I canna take the thatch in exchange," she told him. "So, we'll smooth out the thatch that's here with the leggett, and do a little trimmin' with the knives around the apex and the eaves. That should be enough so that when I tell them we repaired their roof, it willna be a lie."

"Whatever ye say." Nash started using the leggett to hit the ends of the straw, pushing them upward to create a pitch on the roof. Kellina worked quickly trimming the edges. After an hour or two, there was really nothing else they could possibly do. They had touched up both the roofs of the mews and the kennels.

"I think we're done," he told her.

"Done with the roofs, at least." She looked over at him and smiled. His heart picked up a beat.

"I think bein' here is doin' wonders for yer disposition, Wife."

"What did ye say?" She didn't sound happy.

"I'm sorry. I shouldna have said that. I just meant, it's nice to see ye smile and laugh. I didna mean ye have a sour disposition or anythin' like that."

"I was talkin' about ye callin' me Wife. I dinna like it. Can ye just call me Kellina instead?"

"Och, is that all? Certainly, Kellina." He held out his hand and helped her to the ladder.

"I suppose if there's really no work to be done, we should load the wagon and head back tomorrow," she told him.

"Oh, there's work to be done," he assured her, thinking of coupling with his new wife. "But no one said it had a thing to do with roofs."

⧽⧽⧽✕⧼⧼⧼

"EGADS, YE STINK!" North told Nash an hour later, right when Nash was getting ready to join Kellina for a walk, and hopefully to make love.

"What? I do?" Nash held up one arm and then the other, sniffing his armpits. "Bid the devil, ye're right. I do stink. This canna be happenin'. No' now. I'm goin' for a walk with Kellina and then we're supposed to make love."

"Really?" North looked as if he didn't believe him.

Nash helped North brush down the horses in the stable. "Ye heard what I said."

"Did ye two actually schedule the act of couplin'? Isna that supposed to be more . . . I dinna ken . . . more spontaneous?" North looked horrified at the thought of it.

"Probably, but it was her idea and I wasna about to shoot it down," Nash told him, running his hand over the horse's neck, snuggling his face up to it, giving it a quick kiss.

"Ye dolt! That's a horse, no' yer wife," spat North. "What are ye doin'? Practicin' kissin' a mare?"

"Nay, of course, no'. I just like animals, that's all."

"If ye're that hot and bothered that now ye're kissin' horses, ye'd better go cool off in the loch, Brathair."

"Guid idea." Nash put down the brush, and gave the horse one last pat on the side.

"God's eyes, really?"

"I mean – no' that I'm hot and bothered," explained Nash. "I'm goin' to jump in the loch to wash off the stench. If no', Kellina will never get close enough to me to make love. If ye see her, tell her I'll meet her down at the loch in fifteen minutes."

"All right. Whatever ye say."

Nash could hear his brother laughing as he hurried down to the water.

The lake was far enough away from the castle that no one would see him if he went fast. Looking around, he spied the children just outside the castle walls using their bows and arrows, shooting at a target that looked like a man made of straw. There were a few women in the fields, picking vegetables, and some of the men were taking care of the cattle up on the hill. No one was watching him, so he stripped off his clothes and jumped into the water with a splash.

KELLINA BROKE THE surface of the water, opening her eyes and seeing the bright blue sky smiling down at her. The rainbow was gone now. But on the edge of the water was some sort of little fishing shed. She wondered if this was where the rainbow had ended earlier. It was only when she walked down to look at it that she decided she felt hot and sweaty and needed to wash. This was the big night when she was going to consummate her marriage. She didn't want to stink when she finally did it. She figured that she had just enough time to go for a swim and wash off before Nash met her here.

She was swimming back to shore when she heard a big splash and looked up to see something in the water. At first, she thought it was some sort of animal, and it frightened her. Then she saw the head of a person, and realized someone else was going for a swim, too.

"God's teeth, I dinna want them to see me naked." She swam to the shore, running across the rocks and brush, trying to remember where she'd left her clothes.

"Kellina?" she heard someone call out. It sounded like Nash. God help her, she couldn't find her clothes! "Kellina is that ye, lass?"

Finally spotting her clothes, she turned and ran for them, hearing the sloshing of Nash as he exited the water and followed.

"Nay, no' yet, Nash. I'm no' ready." Her fingers fumbled with the ties on her tunic, but she only managed to make a knot. She'd never be able to get it over her head now.

"I guess we both had the same idea," he said, sounding jovial, walking up next to her with his clothes in his hand.

She was down on her knees, but dared to turn her head to look at him. Water dripped down his broad chest, past the rigid peaks of his nipples. It was a warm day, but the water had been cold. She could see raised gooseflesh on his arms. Then her gaze roamed lower, and stopped beneath his waist. Expecting his manhood to be hard and as straight as an arrow, it surprised her when it wasn't.

"Oh," she said, her head snapping back the other way. She picked up her tunic, holding it to her chest. "Just turn around while I dress. And please put yer clothes on, too."

"Dinna be silly." He walked up next to her and she found herself looking down at his bare feet. "Kellina, we've already seen each other naked. Ye dinna have to be shy, lass."

"That was when we were alone. And in the dark." She didn't look at him when she spoke. Becoming self-conscious, she held her clothes closer to hide her nakedness.

"We're alone," he said, looking around. "And the sun is startin' to set, so it'll be dark soon."

"Ye ken what I mean, Nash. Now turn around, please."

"Nay," he said, taking her arm and yanking her up to a standing position. "I dinna mean to disrespect ye, but must I remind ye that we are married now? We planned on making love, and it is long past due."

He pulled her into his arms and kissed her, letting his tongue slip into her mouth, surprising her with his action. She moaned.

"Did ye like that, lass?" He brushed back a lock of her wet hair. "Because I have so much more to teach ye."

"Please, I dinna want to touch myself again," she told him in a breathy whisper, coming to life just from his kiss.

"And neither will ye have to. I'll do all the touchin' this time, I promise."

"Nash, I dinna ken if it will work."

"Why no'?" he asked.

"Because ye're no' . . ." She looked down to his flaccid manhood.

"Oh, that," he said with a chuckle. "I assure ye, it is no' broken, if that is what's worryin' ye. It is just that I was swimmin' in the cold loch. Give me another kiss or two, and things will be back to where we need them."

Before she knew it, she was in his arms again. Their lips were locked and the kissing continued. One of his hands slipped around to cup her bare bottom. The other slid upward, closing around one breast. His fingers flicked at her nipple, causing it to go taut. Then she felt something pushing against her, and looked down. Sure enough, it hadn't taken much, but Nash was hard, hot and ready.

"Nash, I dinna want to do this out here. What if my little brathair sees us?"

"All right. How about we go into that little shed?" He nodded toward the one that she supposed the rainbow had touched earlier.

"That's a guid idea."

With their clothes in hand, they hurried to the shed. Nash slowly pushed the door open while Kellina checked their surroundings, hoping no one was watching.

"It looks like a shed for storage, but there isna much in here," said Nash in a muffled voice, since his head was inside the small enclosure. "It's dark in the shed, but there is still some light coming through the cracks in the roof."

"There's Caitlin," said Kellina, seeing her sister back by the castle with a bow in her hands. "And yer brathair and Leod are headin' this way with fishin' poles in their hands. Hurry, get inside."

Once inside, they quickly closed the door.

"Well, we're here," said Nash, in a sultry voice. "Since there isna a bed, we can lay on my plaid if ye'd like." He threw down his plaid and spread it out with his foot. She still clutched her clothes in front of her, feeling her body tremble.

"Mayhap we should wait," she said, feeling apprehensive about this now.

"Nay. We're married now, and we've agreed to consummate the marriage. I willna let ye back away again, Kellina. We've decided to do this."

"Well, I think I've changed my mind."

"It's for the guid of both our clans. Now, stop bein' so scared. It's verra enjoyable, I assure ye, if only ye'd give it a chance."

She started thinking about how enjoyable it had been last time, and wondered how it would feel if Nash entered her this time, instead of her having to use her own fingers.

"All right," she finally agreed, feeling the rapid beating of her heart. "Tell me what to do."

"Well, the first thing ye need to do is to let go of these clothes, sweetheart." He gently pried her fingers open and the clothes she was holding fell to the ground at her feet. "That's better. Now, just relax."

"I canna," she said. "I'm shiverin'. I think it's from the swim in the cold water."

"Then we need to do whatever we can to warm ye up."

"Like what?" she asked, her teeth chattering together now, making a clicking sound.

"Let me take care of that. I've been kent to start a few fires in my time, I'm proud to say. Ye just sit right here, and I'll show ye." He helped her to sit atop the plaid.

"Nash, ye're boastin' again. It's no' becomin' to talk about startin' fires in other lassies when ye're with yer wife."

"Who's talkin' about other lassies?" She heard a scratching noise and then saw light. She turned to see that Nash had started a small fire in a metal brazier that was on the floor behind them.

"My mistake," she said with a giggle. "But dinna burn the place down, Nash. After all, it's been said that ye are guid at that, too."

"Only in the Horn and Hoof Tavern, and I put out the fire before it burned the place down. Dinna worry, there is a smoke hole under the eaves. Besides, I'll keep the fire small. Just enough to warm us, that's all."

"All right, then."

He played with the fire, stacking a few dry sticks onto it that he found inside the shed. "There isna much kindlin' so this fire willna last long."

"How long will we need?" she asked, her teeth still chattering.

"However long it takes to make my wife happy."

Kellina looked up at Nash staring down at her, and something inside made her feel very lucky to have him, just like her sister had said. He was handsome and kind, always thinking of others before himself. When he wasn't boasting, that is. Still, she didn't mind. Kellina liked a man who had confidence.

"I . . . see that ye're ready now," she said, her eyes fastening to his aroused form. It made her randy.

He knelt down behind her, leaning over, letting his hands slip up around her breasts. Her heart jumped and her shivering stopped as he fondled her and rolled her nipples. Her head fell back and her spine arched.

"I think I'm warmin' up a little," she told him.

"That's what I like to hear." Nash sat down and pulled her atop his lap, spreading her legs. Her womanhood pressed up against his erection. "Just relax. I'll do all the work, lass. I want ye to experience elation, and see just how wonderful makin' love can really be."

Before she could say a word, he was suckling at her breast like a nursing baby. She liked the feeling. It excited her. Her hands slipped around his head and she pulled him closer, feeling vibrations starting up between her thighs.

"Can I touch ye?" she asked, her fingers slipping around his hardened form.

"I'm no' stoppin' ye," he answered.

"So soft, yet hard at the same time. Like silk over steel," she said, running her hand up and down his length. She heard him suck in a breath.

"Mayhap that's enough of that right now." He took her hand off of him. "If ye keep that up, I'll be finished before ye begin. Mayhap for now, I'll do the touchin'."

They kissed some more, and his fingers found their way between her legs.

"Oooooh," she moaned as he slid one finger into her, and then two. She felt her own liquid passion as he readied her, and her body vibrated, coming to life.

"Do ye like that, lass?" he whispered, grabbing on to her hips now.

"I do. But I want to feel ye in me. All of ye, Nash."

"And so ye shall." He lifted her hips and lowered her down over his shaft, sliding into her little by little. "Now, ye can help a little by moving yer hips," he told her.

She breathed out a deep breath, feeling him enter her completely. It was perfect, like the warmth of wearing a snug-fitting glove.

"Are ye sure I'm no' supposed to be on my back?" she asked.

"There are many ways to do it, and we're goin' to try them all," he promised.

He helped her move her hips, then laid back, pulling her atop him. As they did the dance of love, Kellina heard a delightful, naughty squealing. She realized it was her making those noises as she came closer and closer to her peak.

"Somethin' is happenin'," she told him. "I'm almost there."

His breathing became labored and she felt perspiration on his skin. She was getting very hot as well. With her eyes closed, she swore she could see bright light right through her lids. Then he rolled over, putting her on the bottom and thrust into her from atop, making love the usual way. She liked each way he did it. It didn't hurt like she thought it would. Nash was gentle, yet still aggressive, and she liked that as well.

Kellina started thinking about babies, and realized they might very well be making one right now. After seeing how happy Spring and Shaw were with their baby, she wanted to feel that way, too.

"I want a baby, Nash," she told him as he moved his hips, entering her and then sliding out over and over again. "Let's make a baby. Please."

That seemed to excite him as well, because he started grunting like a bear, and being a little more forceful now. She didn't care. When she made love, she wanted to feel it, and she wasn't afraid any longer.

"Take me!" she cried, feeling her body climbing higher and higher with each thrust from her husband as he strived to release his seed. "Ooooh, yes," she cried, releasing all her pent-up emotions, finding her climax, wrapping her legs around his back at the same time.

He kneeled above her, holding her hips, pumping into her while she squealed and cried out from beneath him. This felt so much better than pleasuring herself.

"More, more, more," she cried out, feeling greedy for this kind of pleasure, and feeling no shame. "Plant yer seed within me,

Nash. Let's create a new life, the two of us.

"Arrrrgh, aaaaaah," he cried out, releasing his seed into her, falling to his back and pulling her atop him. Their hot bodies melded into one.

"I canna stop," she told him, crawling atop him, just rubbing up against him, and having another orgasm without his help. By the rood, this was so much better than she ever thought it could be. She never knew it could happen more than once.

"Ye're goin' to kill me," he mumbled from beneath her.

"Nay, I do no' want to kill ye any longer. Honest, Nash."

"I meant with all the couplin'," he told her with a chuckle. "Ye are a vixen in bed, lass. It is somethin' I never expected from ye at all."

"Neither did I," she told him, kissing him, thinking she smelled something burning. "What is that smell?" she asked, lifting her head and sniffing the air.

"I bathed in the loch, honest I did. I am sorry if I worked up a sweat, but ye are vigorous in bed."

"Nay, no' that." She sniffed the air again and looked up, and screamed. "Nash! The roof is on fire!"

$$\cdots\!\diamond\!\circ\!\diamond\!\circ\!\diamond\!\cdots$$

CHAPTER FOURTEEN

"WHAT THE HELL were ye doin' in the shed in the first place, Nash?" North dropped the empty water bucket on the ground at Nash's feet. Thankfully, North had been fishing with Leod when they noticed smoke coming from the shed and hurried over to check it out. They, along with Nash and Kellina, had managed to put out the fire on the roof before the whole thing was consumed.

"What do ye think I was doin'?" mumbled Nash, wiping his brow. He stood there in just his long tunic and bare feet, not having had time to don his plaid.

"Here, Nash, put it on quickly." Kellina handed his plaid to him. She'd dressed in her tunic and braies, still not wearing a skirt like the rest of them. "I see my sister and brathair comin' along with some of the other clansmembers."

"I should have warned ye about the love shed," said Leod with a chuckle. "It's no' exactly the safest place to be."

"The love shed?" asked Kellina, blinking and looking very embarrassed. "Why, I dinna ken what ye mean, Leod."

"Dinna worry, lass, yer secret is safe with me." Leod looked at her from the corners of his eyes, grinning. "I've often used this fishin' shed for the same purpose. However, I kent the roof was fallin' in, so I was never foolish enough to light a fire in there."

"Now ye tell me," mumbled Nash, pulling his clothes back into place.

"We saw smoke," said Jamie, the first one to run up to join them as a group of children headed toward them.

"And flames," added Caitlin, on his heels. Some of the adult clansmembers ran after them from the castle, crowding around now, curious as to what happened.

"Is anyone hurt? Let me through. Move aside." Shaw pushed his way to the front of the crowd. Spring was right behind him with her baby in the crook of one arm.

"Nay, everyone's fine," Leod called out to his brother. "The fire is out and there's no real damage except to the roof of the shed."

"We're sorry, and we promise to fix the roof right away." Kellina ran a hand over her hair, looking at the ground rather than directly at anyone. She felt more embarrassed than she ever had in her entire life. There was no doubt everyone would figure out what they were doing in there, if they didn't already know. God's eyes, she hoped Jamie and the rest of the children wouldn't realize what she had just done.

"Well, if no one was harmed, I guess there's no real damage done then," said Shaw. "And I willna even ask how the fire got started, since I think I can figure it out." He looked at Nash and Kellina when he said it. "There are times and places for every-thin', and this is no' one of them, I assure ye."

"Husband," Spring said in a low voice, in an obvious warning not to say anything more.

"They are our guests, so dinna be too hard on them, Brathair," said Leod.

"Shaw, I told ye about that roof months ago," Spring scolded him. "At least now it will get fixed before winter. I am sure Kellina and Nash wouldna mind repairin' it. Would ye?" she asked them.

"Nay, of course no'," said Nash.

"Like I said, we would be more than happy to fix the roof for ye," added Kellina.

"All right, then. There is plenty of thatch in the back room of the stable," Shaw instructed. "I suggest ye get started on it right away."

"Thank ye. Of course, we'd be happy to," said Nash, straightening his sash.

"Caitlin, can ye watch the baby for me?" Spring asked. "I'd like to stay and talk to yer sister.

"I can hold the baby?" asked Caitlin excitedly. "Oh, yes! I would love to, thank ye." She took the baby boy, fussing over him, smiling from ear to ear. She and the group of children and younger clansmembers headed back to the camp along with the rest of the group.

"I'll meet ye at the stable," Nash told Kellina with a quick wave. "North and Leod, would ye mind givin' me a hand gettin' the supplies?"

"Why no'?" asked Leod. "I've been meanin' to fix that roof for some time now anyway."

"The fishin' was no guid today, so I'll help, too," added North. The men walked away, talking about fish and roofs and women.

KELLINA KNEW WHAT Spring was going to say even before she said it. Still, she waited patiently for the men to leave, and for Lady Spring to start the conversation.

"Ye were in there makin' love in the shed, werena ye?" asked Spring, even though it was more than clear that she knew the truth. It made Kellina wonder why she was even asking.

"Aye," Kellina answered truthfully with a sigh. "I am sorry we were so careless. We never meant to almost burn it down."

"Nay, I am no' askin' ye this to reprimand ye for what ye did," Spring assured here. "I am happy for ye that ye finally consummated the marriage. How do ye feel about it, Kellina?"

"I'm no' sure. I'm still confused." Kellina tied back her hair. "I still feel anger toward the MacKeefes for killin' my parents but, at the same time, I feel something special for Nash, deep inside. I honestly think I want to have his baby, although I never thought

I'd say it. I just see ye and Shaw with the baby and realize how happy ye two are. I want to feel that same kind of happiness. It is what I want more than anything in life right now."

"Aye, a baby is a wonderful way to bring two people together," said Spring. "However . . . if ye two are no' ready to start a family, it could be considerably tryin'. It might also end up tearin' ye apart if ye are no' both willin' to make the sacrifices that might be needed."

"What do ye mean?" asked Kellina.

"I mean that it is a lot of work on both yer parts to raise a family. I couldna even begin to tell ye what trouble Shaw's three children gave him, as well as me at first, before they accepted me as their mathair. Still, it is the best feelin' in the world when they tell ye they love ye."

"Speakin' of love, I think we made love today, no' just coupled," Kellina said shyly, but wanting Spring to know. "It was different than just couplin', I think. Just like ye said."

"Oh, did Nash say he loved ye?" she asked with a smile. "How nice."

"Well, nay." Kellina started thinking she must have misunderstood what Spring meant when she talked about making love versus coupling. "He did no' say that, actually."

"I see. Ye told him that ye love him, then? Well, that is a guid start."

"Uh . . . nay. I didna say I loved him, either. But I'm sure we will both tell each other that soon."

Spring put her arm around Kellina's shoulders as they walked. "All in guid time, Kellina. These things canna be rushed."

"I'm sorry about the roof," apologized Kellina.

"I'm no'," Spring answered. "Sometimes one wall – or roof – needs to come down before another can be built. I just hope that ye and Nash can work out yer differences before ye have a bairn together. If no', those walls might just become higher than ever."

THE ROOF WAS an easy fix, and Nash cherished the time that he and Kellina spent working on it together. A fresh breeze blew past his face, making him feel alive more than ever. He'd enjoyed finally consummating his marriage, as he had been starting to think that it was never going to happen. Kellina seemed to finally relax and accept him, and that was good. But still, something was bothering him. His new wife seemed so insistent on getting pregnant, and that surprised as well as confused him. He found her wanting for a baby an odd thing. After all, she didn't want anything to do with him just a few days ago. It made him feel uneasy and suspicious. He didn't think she was up to anything devious, but her eagerness to get pregnant so quickly made him feel on edge.

"That looks guid," said Kellina, putting on the finishing touches, and sitting down atop the shed. She looked out over the water of the loch with a smile. Nash wondered if she was thinking about their swim in the cold water that led to coupling to warm up, in the end.

"Aye, it does look guid," he said, sitting next to her. He reached out to stroke her cheek, looking at her instead of at the roof. God's eyes, she was beautiful. They'd been so busy fighting with one another that he hadn't really taken the time to drink her in. She was his wife now, he reminded himself. And, she wanted a baby, quickly. The knot in his stomach returned at the thought. When she leaned in closer, meaning to kiss him, he pulled away.

"What's the matter, Nash?" She looked bewildered why he would do such a thing.

"Let's just look at the sky for a while. It's such a nice day." He laid back, staring up at the sky. Big, puffy, white clouds hovered over them while the scent of heather drifted past on the breeze. It would all have seemed so perfect . . . if he hadn't been worried about being a father. His head was still in a tizzy from being told he had to marry a woman he hadn't chosen for himself. Then he was told he had to consummate the marriage – which he understood. But now, Kellina insisting they conceive a baby, especially the first time they made love, had him concerned. He hadn't even gotten used to the fact that he had wife yet. The last thing he wanted was to add a baby to the mix. He and Kellina needed to work out their differences first.

"Ye didna like makin' love with me, did ye?" Kellina sighed and laid on her back looking at the sky as well.

"Nay, that's no' true, lass. I enjoyed it immensely," he said, taking her hand and gently stroking her arm with two fingers, in deep thought.

"Then what is botherin' ye, Nash? Dinna lie to me, please. I can tell there is some sort of wall between us, and I want to ken what it is."

"I guess I was just curious about somethin'."

"About what?" she asked.

"Ye didna even want me to touch ye before today. Now, ye accepted the couplin' easily, and kept tellin' me ye wanted a bairn."

"Aye, I do want a bairn, Nash. Spring has been talkin' with me, and she helped me realize things I hadna thought of before."

"Like what? I dinna understand."

"It doesna matter. All that matters is that we are happy together." She sat up and looked down at him. "Spring and Shaw seem so happy with their children, Nash. It looks like a perfect life to me. I want that, too. More than anything. Dinna ye want to have children? Dinna ye want to have a family with me, and be happy like they are?"

"Well, of course, I want to be happy. Who doesna?" Nash sat up. "And about the bairn . . . aye, I guess I want one. Someday."

"What?" She blinked twice and bit her lip. "Ye dinna sound sure about it, Nash. That is scarin' me. Ye dinna want to have a family with me."

"That's no' true. I want children, Kellina, honest I do. But someday . . . no' right now. We dinna even really ken each other yet. Everythin' is happenin' so fast."

"What does that mean? We ken each other well now since we've been intimate together."

"I'm no' talkin' about just couplin'. I dinna feel that I ken who ye are, really. Or who I am, for that matter."

"Nash, ye are confusin' me. Why dinna ye just come right out and say what ye mean instead of playin' these doitit word games with me?"

"Aye, I will. Kellina, ye were verra angry about the MacKeefes killin' yer parents, and had no qualms in lettin' me ken that."

"I still am! We're talkin' about my parents' lives, Nash. How could I no' be angry?"

"But . . . I'm a MacKeefe, lass. If ye dinna get over this soon, it will always come between us."

"Nay. That's no' true. Ye're my husband. That is different."

"True, we are married. But what is goin' to happen when we go back to live with the MacKeefes? How will ye feel about them then?"

"Live with the MacKeefes?" Her brows dipped. "Why would we do that?"

"Kellina, I am goin' home sooner or later. Ye had to have realized that. I am only here for a short while to work off my punishment. I want to be accepted once again back into my clan."

"But I – I just thought we'd live with the MacKenzies now that we're married. This is where I belong."

"Mayhap, but it is no' where I belong," he told her, seeing her disposition starting to darken. "I am goin' back to the MacKeefes soon. I canna leave my clan."

"Nash, I dinna ken if I can do that." She started to look panicked now. "How can I live with the people who murdered my parents? How can ye even think I would?"

"Ye just have to accept it, Kellina. These things happen, unfortunately, but our clans have an alliance now because of our marriage. Ye canna let it affect ye the rest of yer life."

"How can ye be so insensitive?" she snapped. "If ye were in my position, ye would feel the same way."

"Would I?" he asked, feeling perturbed by her lack of sensitivity now. "My parents were killed as well, Kellina. I ken verra well what ye are feelin', so dinna ever say that."

"I'm sorry. I didna ken yer parents were dead. Still, it is different, Nash. It's no' like ye're marryin' someone from the murderin' side, the way I was forced to do."

Before Nash could respond, loud voices could be heard from down below.

"Somethin's wrong," said Nash, getting up and looking out over the hills. "I think someone from yer clan has arrived at the gates."

"My clan?" Kellina got up and looked down, squinting her eyes to see. "That is Fergus, Tomas' guid friend. I wonder why he's here."

"Let's go find out." They made their way off the roof, and ran back to camp to find Fergus talking with Shaw.

"Ah, there ye are," said Fergus, running over to meet them. "Kellina, ye must come back at once."

"Why?" she asked. "Has somethin' happened to our camp? Have we been attacked again?"

"Yer uncle has taken a turn for the worse," he informed her. "I think his leg as well as his side is infected from his wounds. The infection seems to have spread through his body and made its way to his lungs as well. He is spittin' up blood and the life drains from him quickly."

"Och, nay!" cried Kellina, putting her hand to her mouth. When she pulled it away, Nash saw her bottom lip trembling. "Jamie, Caitlin," she shouted. "Get our things together, quickly. We must leave right away."

"My men have already loaded the wagon with the thatch for ye," said Shaw. "I will have a few men from my clan escort ye back to yer camp as well."

"There's no need for that," said Nash. "My brathair and I will protect Kellina and her siblin's. Plus, we'll have Fergus to watch our backs. We'll take the trail Spring showed us, and there shouldna be any problems at all."

"What's happenin'?" asked North, walking up, munching on an apple.

"North, we need to return to the MacKenzie Clan right away," Nash told him. "It seems their chieftain is dyin'."

"He's dyin' and he insisted on talkin' to ye two before he passes," Fergus told Kellina and Nash.

"Us?" asked Nash. "Whatever would he want to talk to me for?"

"I dinna ken," Fergus answered. "He told me to hurry. He said that if he died before he could talk to ye two, then there would never be peace between the MacKenzies and the MacKeefes."

"That's an odd thing to say," commented Spring. "After all, there should already be peace since Kellina and Nash married to form an alliance."

"I have a suspicion that there is more behind this alliance than the chieftain led ye two to believe," said Fergus.

"What does that mean?" asked Kellina.

"I think it has to do with the deaths of yer parents, but I'm no' certain."

"Our parents?" asked Kellina. "I'm confused."

Fergus' eyes roamed over to Nash. "Doesna she ken?"

"Ken what?" asked Kellina.

"I tried to tell her, but it isna easy to get a word in edgewise with her," said Nash.

"Tell me what?" asked Kellina. "Nash, what is goin' on?"

"I'm no' sure exactly what the chieftain wants with us, lass," answered Nash. "However, I have to guess that this all has somethin' to do with the fact that my parents were killed in the same battle that took yer parents' lives."

"They were?" asked Kellina, looking shocked.

"Aye. My parents were killed on the same day as yers," Nash continued.

"I didna ken this," said Kellina. "Then ye are sayin' that –"

"That's right," said Nash with a slight nod. "Yer parents were killed by MacKeefes, but my parents were killed by the MacKenzies. Now, ye see that I ken exactly how ye feel."

✦•◦◇◦•✦

CHAPTER FIFTEEN

"I CANNA BELIEVE that ye never told me yer parents were killed by my clan." Kellina sat on the bench seat of the wagon next to Nash as they headed home. Since the wagon was loaded down with thatch, their things were secured on Nash's horse. The horse's reins were tied to the back of the wagon. Caitlin rode double with North, and Jamie was with Fergus.

"Ye never asked me," he answered nonchalantly.

"Well, ye could have offered the information. After all, I'd think it was important to ye to let me ken."

"Aye, it is important," he told her. "But ye were so busy goin' on and on about how much ye hated the MacKeefes for what they did that I didna see any point even bringin' it up."

"Ye saw no point in it?" She was back to blinking those damned long lashes again. "Nash, ye sound as if ye dinna even care."

"Of course, I do," he spat. "I buried my parents the same as ye did, no' even bein' able to do anythin' to stop them from dyin'."

"Where were ye? When it happened?" she asked.

"North and I were tendin' the sheep that day. I kent somethin' was amiss because my parents left quickly without even sayin' guidbye. The next thing I kent, the chieftain told me my parents were dead."

Nash slipped back into his thoughts of that horrible day when he was only twelve years old.

"That's the last of the sheep," Nash told his brother. "Now, they're all safe in the pen. Let's go and tell Mathair and Da. They said when we completed our chores we were goin' to spend the rest of the day as a family, and I canna wait."

"Ye just want to show Faither how guid ye're gettin' with the sword he gave ye," said North. "Even though we both ken ye're just braggin'. I can beat ye with a blade any day."

"Ye canna."

"I can so."

"I think ye just wanted the sword I got but Faither let me choose first since I am his favorite and was the firstborn twin."

"Ye might be Faither's favorite, but I've always held Mathair's heart," said North.

"Well, let's go ask them, shall we?"

"I think that is a guid idea."

They turned to start down the hill, but stopped in their tracks.

"Why are Mathair and Da leavin' without us?" asked North as he and Nash saw their parents on horseback, leaving camp.

"Wait for us!" Nash called out, waving his hand above his head.

His father didn't stop, but kept on riding. Their mother stopped and looked back at them, but didn't say a word. Nash felt it in his heart that something was very wrong. His mother had such a sad look on her face that it almost made Nash want to cry.

"Wait! We're done with our chores. We'll come with ye," called out North, but their parents did not heed the request.

"Somethin' is wrong," said Nash. "I feel it deep inside. We are never goin' to see our parents again."

Their father called out to their mother, and she turned around and headed out of camp, never saying a word to them.

"Where are they goin'?" cried North. "We were supposed to spend time together as a family. I've got to stop them."

He started to run, but Nash grabbed his arm.

"It's too late, North. They left, and we will never see them again."

"Dinna say that. Ye lie," bellowed North, breaking away and running down the hill.

"Guidbye, Mathair. Guidbye, Faither," whispered Nash, running after his brother, knowing that they were too late. That was the last time

they would ever see their parents alive.

"Och, I'm so sorry, Nash," said Kellina. "I kent the battle happened on the road somewhere, but I was young at the time. No one ever told me exactly how it happened or who was involved. All I kent was that it was the MacKeefes."

"I'm no' sure anyone kens for sure how their lives were lost. I only wish North and I would have taken horses and followed them that day. But one of our clansmembers stopped us, sayin' it was by our faither's orders that we were to stay there and wait for them to return." Nash's eyes teared up and he shook his head. "I kent they werena goin' to return. I just felt it in my heart."

"Oh, Nash," she whispered, feeling so sorry for him now.

He cleared his throat and seemed to regain his composure. "Well, now ye see, Kellina, that I am no' such a cold-hearted, insensitive monster after all."

Kellina reached out and took Nash's hand. She saw Nash's eyes getting wet and knew he was holding back his tears. She had been too soon to judge her husband, and she realized that now. Nash had feelings as well as she did, only he had been holding them all inside and not letting them out.

"I could never think ye are a monster, Nash. Ye are the kindest person I have ever met."

"Except that I'm a MacKeefe. And responsible for yer parents' deaths. Or so ye seem to think, since every MacKeefe is to pay for it for the rest of yer life." His jaw was firm and he looked straight ahead. Kellina had never seen Nash look so upset, or so serious before.

"I'm sorry if ye dinna think much of me right now, but I canna help the way I feel."

"I've been ignorin' my true feelin's all this time, but mayhap I shouldna anymore." He pulled his hand away from her, still looking straight ahead as they rode.

Kellina decided it was better not to talk about their parents right now. Her heart ached for Nash, but she didn't know how to ease the pain he'd locked away inside himself for all these years. She felt so selfish now, since she never realized that he was in the same position as she was. Kellina kept thinking of Spring's words, and how Spring told her to try to bring down those walls between them before ones were built that were too high to ever be removed.

She did want to bring down those walls, but didn't know how to do it. Now, it seemed that Nash had put up a new wall and, this time, it was done specifically to keep her out.

NASH HADN'T FELT like talking with Kellina because if he did, he would probably say things he would end up regretting. He had buried inside him long ago the memories of his parents and the events of the day they'd died. Even when Kellina kept going on and on about her parents being killed by MacKeefes, he hadn't said anything because he didn't want to remember. It hurt too much. He didn't want to feel the pain of him and his brother being orphans at such a young age.

Nash loved his parents, and never understood why they had to die. Some battle between the clans took place on the road one day, claiming their lives, was all he knew. There were dead from both sides, but no one knew details, nor did they seem to want to talk about it.

They rode into camp, and Nash jumped off the wagon and started walking, not even helping Kellina dismount. He didn't want to see her right now. He couldn't. It wasn't that he blamed her for his parents' deaths, that wasn't it at all. It was just that she had stirred up feelings inside him having to do with that awful day that he never wanted to feel again.

"Brathair, are ye all right?" North met up with Nash and they stopped. "I ken ye're upset with all this, and rightly so. I am, too."

"Ye're damned right I'm upset," snapped Nash. "I didna ever

want to think about that awful day again, and now I'm bein' forced to."

"I understand. I feel the same way. Mayhap we should just leave and go back to our own clan. This was a bad idea for the MacKeefes to send us here, of all places."

"Nay. I canna run from this problem, Brathair. Kellina is my wife now, and I am married unless ye've forgotten. I just have to deal with it."

"Mayhap we can get ye a divorce."

"I dinna want a divorce," he ground out. "I want –" He looked over his shoulder and saw Tomas talking with Kellina. Caitlin and Jamie were both crying. Then Kellina took her siblings and headed to the chieftain's hut. "I dinna ken what I want," he answered, closing his eyes. "I think I have feelin's for Kellina, and I canna just walk away from her."

"Then bring her with ye, Brathair. She can live with the MacKeefes from now on as yer wife."

"I wish it was that easy. She doesna want to live with our clan, and I dinna want to live with hers."

"Then what are ye goin' to do?" asked North.

"I dinna ken," he answered, watching as Caitlin and Jamie exited the hut. A woman of the clan escorted them away. Tomas spied Nash, and rushed over.

"Nash, the chieftain is about to die. He wants to talk to ye and yer brathair, too," Tomas informed them.

"Me?" asked North. "What for?"

"Well, this has to do with yer parents, and ye are twins, so it concerns both of ye," answered Tomas.

"Our parents?" This was the last thing Nash wanted to hear right now. "Fine then. Let's go, North." Nash led the way, ducking to enter the small hut, taking a moment for his eyes to grow accustomed to the dark.

There were two candles burning, one of each side of Ciaran's bed. The man lay there with his eyes closed and his mouth gaping open, looking as if he were already dead and his spirit had fled his body. Kellina sat on the bed next to him, holding his hands in hers.

"Are we . . . too late?" Nash looked over to Tomas who shook his head slowly.

"Nash, come here quickly," said Kellina with a sniffle. "Uncle says he wants to tell us somethin' important. Ye, too, North and Tomas. He wants ye all to hear what he has to say."

"We're here, Chieftain," Tomas informed his leader, stepping around the twins and leading the way to the bed.

"I'm sorry," said the chieftain in a soft whisper.

"What did he say?" asked North. "I canna hear him. He is speakin' too softly."

"Get closer. All of ye." Kellina moved over, making room for Nash to sit next to her on the bed. North and Tomas went around the other side of the pallet.

"Go ahead, Uncle. We can all hear ye now," Kellina urged him to speak.

The man opened his eyes slowly, then used what little breath he had left to tell them a story that Nash would never forget for the rest of his life.

"It was no one's fault but my own that yer parents are dead. Both yers, Kellina, and yers, too, Nash and North." He coughed, spitting up blood onto a rag.

"Yer fault?" asked Kellina, taking the cloth and giving him a fresh one. "What do ye mean?"

"Kellina and Nash, yer parents were . . . friends . . . at first. It all started when I drank too much Mountain Magic . . . one night in the . . . Horn and Hoof."

"I ken the feelin'," said North with a snort. "I've done that on occasion and couldna remember a thing afterwards."

"Shhh," Nash silenced his brother. "Go on, Chieftain. Tell us what happened."

"I didna ever want to tell this story aloud . . . but now I must. I willna . . . go to my death lettin' the MacKeefes and the MacKenzies be . . . enemies."

"What happened?" Kellina asked him again.

"Och, I dinna want to say." The man closed his eyes and turned his head, looking as if he were disgusted with himself.

"Uncle, ye called us here, so please tell us," said Kellina. "If ye have somethin' weighin' heavy on yer soul, then confess it before ye die."

"All right," the man said, coughing a few more times, looking weaker by the moment. "I am a lustful cur, and I was . . . attracted to both . . . yer mathairs."

"What!" snapped Nash, ready to take off the man's head.

"Uncle, ye had a wife. And children," cried Kellina. "I dinna understand this kind of talk at all."

"I didna . . . understand either. I wish to God I didna do it."

"Do what?" Nash demanded to know. "If ye touched my mathair at all, ye willna have to suffer any longer from yer wounds because I will kill ye right here in yer bed."

"Nash, please," begged Kellina. "Let the dyin' man speak."

"Go on," said Nash, biting his tongue before he said things not fit for Kellina's ears.

"It was a celebration that night . . . I dinna remember what for. I had to piss . . . so I borrowed yer faither's cloak, Nash, and went outside. That's when I saw Robena."

"My mathair," Kellina told Nash.

"She was by herself . . . and I had to have her."

"God's eyes, nay!" Kellina gasped and held her hand to her mouth. "Ye raped my mathair?"

"Nay, lass. But I might have if things had gone differently. I grabbed her from behind and kissed her. She . . . fought me. And she called for Avery, to tell him . . . Bram accosted her."

"Bram?" asked Kellina.

"That's who she thought ye were, right?" asked Nash. "Ye were wearin' my faither's cloak and it was dark."

"Aye," the chieftain admitted.

"I canna listen to this any longer." Nash started to stand up, but North reached across the bed, putting his hand on Nash's shoulder and pushing him back down to sit.

"Stay and listen, Nash," said North. "We need to ken what really happened, no matter how awful the truth is."

"Go on, Chieftain," said Tomas, listening intently.

"Bram didna hear her cries for help, but Una did."

"My mathair," Nash told Kellina.

"The two women fought about the accusations, but didna tell their husbands about it until the next day."

"That's when they met at the crossroads?" asked Kellina.

"Aye. I sent each of the couples a missive, pretendin' it was from the other," the chieftain continued, wiping his brow. "I wrote . . . I wrote that they wanted peace. To be friends again, like they once were. They were to meet at the crossroads to settle this once and for all."

"God's eyes, why would ye do that?" spat Nash. "Did ye really think they would make amends after what they thought had happened?"

"I was goin' to tell them the truth . . . that it was me," the chieftain told them. "I wanted them to ken . . . I was drunk . . . and sorry. That's why I went to the crossroads as well." Ciaran coughed and cleared his throat, and Kellina gave him a sip of ale.

"So, this didna involve both our clans at all?" asked North.

"Nay. Just the four of them, and no others," answered Ciaran.

"That's where they died. At the crossroads," said Nash.

"Because ye let them fight and didna stop them!" North's anger was showing now.

"Aye. I am ashamed to say, that is true." The chieftain closed his eyes again, and looked like he was about to sleep.

"Wake up, Uncle." Kellina reached out and shook him. "Ye need to tell us the rest."

"Did they ken ye were there?" asked North. "Did our parents even see ye?"

"No' at first, they didna," said the chieftain in a soft voice. "I was late in arrivin' . . . and I saw them . . . startin' to fight. I kent I had to intervene. Avery wanted to kill Bram . . . for touchin' his wife."

"God's teeth, why didna ye tell them the truth?" asked Nash.

"Because he kent they'd kill him, that's why," growled North. "This man is naught but a coward."

"Nay, I tried to tell them, but they didna hear me," protested the chieftain. "Both the men were angry. They . . . pulled their swords and . . . started to fight."

"What did our mathairs do?" asked Nash.

"When Avery was about to kill Bram . . . Una rushed forward and . . . stabbed Avery from behind."

"Nay! My mathair killed someone? I dinna believe it," spat Nash, shocked to hear this information.

"Me neither," added North. "She was a kind and gentle soul."

"It's . . . true, I'm sad to say." The chieftain coughed up more blood, looking very pale now, as if his face was turning white like a ghost.

Nash saw Kellina's body stiffen at hearing this last part. "So, my faither was killed by no' just any MacKeefe, but yer mathair, Nash?" She moved away from Nash, looking disgusted and appalled.

"Ye heard the chieftain, Kellina. Yer faither was about to kill mine," spat Nash. "My mathair was only tryin' to protect the man she loved."

"Haud yer wheesht. Both of ye," commanded the chieftain, using all his strength to shut them up. "When Robena saw Una kill her husband, she rushed forward with her dagger and stabbed Bram to death. She went crazy, and wanted . . . Una to pay for what she'd done."

"Nay!" screamed Kellina. "I dinna believe this at all."

"So, it seems that no' just any MacKenzie killed my faither, but it was yer mathair, Kellina." Nash glared at Kellina now.

"What I want to ken is what the hell were ye doin' while all this was goin' on?" growled North.

"Aye, Chieftain. Why didna ye stop the women?" asked Tomas. "Ye said ye were there."

"I was too shocked by what I saw to even move," said Kellina's uncle. "I was also . . . verra drunk . . . but already regrettin' my actions."

"God's eyes, Uncle. Ye could have stopped them all from dyin' and ye didna do a thing," Kellina all but shouted. "Their deaths are all because of ye!"

"How did the women die?" Tomas interrupted.

"I called out to them," said the chieftain. "When Una turned to look at me . . . Robena killed her, too."

"My mathair wasna a murderer! I refuse to believe it." Kellina started crying.

"Kellina," said Nash, putting his arm around her, but she pushed it away.

"Finish the damned story, and then die already, Uncle." A dark side of Kellina was coming to the surface that Nash didn't like to see. "I think ye killed them all and are just makin' this up to cover yer arse."

"Kellina, the man is confessin' on his deathbed," said Nash. "Let him talk. Afterwards, I will personally kill him for what he's done."

"Stop it! Both of ye," commanded Tomas. "I willna let ye touch him." Tomas' hand went to the hilt of his sword.

"Nay, Tomas, it's all right," North told him. His hand wavered above his sword as he spoke. "They are upset, as am I. This is hard to hear."

"But it's the truth," said the chieftain. "I hid the truth . . . because I didna want anyone to ken. The clans would battle . . . if they kent it was me. And I could no' bear to let Lorna and the girls . . . ken what kind of man I . . . really was. Still, I had no choice. I was goin' to . . . tell them, I swear."

"How did Kellina's mathair die, since she was the last one standin'?" asked Nash. "The only one left to kill her was ye."

Kellina's head snapped around and her eyes bore fire. "Did ye kill her, Uncle? Tell me! I have to ken the truth. Did ye kill my mathair or no'?" Kellina wiped away a tear.

"Nay, I didna . . . kill her." Ciaran spat up more blood and had a coughing fit before he continued. "Kellina, Daughter, I am . . . sorry."

"Stop callin' me Daughter. I am no' yer daughter."

"Aye . . . ye are."

"What?" Both Kellina and Nash said together.

"I did have yer mathair, but no' that awful night. Instead, it happened earlier . . . right after she married Avery."

"Ye disgust me!" Kellina shouted, jumping up, but Nash pulled her back down, and put his arm around her to hold her still. "It's no' true," cried Kellina. "My mathair would have told me."

"She couldna, lass. She kept it a secret because she loved Avery and . . . didna want to lose him," the chieftain continued. "She also kent it would mean Avery would try to kill me."

"Aye, Avery would have killed ye, my laird, if he had kent," agreed Tomas. "And then he would have been killed in return."

"I'm no' yer child," spat Kellina. "I canna be. My mathair was married . . . I'm Avery's daughter."

"Perhaps," said Ciaran. "But I dinna think so. Ye . . . dinna look like Jamie or Caitlin with their dark hair. Ye look more like Sileas and Eilidh, with blond hair and blue eyes instead," he said, speaking of his daughters who had died in the battle with the Sutherlands.

"Ye killed my mathair, didna ye?" cried Kellina. "Ye did it to keep her quiet."

"Nay. She took her own life, right in . . . front of my eyes."

"S-she did?" Kellina's body shook and Nash had to hold her tighter to comfort her.

"Robena said she . . . didna want to live . . . no' after murderin' her friends, and without her husband. She . . . went crazy with guilt."

"Why didna our chieftain tell us there were only four people involved?" asked Nash.

"I told him it was a lover's spat . . . between them," said the chieftain, fighting for breath. "Neither side . . . would fight that way. But I asked him . . . to keep silent. For the sake of the children . . . all of ye."

"So, that is why our clans were enemies, but never actually went to battle, beyond this occasion," said Tomas, understanding now.

"Aye," said Ciaran. "That is . . . why."

"Why are ye tellin' us this now?" Kellina's nostrils flared and her jaw ticked. "Why no' just take yer horrid secrets to the grave with ye? Ye are a terrible man, and I hate ye! No matter if ye are my faither or no'."

"He'll get what's due to him . . . in hell," spat North.

"I have already been punished . . . more than ye ken." The chieftain coughed some more and his eyes started closing. He didn't look like he could speak or even breathe much longer. "The Sutherlands killed my wife and daughters . . . so I have been punished . . . by the hand of God for my mistakes."

"Why did ye even have to tell us this at all?" spat Nash. "Are ye purposely tryin' to ruin the marriage between me and Kellina?"

"Nay. I wanted . . . an alliance between . . . yer clans. That was . . . the only way . . . I could . . . do it." He looked over to Tomas next. "Tomas, ye are . . . chieftain now. Please, keep the alliance strong . . . between the MacKeefes and . . . our clan . . . forever."

With that, his breathing stopped, and his open eyes stared up at the ceiling, and the man died. Everyone stayed silent for a minute, not knowing how to respond to what they'd just heard. This confession was life-changing, and could bring about peace . . . or most likely trouble. The truth was out, and now they had to decide just what to do with the confession they'd just witnessed. It wasn't going to be an easy choice.

"What do we do now?" North finally spoke, saying exactly what they were all thinking.

"I suppose I'll need to tell the clan, and ye'll need to tell the

MacKeefes what really transpired," stated Tomas. "Although, I'm no' sure how everyone is goin' to take it."

"Nay, no one will say a word," said Kellina, standing up, looking stronger than Nash had expected, especially after hearing this. "No matter what my mathair did, I willna have her name and image dragged through the mud and sullied. It seems to me that she's been through enough, havin' to keep the secret of what our chieftain did to her. I canna even imagine how horrible that must have been for her. I'm surprised she didna take her life years ago. I think I might have."

"Kellina, yer mathair isna at fault for that, and no one would blame her for what the chieftain did," said Nash.

"If Avery had kent, he would have killed Ciaran, and battle would have broken out within our clan," Tomas pointed out.

"She did the right thing by stayin' quiet then," said North. "She did it for the guid of the clan."

"I canna say I agree with her silence, but I suppose I understand now why she never told me that Ciaran might be my faither." Kellina paced back and forth in thought.

"There's still a chance, he's no' yer faither," said Nash. "Nobody kens for sure, lass."

"Either way, I dinna want my brathair and sister to ever ken the truth about any of this." She started pacing faster. "They can never ken."

"I agree," said Tomas. He looked down at the dead man on the bed as he spoke. "Laird Ciaran didn't have to tell us any of this, but he did. He could have gone to his death with everyone still admirin' him, but he chose to tell the truth."

"A little late as far as I'm concerned." Nash stood up.

"He wanted to clear his conscience," said North. "Even if he will burn in hell for the things he's done."

"Aye, mayhap," Nash answered.

"Ye heard him," said Tomas. "Ciaran told the truth because he wants peace between our clans. He doesna want the loss of any other lives."

"Peace, meanin' he wants us to stop blamin' each other's clan for the deaths of our parents." Nash looked over to Kellina when he said it.

Kellina's body stilled. "The fact still remains, that our parents are dead," she answered with a stiff upper lip.

"But now we ken that it was the chieftain's actions that caused the reactions of our parents," added North. "I dinna think either clan will feel settled hearin' that!"

"The MacKeefes could attack us if they find out," added Tomas.

"No more lives will be lost over this," said Nash. "This needs to stop, right here, right now."

"Then mayhap it is best for all of us to forget what was said here today, and never mention it again." Tomas walked over and closed the chieftain's eyes. "I will see to his burial, and then I will take over as chieftain of this clan as he instructed. I think only more anger and problems would arise if we told the clans what really happened. The MacKenzies admired Ciaran. I would hate for them to lose trust over this."

"As much as I hate to agree, I think he's right," said North. "Our clans are aligned by yer marriage to Kellina, Nash. We are allies, so it is done and over."

"I'll agree to stay silent," said Nash with a nod. "We canna change the past, and neither should we try to. Kellina? What do ye say?"

They all stood staring at Kellina, waiting for her answer. She would be the only one to give them trouble.

She took a moment to respond, letting out a deep sigh before giving her answer. "This secret will go to our graves with us," said Kellina. "But I will never forgive my uncle . . . my faither . . . or whoever he was . . . for ruinin' my life."

"It's no' ruined, lass." Nash reached out for her, but she backed away. "We are married now, Kellina, and I love ye."

She looked at him in shock, shaking her head. "How can ye say ye love me now, Nash?" she asked, tears flowing down her cheeks. "My parents killed yers."

"And mine, yers," he said.

"But I am naught but a bastard, spawned by the devil, with a murderer for a mathair. Nay, Nash, we canna stay married. It isna right." She rushed out the door, crying.

"Kellina, wait!" Nash started to go after her, but North held him back.

"Give her some time alone, Nash," said North. "She has a lot to think about. Give her some space."

Nash watched Kellina running to the stable, then saw her riding out of the camp atop a horse. His heart broke for her. The last thing he wanted was to leave her alone. She needed someone – she needed him now, more than anything. He would not abandon her in her dark hour.

"Nay, North. I canna give her space, because she is my wife now. I've got to go after her," said Nash, ignoring his brother and heading out the door. "I will no' let the woman I love go through this alone."

✦•◦◇◦•✦

CHAPTER SIXTEEN

"KELLINA? KELLINA, WHERE are ye?" called out Nash, but Kellina didn't answer. She sat atop her horse at the crossroads where her parents were killed, staring into space, not knowing how to feel.

"Kellina, there ye are, lass," said Nash, riding up next to her. "I was callin' ye. Why didna ye answer?"

"I wish I had been here when it happened. I would have done somethin' to stop them from dyin'," she said, staring at the ground where she knew the lifeblood had slipped from the bodies of their parents.

"Listen to yerself. Ye dinna ken what ye're sayin'. Ye were naught but a child and couldna have done anythin' to make a difference. Ye would have died, too, if ye were here, and ye ken it."

"How could Ciaran have done nothin' to stop it all? Especially when he was the one to start it? He is a horrible man and I hate him."

"It's over now, Kellina. Let it go."

"How could my mathair be a murderer? I canna believe it, Nash. She was always so kind and gentle and sweet. I dinna understand any of this at all. I feel like I'm in a bad dream and I just want to wake up, and canna."

"When people are upset, they say and do things they dinna mean," said Nash, trying to comfort Kellina.

"Hah! Or drunk?" she asked, thinking about Ciaran.

"I suppose so."

"Och, now it makes sense why my uncle always called me Daughter."

"Ye mean . . . yer faither," he corrected her, realizing immediately the mistake he'd made. "I mean . . . mayhap he was yer faither. We dinna ken for sure, of course."

Her head turned and she glared at him, feeling angry to hear him say this.

"He's no' my faither, Nash, and I never want to hear ye say that again. My parents are Avery and Robena. Do ye understand me?"

"Come back to camp with me, Wife," he said. "Ye need to rest."

"I canna be yer wife, Nash. I am tainted, and I ken it now."

"Dinna be silly. We are married now, and none of this should affect our marriage, Kellina."

"I dinna want to be a mathair anymore, Nash. I canna be a mathair." Her hand went to her belly. "God's eyes, I pray I am no' pregnant now."

"Kellina, stop it! Ye'll make a great mathair someday."

"But what if I murder someone like my mathair did? Oh, Nash, I am so frightened."

"Ye are no' goin' to murder anyone, now stop that. Stay there," he told her, getting off his horse and mounting her horse, right behind her. He tied the reins of his horse to hers. "I love ye, Kellina, and I ken ye are havin' a hard time right now. I want nothin' more than to help ye get through it."

"Nash, my mathair killed both yer parents. How can ye say ye love me?" she cried. "Ye should hate me right now."

"And my mathair killed yer faither," he answered. "We are in the same boat, so to speak."

"But it might no' really be my faither she killed after all. Therefore, ye have every reason to hate me, but I have none to despise ye."

"Ye just told me Avery is yer faither, and that is what we are both goin' to believe. Now, no more! We're goin' home," said Nash, holding her tightly, directing the horse back to the MacKenzie camp. "I willna hear another word about hatin' each other. We are married now, and we need to get along. Besides, I could never hate ye."

"How can ye sound so calm, Nash? Doesna any of this bother ye?"

"Of course, it does. How can ye even think it doesna? However, even though I'm upset by what happened to our parents, it bothers me more that ye are blamin' yerself now for somethin' that ye couldna have stopped from happenin'. We canna control the lives and actions of others, and neither should we try. All we can do is control our reactions. That is what makes us strong, Kellina. Ye are strong – one of the strongest lassies I have ever met. Dinna forget that. None of this has anythin' to do with either of us, lass. We are naught but victims of circumstance. It was all between the chieftain and our parents."

"I suppose ye're right. I just wish things could have been different, that's all."

"Ye need to forgive and forget about what happened, and move on with yer life, Kellina, before it destroys ye. Yer parents are no' who ye are, and ye need to remember that."

"I have to talk to Caitlin and Jamie."

Nash's head snapped up. "I thought ye werena goin' to tell them what happened."

"I'm no'. I canna. No' now, anyway. Mayhap when they are much older, I'll change my mind. Right now, if they kent, it would scar them for life, I'm sure. They never really kent our parents, but they admired Ciaran and Lorna and thought of them as their parents after the deaths of ours."

"I think it's the right decision to keep silent. No guid can come from exposin' the nasty truth now, lass. What's done is in the past, and we canna change that. Let us focus on the present. However, I do believe we can change our future, and I think we need to do so."

"Change our future? How? I hate Ciaran! Dinna ye hate him, too? This was all his fault."

"Despisin' a man who is deceased, isna goin' to bring our parents back from the dead. All we can do is learn from his mistakes. We need to be sure to be better people – better parents – than he was. Ye've got to move on, Kellina. We all do. At least we ken the truth now about what happened, no matter how much it really hurts. So now we can put it to rest, and no' live the rest of our lives wonderin' what and how it happened."

"I will spit on Ciaran's grave until the day I die," she ground out. "But I will also be strong – for Caitlin and Jamie . . . even if they might no' really be my siblin's after all."

She hung her head in sadness, and Nash felt her anguish and her pain.

"Will ye be all right, love?" he whispered in her ear, kissing the back of her neck as he held her closely in his arms as they rode.

Kellina let out a deep sigh. "I will move on, as ye suggest, Nash. I ken it is for the best. However, I canna forgive Ciaran for what he did, and I will never, ever forget!"

NASH CLOSED THE door to the infirmary, and made his way over to the fire where his brother was drinking whisky with Tomas. The rest of the clan was sleeping for the night. The sun had set hours ago, filling the vast sky with beautiful streaks of orange and red as the fiery ball slipped down below the horizon.

Earlier, they'd buried the chieftain's body up on the hill next to his wife and daughters. The clan didn't know all the information that Nash was privy to, so they felt the pain of the loss of their chieftain. Spirits were solemn on this night. A clan had lost the life of their leader. Nash, Tomas, and the rest let them mourn as was proper. Everyone was quiet and kept to themselves, thinking about the dead.

"How is Kellina?" asked North, handing Nash a tankard of whisky.

"She's finally sleepin'," Nash reported, sitting down on a stump by the fire. "Caitlin and Jamie were havin' a hard time with their uncle's death. Kellina let them both sleep in the box bed with her. They closed the curtains for privacy from the rest of the clan. I heard a lot of cryin'."

"This was a hard day for everyone," said Tomas. "Especially, comin' so close to the Sutherlands' last attack."

"Aye, it was hard." Nash took a drink of whisky, smacking his lips and looking over to his brother. "Is this Mountain Magic?" he asked, his spirits suddenly rising.

"It is," confirmed North with a smile.

"Where did it come from?"

"Shaw and Spring sent it with the thatch," he told him. "I guess they thought we might need it, with the chieftain dyin' and all."

"Well, they were right. It's just what I need after a day like today." Nash took a long draw and let out a satisfied sigh.

"I sent a missive to the MacKeefe camp, lettin' them ken that our chieftain has died, and that I am the new chieftain of the MacKenzie Clan," said Tomas. "I also told them that I honor and cherish the new alliance between our clans brought on by the marriage of Nash and Kellina."

"Guid," said North, taking another swig of Mountain Magic. "Mayhap Old Callum will feel pity on us, and let us come home now."

"Nay." Nash shook his head. "I willna leave until all the roofs are thatched. It is what I was sent here to do, and I will finish my sentence. Besides, I want to do it, to help rebuild the camp for the clan."

"But that could take quite a while," complained North, breaking up a stick and tossing it into the fire. "I'm really tired of bein' here, are no' ye?"

"Ye have no idea," Nash mumbled into his cup. "However, I willna leave without Kellina, and I'm no' sure she wants to live with the MacKeefes."

"Well, ye're no' stayin' here are ye?" asked his brother. "Nash, we've always been together, ever since bein' in our mathair's womb."

"I dinna want to leave the MacKeefes," said Nash. "They are my family. But I dinna want Kellina to have to leave her family either."

"She doesna seem to have any family left," said North, pouring himself some more whisky. "I mean, besides Caitlin and Jamie. Mayhap. We dinna even ken that for sure."

"North, please," said Nash, looking around, not wanting anyone to hear about the fact that Kellina might be the chieftain's daughter. "I'll let her decide where we'll go, but I willna abandon my wife. I think she needs to get her mind off of all this, but I dinna ken how to help her."

"I have an idea," said Tomas.

"What's that?" asked Nash.

"I ken how to thatch roofs. I will no' only help, but will also teach the rest of the clan to do so. I want to be a guid leader now, as clan chieftain. This will also bring everyone together. North, if ye'll work with me, it'll allow Kellina and Nash time to get away for a few days. Nash, take her to the marketplace, and stay the night at an inn. Celebrate yer marriage, since ye havena had time to really do that yet. Ye two need to get away from here and relax. Mayhap it would help, after everythin' ye've been through lately."

"I like the sound of that," said Nash, thinking it sounded like heaven. "What do ye say, Brathair?"

"I've been through just as much as ye – regardin' our parents." North didn't look at all happy with this proposal.

"That's true," said Nash. "I suppose it wouldna be fair of me to ask this of ye. Ye have already helped me out so much, and I thank ye."

"I also think this sounds like I'll be doin' yer punishment while ye're out havin' a guid time," North continued. "I dinna like it at all."

"Well, what if I promise to go with ye and help out when ye get yer sentence?" asked Nash. "Then would ye do it? Please?"

North took a big swig of whisky, then sighed loudly, looking over to Nash. "Sure," he said with a snort. "Even if I dinna believe for one minute that ye're goin' to leave yer new wife to come with me when I get my sentence."

"I've never broken a promise to ye before, have I, Brathair?"

North thought for a moment and then shrugged. "I guess no'."

"I'll bring ye somethin' back from the market as well," Nash promised.

"I'll do even better than that," said Tomas with a chuckle. "Nash, as soon as the roofs are all thatched, I'll write a missive personally to that old bat, Callum MacKeefe. I'll tell him yer punishment is completed and that ye are no longer needed here. After all, ye will have done everythin' he wanted, now that ye're married to Kellina as well."

"I'd like that," said Nash with a nod, looking over at his brother. "Well? Is it settled then?"

"Will ye bring me back somethin' made of silver?" asked North, always wanting nice things that others had and he couldn't afford. "I like silver, ye ken."

"I'll do my best," Nash promised.

"Then ye've got a deal." North raised his tankard in the air and the three of them drank together. "This way, I'll get my punishment quicker. God kens, I've waited long enough, and had to feel the wrath of each of yer punishments so far. It's about time that things are just about me."

"Ye're the best, Brathair." Nash laughed, starting to feel more and more relaxed with each sip of Mountain Magic he took. "The best part is, all our worries are behind us now, and the worst is over."

"Somethin' tells me, it's never over," said North, burying his nose in his tankard.

No one knew how true North's assumption was going to prove to be.

CHAPTER SEVENTEEN

"NASH, I FEEL guilty bein' here instead of back at camp helpin' the others thatch the roofs," said Kellina the next day as they strolled hand in hand through Kilfinnan after riding for several hours to get here. They'd stabled their horses and were proceeding on foot.

"Dinna feel guilty." Nash reached over and kissed her on the cheek, making her blush. "Ye have had a hard time lately and deserve some time away. Now, all ye need to do is relax, lass."

"Och, look at that," said Kellina, stopping in front of the window of a clothier's shop. Dresses were displayed in the window, and one of them had caught Kellina's eye. It was a long skirt, made of wool dyed in bright, colorful orange tones. A white tunic with billowy sleeves and a low neckline was shown with it. "It's so bonnie."

"Do ye like it?" asked Nash.

"I do." Kellina couldn't take her eyes off of it.

"Then I say we buy it for ye."

"What?" Her head snapped around and her mouth fell open. "Nay, it's no' necessary. I dinna need new clothes." She acted so humble when she didn't need to.

Nash made a big show of looking her up and down. She was still dressed in her tunic and braies and boots.

"I think ye do need new clothes, lass. Besides, I would like to see my wife in a skirt, and no' have her be wearin' the braies of the family."

They both laughed.

"It is so bonnie, but I should be wearin' my clan colors," she told him.

"Ye're a MacKeefe now, Kellina. Ye can wear this skirt and the MacKeefe plaid as a sash or shawl over the tunic. I'll have the weaver back at the MacKeefe camp make one for ye as soon as I can."

She looked at the outfit in the window again, cocking her head and thinking about it. "All right," she said. "I think I would like it then."

"Well, we'd better hurry," suggested Nash. "They are closin' the shops early since the market is about to start."

On market days, the shops in town were required to close and sell their wares from a stall in the marketplace instead. Farmers, peasants, merchants and tradesmen came from towns all around, bringing their wares. They traveled by cart, horseback or on foot, sometimes taking several days just to get there. This wasn't as large or as elaborate as a trade fair, but was still a prosperous and busy place.

It didn't take long to buy the clothes, and for Kellina to change into them. She did a quick twirl to show off her new outfit to Nash. He loved it.

"Ye are the bonniest lass at the market today," he told her.

"I ken ye are just sayin' that because we havena even been to the market yet, so how could ye come up with that decision?"

"I might be a little biased, since ye are my wife." Smiling widely, Nash perused his wife, loving the way she looked in these nice clothes. She deserved something good in her life, and he was happy for her.

"I'm sorry, but we are closin' now, and ye'll have to leave," said the shop owner. "I have to join my husband at the market to help him set up our stall."

"Thank ye," Kellina told the woman, taking her old clothes and shoving them into the leather bag she carried. Wearing the outfit out of the store, Kellina and Nash followed the crowd, heading over to the marketplace next.

"Look, everyone is settin' up around the mercat cross," Nash told her, pointing in the direction that the crowd was heading.

The mercat cross – or market cross, was a round, stone pavilion with a tall stone spire in the center with a cross at the top. This structure denoted that the town had the right to hold a regular market or fair, granted by the king, a bishop, or a baron. There was a church nearby, and streets all around them, lined with the town's shops.

All the vendors set up their stalls around the mercat cross, hoping to attract buyers to their wares. Farmers came from towns all around, wheeling their carts and carrying their baskets of vegetables to sell. Livestock filled the streets, as sheep, chickens, and even cattle were for sale as well.

"Be careful where ye step, and hold up that new skirt high," Nash warned Kellina, since the ground was not only muddy with ruts in the road, but also littered with spoiled food and animal feces.

"Och, I wish I had a pair of pattens now," said Kellina, speaking of the wooden platforms that one wore over their shoes in muddy areas to protect them.

"If I have to carry ye, I will, love." Nash went to pick her up, but she stopped him, laughing at his attempt.

"I appreciate it, Husband, but I think that would make us too much of a spectacle. I'll just walk instead."

"Fresh fruit hand pies for sale. Hot from the oven," shouted a man, waving them over to his stall.

"Are ye hungry, lass?" asked Nash.

"Mmmm, they do smell delicious."

"We'll take two," said Nash, laying his coin on the table and collecting the warm pies that fit in the palms of their hands.

One bite of the bilberry pie, and flavor exploded in Kellina's mouth, bringing her to life. "These are delicious," she said, licking her lips. "I'm goin' to learn to make them for ye, Nash."

"I'd like that. And mayhap ye can learn to make haggis, too?"

"I hope to experience many new things, bein' yer wife now." Kellina really seemed to be relaxing, and also accepting of their marriage. Nash had started to feel like a husband and was thinking that, in time, he would enjoy being a father, too.

"I think I'd like five or six children," he blurted out, almost making her choke on the pie. "Four lads and two lassies would be guid. Dinna ye think?"

"I thought ye said ye wanted to wait to make a family."

"I've changed my mind."

"Well," she said, finishing the pie and licking off her fingers. "Six sounds like a lot to me. How about if we have one first, and see how it fares with both of us?"

"Then ye're no' against bein' a mathair? I mean . . . ye sounded like ye didna want to have bairns anymore."

"I think bein' away from the clan is really helpin' me to clear my head," she told him. "I see now that ye are right. We need to look to our future, and no' the past."

As they continued strolling through the marketplace, they saw baskets of beets and white and purple carrots as long as one's forearm. The aroma of freshly baked brown bread wafted up into the air, helping to disguise the stink of the town and all the livestock in the streets.

Brown eggs were piled up in baskets and set on tables, waiting to be bought. A man who looked to be a tailor cut bolts of cloth and wrapped the pieces in brown paper for his customers to take with them to make clothes. Minstrels strolled through the streets playing lutes and panpipes, carrying small baskets at their sides for coins they collected from the customers who enjoyed their music.

Small children ran through the streets chasing barking dogs. One hound stole a string of sausage and ran through the street dragging it, with a half-dozen other dogs following, trying to get it. A man at a stall with grapes on his sign poured wine into cups from a spigot in a wooden barrel.

"Can ye fill this up?" asked Nash, handing the man his empty wineskin along with another coin.

"Aye," said the man, slipping the coin into his pocket, and taking the wineskin from Nash. His wife and young son sat behind him at a table with a basket of kittens underneath it.

"Would ye like to buy yer lass a kitten?" called out the woman. "My son's stray cat just had a litter a few weeks ago and we canna keep them all. They will hunt down rats twice their size."

"No, thank ye," said Nash, but Kellina loved animals and didn't feel the same about it. Actually, Nash loved animals, too, but didn't know what they'd do with a kitten right now.

"How much?" asked Kellina.

"Five pence each," said the woman, making Nash almost choke on his spit.

"Five pence? Ye've got to be jestin'," snorted Nash. "Why in heaven's name would someone pay that high of a price for a cat?"

Kellina stepped around the front of the stall, hunkering down to pet the kittens. "They are so cute, Nash. Can ye come here and look at them at least?"

"If ye need me to, I guess," said Nash, taking his wineskin back from the woman's husband.

KELLINA WAS ON her knees now, and several kittens had climbed up onto her lap. She picked up one and then another, peeking into the basket at the rest.

Kellina's heart went out to the little kittens that were all brown and white, except for one that seemed to be the runt of the litter and was black with a white ring around one eye.

"They are so precious," said Kellina, picking one up and cuddling it to her chest.

"And most likely loaded with fleas." Nash took the kitten from her and placed it back in the basket. "Come along, Kellina, there is more to see."

"I like the kittens," she told him, still staring at the basket.

"We are no' payin' the wench that price for a cat. We can find a stray one along the road if ye really need one."

"I'm sorry, but we willna be able to buy one," Kellina told the little boy, turning and walking away with Nash.

"Wait," called out the lad, running up to them, holding the scrawny black kitten out to her. "My mathair wants to get rid of this one," said the boy. "She said since it's black, it is bad luck and spawned by the devil. She wants to drown it, but I dinna want her to kill it. Please, take it with ye for free."

"Oh, I dinna ken." Kellina looked up to Nash. "Can we?"

Nash let out a sigh. "Well, I'm never goin' to hear the end of it if I'm the cause for the kitten bein' killed. Go on, Kellina. Take it from him," he told her.

"Thank ye," said Kellina, cuddling the kitten. When Nash turned to leave, she reached into her pouch and pulled out a penny and gave it to the boy. "Buy yerself a fruit hand pie. They're guid," she said with a wink, watching the boy's eyes light up.

"Thank ye!" he cried, running toward the pie vendor's stall. Kellina turned around, only to bump right into Nash's chest.

"Och, I dinna ken ye were there," she told him, almost dropping the little kitten.

"Obviously no', or ye wouldna have given that lad money for this bag of fleas."

"Blethers, Nash, it made the lad's day. Did ye see his eyes light up when I gave him the coin and mentioned the fruit pies? I'm sure I made him happy."

"I'm sure ye did."

Kellina looked down at the purring kitten, smiling, and scratching it behind its ears. "Besides, it was the least I could do after the lad saved Midnight's life."

"Midnight? Is that what ye named the cat?"

"Aye. I think it is fittin', being dark like a starless night."

"Mayhap we can dunk it in the loch and wash off its fleas," suggested Nash.

"It doesna have fleas," she retorted. "Now, let's go find

someone sellin' cream, because Midnight will be hungry."

NASH MOANED AS they headed for the livestock, wondering how much this new addition to the family was going to cost before Kellina was done. He didn't particularly like cats all that much. He liked dogs and sheep and even chickens better. Cats always seemed so finicky, and were worthless except for catching rats, like the woman said. He'd rather have a hound someday who could travel with him and help hunt as well. Then again, he wouldn't even consider getting a dog until he convinced Kellina to move to the MacKeefe Clan with him.

"We need to stop at the silversmith," Nash told Kellina after they spent most of the day buying things to eat, or looking at the wares. "I promised I would buy somethin' made of silver for North."

"And what is that goin' to cost?" she asked with a smile, since he'd been complaining to her that the kitten was draining him dry of money after she insisted on buying herring for it to eat as well as the cream.

"It is no' costin' me a thing, when ye weigh out the fact that the only reason we're here is because my brathiar agreed to thatch roofs for us so we could get away."

"Ye're right. I'm sorry," she said, cuddling the kitten in one arm and taking his hand. "What will ye buy North?"

"I'm no' sure. Hopefully, somethin' that looks expensive but costs little," he said with a chuckle as they headed over to the silversmith's stall next.

The silversmith pounded his hammer against the item on the anvil, filling the air with noise. Nash stopped at the table, being watched over by the man's wife. He looked down to see many beautiful items all made from silver. Bracelets, ladies' head circlets, and ornate buckles for belts were all spread out on the table, looking very impressive to Nash. And expensive. He wasn't sure he could afford any of these things for his brother. Now, he was starting to regret his promise. Still, he couldn't go back empty-handed. He'd never broken a promise to North and wasn't going to start doing that now. Not when he owed his brother so much for all the help and support he'd given him.

"Oh, this is beautiful," said Kellina, picking up a silver, ornate, etched goblet in one hand, still holding on to the kitten with the other. The goblet reminded Nash of the one North borrowed at the Horn and Hoof Tavern, and then it was stolen by thieves. It was their chieftain Storm's chalice given to him by the king.

"North isna gettin' that," said Nash, snatching it away from her and placing it back down. "What have ye got that is small and inexpensive?"

"The only small things are the rings, or mayhap this." The woman held up a silver cross with a link on the top. It was made to wear on a chain or cord around the neck.

"I'm goin' to put the kitten down over there," said Kellina, nodding to an area. "I think it needs to relieve itself," she whispered.

"All right. I'll be right there," said Nash, looking back at the table.

"Do ye want the silver cross?" asked the woman.

"Mayhap." Nash picked up a silver ring, inspecting it closely.

"All our rings can be engraved for an extra price," the woman's husband called out.

"Really," said Nash, having an idea. "All right, then. I'll take the silver cross, but only if I can make a deal for it and the ring, both. And I want the ring engraved."

KELLINA HAD JUST put the kitten on the ground when a pair of booted feet stomped up and stopped in front of her nose. She looked up, and her heart almost stopped. In the sunlight, she saw the undeniable colors of the Sutherland plaid!

$$\blacktriangleright\!\cdot\!\circ\!\diamond\!\circ\!\cdot\!\blacktriangleleft$$

CHAPTER EIGHTEEN

KELLINA GASPED, AND jumped to her feet. Sure enough, she was staring straight into the eyes of a Sutherland. The man had rugged skin, blackened teeth, and long, scraggly hair. The most distinctive thing about his appearance was the long, fresh scar across his cheek. She remembered him well, since she'd been the one to give him that scar with her sword.

"Ye bastard," she spat through gritted teeth, grabbing for her sword, but she didn't have it. When they'd left on their trip, Nash had convinced her not to bring it with her. She didn't even have a dagger on her now, and regretted it. If she had, she'd kill this man right where he stood.

"What's this?" said the man, picking up the kitten by the scruff of its neck. "Only witches have black cats. I'm goin' to have to kill it." He pulled his dagger from his side.

"Ye willna harm my kitten. Now give it back!" When she tried to reach for it, he pushed her hands out of the way and held the kitten higher.

"If ye try to stop me, Witch, I'll kill ye as well."

"Nay!" screamed Kellina as he pointed his dagger at the kitten. The sound of a sword being unsheathed, and Nash's voice stopped his action.

"I've got my sword aimed right at yer heart," Nash warned the man from behind. "If ye so much as harm a hair on that kitten or my wife, ye'll feel this blade goin' through ye like butter."

"Yer wife?" the man asked, stilling his actions. "Argh," he grunted. "Now I remember her. She's a stinkin' MacKenzie – the one who gave me this scar." He ran his hand down the side of his face. "Do ye two ken who I am?"

"Ye're a Sutherland, and that is all I need to ken," growled Nash.

"I'm Iver Sutherland – chieftain of my clan. Yer wife here almost killed me."

"I wish I had!" spat Kellina. "I should have killed ye when I had the chance, ye filthy bastard! Dinna close yer eyes at night, because if ye do, I'll gouge them from yer head for what ye did to my clan, killin' our chieftain's innocent wife and daughters," growled Kellina.

NASH HAD TO look around the man, just to make sure it was really his wife he was hearing. She sounded so tough, so mean. And downright threatening. This was a side of Kellina that he had yet to see.

"Yer chieftain is the one we were after," spat Iver. "He has a roamin' eye, and canna keep his hands off the women – even of our clan."

"God's eyes, nay," whispered Kellina. Nash could almost hear the thoughts going through her head, wondering how many more bastard children her uncle had.

"Put down the kitten, and get the hell out of here, Sutherland," spat Nash, not wanting to kill him right here at the market. If he did, he couldn't be sure that more innocent people wouldn't die if Sutherland's men came to help him. It was much too crowded, with too many children around to even attempt it.

"I dinna want to touch this cursed thing anyway." Iver Sutherland tossed the kitten, and Kellina screamed, reaching out and catching it before it hit the ground.

"Remove yer blade from my back," the man demanded.

"No' until ye put away yer dagger," warned Nash.

The man did so, and slowly turned around with his empty

hands in the air. Nash lowered his sword as well.

"Ye're a MacKeefe!" he spat, looking at Nash's plaid. "Since when are ye allies with the MacKenzies?"

"Since I married one," Nash ground out. "Now get the hell away from my wife, and I dinna want to see yer sorry face again."

The man snorted. "If MacKeefes are allies of the MacKenzies, then ye're our enemies now, too."

"I guess so," Nash called out to the man's back as he hurried away.

Nash sheathed his sword and ran over to Kellina.

"Are ye all right, lass?" he asked, his arms going around her for comfort.

"Aye," she said, holding the kitten protectively to her chest. She was on the ground, having fallen when she dove to catch the kitten. "I wish I'd had my sword with me, Nash. I would have killed him, I swear I would have." Her eyes blazed fire and her jaw was clenched. Anger showed in her features as well as her stiffened body.

"I'm glad ye didna, because I dinna want my wife killin' anyone. I'll be the one to do the killin' from now on."

Nash helped Kellina to her feet.

"Och, now I've gone and dirtied my new clothes," pouted Kellina, brushing off her skirt.

"Nash? Is that ye?"

Nash turned around to see Gavin and Cam strolling through the marketplace with tankards of ale grasped in their fists.

"Gavin? Cam? What are ye doin' here?" Nash took a hold of Kellina's arm and walked over to join his friends.

"I think we can ask ye the same," said Cam, lifting his tankard as he spoke.

"And we felt sorry for ye, havin' to thatch all those roofs," said Gavin with a chuckle. "I guess ye pulled a fast one on Old Callum after all, since it doesna look to me as if ye are workin'."

"North is the one ye have to feel sorry for," said Nash. "He is thatchin' the roofs for me, so I can be here with Kellina."

"Yer wife, I am guessin'?" Cam nodded to Kellina.

"Aye. Kellina, these are my guid friends, Cam and Gavin."

"Hello," said Kellina. "I've heard so much about ye."

"We were actually on our way to the MacKenzie camp to help ye thatch roofs," said Cam. "We thought we'd stop here for the night and enjoy a drink."

"Ye were comin' to help me?" asked Nash. "Why?"

"Because ye helped us with our sentences," said Gavin. "However, I'm no' sure ye need us."

"We were goin' to stay a few days, but after what just happened, I think we will head back first thing in the mornin'," said Nash.

"What happened?" Gavin took a swig of ale.

"A Sutherland tried to kill my kitten," said Kellina, before Nash could even answer. "And I swear if Nash hadna convinced me to leave my weapons at home, I would have finished carvin' the man's face, since I'd already started when he raided our camp with his clan."

"Blethers! Ye've got yerself a live one here, Nash," said Cam. "So, the Sutherlands are here at the market?" He looked around, his hand going to the hilt of his sword.

"It was their chieftain," stated Nash. "I think I scared him off, so there shouldna be any more trouble."

"For everyone's sake, let's hope no'," answered Cam.

"Where are ye two stayin' the night?" asked Nash.

"We've got a room at the inn," Cam told him.

"Where are ye two stayin'?" asked Gavin.

"Well, I had hoped to secure a room." Nash looked over at Kellina, who had stepped away again, putting the kitten on the ground to sniff around. "But since I had to buy Nash somethin' made from silver, and then I got this for Kellina, I ran out of money." He held up a silver ring in two fingers, keeping his back toward Kellina so she couldn't see it.

Cam whistled, inspecting the ring that Nash had gotten engraved with a few images on it of nature things. "That's a nice one, Nash. When are ye goin' to give it to her?"

"I dinna ken." He glanced back at Kellina who was now picking up the kitten again. "I guess I was waitin' for the right time. However, I think she's too angry with the Sutherland man now, so I'd better wait."

"If ye want, ye can share a room with us," said Gavin.

"Och, Gavin, give him and the lass the room for themselves. We'll get another for us," said Cam. "After all, they are newly married and might want some time alone."

"Then it's done," said Gavin. "And in the mornin', we'll travel with ye back to the MacKenzies."

"Aye," said Cam. "Mayhap we'll help North finish the thatchin', since he seems to be gettin' the brunt of all of our punishments."

"Thank ye," said Nash, looking back over his shoulder at Kellina. "Kellina has been havin' a hard time lately."

"Since her chieftain died?" asked Cam. "Aye, we got the missive at the MacKeefe camp. That is another reason why we convinced our new wives that we needed to go and help ye."

"Aye. Kellina's upset because of the chieftain's death," said Nash, wanting more than anything to tell his friends everything that had transpired. But he couldn't. He'd made a promise to keep this information to himself, and now he would have to keep it a secret for the rest of his life. Nash didn't like keeping secrets from his friends – from his family. It just didn't seem right. Then again, Kellina was his family now, and he had to adjust to the fact that he might end up staying with the MacKenzies forever, although all he wanted was to return to the MacKeefes once and for all.

Chapter Nineteen

"**W**ELL, I THINK it's time I go up to the room and give Kellina the ring," Nash told his friends later that night. They'd been drinking together at the Soused Grouse Tavern and Inn, and it felt damned good to be back together with his friends again. However, Nash was feeling guilty about leaving his brother back at the MacKenzie camp, doing the work that was really his punishment, not North's.

"I still dinna see why Kellina didna want to drink with us," said Gavin.

"She was in a hurry to get to bed. Right, Nash?" asked Cam with a wink. Cam was always a lady's man, but since he'd married Yvaine, he didn't spend his time with the girls anymore. Even so, he still understood them more than Nash or the others ever would.

"I think Kellina went up to the room early because she was worried about the kitten," explained Nash. "It really shook her up when Sutherland threatened to kill it."

"No' to mention, kill her," added Gavin.

"Aye, we'd better keep an open eye for more angry Sutherlands," said Cam. "Ye never ken where they may be lurkin'."

Gavin downed the rest of his ale and banged the tankard on the table. "Ye should be with her, Nash. She needs ye right now."

"One thing ye'll learn about Kellina is that she really doesna need anyone," Nash told his friends. "She is verra independent.

I'm only glad she didna have a blade on her, or I have no doubt she would have tried to kill Sutherland today, and she might have gotten killed instead."

"All this over a damned cat?" asked Gavin. "I canna understand this."

"It's no' about the kitten," said Nash. "No' really."

"Nay. I'm sure it's about the raid," said Cam, nodding his head, understanding.

"Well . . . aye and nay," Nash answered.

"What does that mean?" asked Gavin. "Ye are makin' no sense, friend."

"I agree. And I also get the feelin' there is somethin' ye are no' tellin' us." Cam put his elbows on the table and leaned forward, waiting. "Well? What is it, Nash? Speak up. It's just us here, and ye ken ye can tell us anythin'."

"Aye. What's botherin' ye, Nash?" asked Gavin, leaning forward as well. "Ye dinna seem to be yerself tonight."

"It's nothin'," said Nash, pushing out his chair and standing up. "I'll tell ye one thing, though. I'm glad I convinced Kellina to give that kitten a bath in the loch. I dinna fancy wakin' up scratchin' from fleas."

IF KELLINA HADN'T been worried about leaving Midnight alone in the room, she swore she would have found a blade and hunted down the Sutherland chieftain and killed him for what he had done. It was not only for almost killing her kitten, but for calling her a witch and threatening to kill her, too. However, she was most angry at the Sutherlands for killing Lorna and the girls. For all she knew, Sileas and Eilidh might really have been her half-sisters.

"Blethers, Midnight, I am sick over all of this," she said, sitting down on the bed with the kitten on her lap. Midnight playfully bit at her fingers, but it didn't hurt half as bad as the news she'd received from Ciaran just before he'd died. "I have to get over it," she said, stroking the kitten. "None of it matters anymore. It's in the past." She repositioned the kitten on her lap. "Jamie and Caitlin are my siblin's, and they will always be."

"That's right," she heard from behind her. Turning her head, she saw Nash standing in the doorway. He had one arm leaning on the door jamb, his other hand still on the latch. He looked handsome in the firelight from the room that lit up his face, but still kept him in shadow at the same time.

"How long have ye been standin' there?" she asked.

"Long enough to ken that ye are still bothered by everythin' that happened lately."

"Well, do ye blame me?"

"Nay," he said, closing the door and walking over to the bed. "I dinna blame ye, lass. I just thought the whole reason for us comin' here was to try to relax and ease our minds. To forget about all the awful things that have happened."

"It's no' easy to forget that our parents killed each other, Nash."

"I ken that." He let out a sigh. "Kellina, it's a horrible thing that happened, and I wish just as much as ye that I could change the events of time. But we canna do that." He sat down on the bed across from her, reaching out and taking her hand. "We are married now, and I dinna want this to ever come between us. We are no' our parents, and neither are we anythin' like Ciaran. Now, we need to pull ourselves up by the bootstraps and get on with our lives. We need to start livin' our lives together – as husband and wife."

"Aye. Ye are right," said Kellina with a sniffle. "I'm sorry, Nash. I dinna want to ruin our special time together."

The cat jumped off her lap and to the ground. She started to reach for it, but Nash's hand shot out and he stopped her.

"Leave it," he said. "There is somethin' I want to say to ye, and that cat is only goin' to distract us."

"What is it, Nash?" she asked, wondering why he sounded so serious all of a sudden.

"When I bought the silver cross for North today, I spent the rest of my money on a present for ye."

"Ye did?" Emotion flowed through her. No one had ever purposely bought her a present before. It made her feel special.

"Aye. I used up all my money but, thankfully, Gavin and Cam gave up their room for us. If no', we'd be sleepin' in the street tonight."

"Oh, Nash, whatever ye bought me sounds expensive. What is it? Please, let me see." Kellina was truly excited about this.

"Close yer eyes," he said, taking something out of his pocket.

"Why?"

"Just do it."

"All right." Kellina closed her eyes, feeling Nash slipping something onto her finger. "Nash, is that what I think it is?"

"Mayhap."

"Can I open my eyes now?"

"Just a minute."

She felt Nash get off the bed. Then she heard the rustling of clothes, followed by the dip of the mattress as Nash settled himself back on the bed again.

"All right. Open yer eyes, lass."

She opened her eyes, looking at her finger, and gasped. She wore a beautiful, silver, engraved ring. Little etchings of birds, clouds, and a sunshine were carved right into the band of the ring.

"It's beautiful!" She couldn't take her eyes off it. Holding up her hand, she inspected the ring closer by moving her hand in different positions.

"I figured it was time to give ye a weddin' ring. I also thought it appropriate to have things etched into it that we both witnessed from the roof while we were thatchin'. Actually, we saw those things while we were lyin' on the roof together, lookin' at the sky. I asked the silversmith to put them on the ring for me."

"It's so nice. I love it. Nay, it is too expensive. Why would ye do this, Nash?" Her eyes remained focused on the ring. It was the prettiest thing she'd ever seen in her life and it meant the world to her. Now, she really felt like a married woman.

"I did it because I love ye, Kellina."

"Oh, Nash! I love it, and I love ye, too. I really love ye." She reached out to hug and kiss him, first noticing that he was lounging back on the bed, stark naked. "Oooooh, Nash," she said with a giggle when her eyes roamed lower and she saw the size of his erection.

"I think it's time ye take yer clothes off, too," he suggested in a sultry whisper.

"Well, I'm no' sure," she said, playfully holding out her hand to look at her ring again. "I think I'd rather just sit here and look at my beautiful ring instead."

"What?" he bolted to an upright position, sitting there with his back as stiff as his manhood. He looked very upset until he saw her smile. "I see," he said, equally as playful. "Then go ahead and look at yer ring, Wife. Dinna let me disturb ye." He started to get off the bed.

"Nash?" she asked, almost thinking he was really leaving. That is, until he knelt at her feet with his hands resting on her knees.

"What are ye doin'?" she asked. "It is too late to propose on bended knee, since we are already married."

"It is because we are married that I am down here, love."

"What? I dinna understand."

With a cocked smile and a quick wink, Nash flipped her skirt up and over his head.

"Nash?" she asked, her heart jumping around in her chest. "W-what are ye doin'?"

"Dinna mind me," he said in a muffled voice from beneath her skirt.

She felt him sliding his hands up her legs little by little, causing her lust as well as her anticipation to swell. Then his fingers closed over her undergarments, untying them and pulling them down her legs. Still, his head remained covered by her skirt.

"Nash," she said again. "Mayhap ye should – oh!" she gasped, feeling his breath between her thighs now. She pulled up her skirt, looking down at the top of Nash's head. His face was buried between her legs, and pressed up against her swollen womanhood. To her surprise, his tongue flicked out and he tasted her . . . right there. It caused her to jerk. She wasn't sure what to do. Her heart beat so furiously now that she wouldn't be surprised if it beat right out of her chest. "W-what are ye doin'?" Her voice hitched and she could barely breathe let alone talk right now. Was this really happening?

"Shhhh," he said, the air from his mouth hitting her moist private parts. That only elevated her excitement and she started tingling everywhere. He kissed her next, the way he did when he kissed her lips. Only this time, he used his tongue a lot more.

Her breath hitched, and when she felt her body coming to life, her head fell back and she let out a moan. It felt . . . surprisingly wonderful. It made her feel randy and sexy, and she wanted him to do more.

"I thought ye were lookin' at yer ring," he said, crawling up her body, pulling off her clothes with his nimble fingers until she was left as naked as he.

"Ye proved to be a little more distractin' than the kitten." Kellina purposely reached down, closing her hand around his shaft, making him gasp this time. Squeezing gently, she ran her fingers up and down his manhood, testing his length, thinking about taking him into her body, fully. When her thumb grazed over his tip, Nash's hand closed over hers and he let out a long, deep moan.

"Ye're makin' me even harder, and I dinna ken how much more of this teasin' I can take." Nash reached out for her, pulling her to him and burying his head between her breasts next. He let his tongue do the exploring. When he licked her, and dragged his tongue across her skin, he managed to fan the flames of her passion. Excitement filled her being, making her climb to that place where she would soon find release. First one, then the other, he flicked his tongue across her nipples, bringing them to hardened peaks.

Kellina gasped in delight, her chest heaving and her back arching as she pulled him closer, pushing herself deeper and deeper into his mouth. This felt amazing. It was so good! Her breathing labored with anticipation of what was yet to come.

"Nash, ye are gettin' me so excited, I can barely breathe, and my body trembles."

His hands slowly slid up her sides and then he laid her back on the bed, looking deeply into her eyes.

"I'm glad ye like it, lass." Nash straddled her as he mounted, climbing between her open legs. His palms covered her breasts, and he gave them a quick squeeze. Then he flicked his thumbs over her nipples, about driving her out of her mind. She moaned some more. "Breathe," he told her. "Deep ... and long," he teased her, pressing his hardened manhood up against her, but being careful not to enter her.

"Ye're teasin' me," she said, kissing him on the mouth. "I canna take any further foreplay, Nash. Please," she begged him, wanting him to take her.

"Breathe. Really," he told her, waiting for her to do it.

"All right." She started breathing deeply, making her breasts move closer to his mouth and then farther away. He took the opportunity to suckle her each time her breast reached him.

"I canna hold back any longer," he told her. "I am so hard I am goin' to burst."

"Then dinna hold back, Nash. And this time, I really mean it. Dinna try to be gentle. Make love to me like ye mean it."

"Are ye – are ye sure, Kellina? I dinna want to hurt ye, lass."

"And neither will ye. I am sure of this, my husband," she whispered, feeling herself already starting to ascend. "I want to feel ye, hard, hot and fast. I want yer full length in me, and I want ye to make love to me in a way that I will never forget for the rest of my life."

"I will," he promised, entering her, pumping her hips as his full length slid in and out, making her more and more excited.

"Aaaah, Nash, this feels so guid. So right," she said, wrapping her legs around his hips as his thrusts got faster and faster. Each time, she brought her hips up to meet him. They did the dance of love, their passions out of control for each other. Kellina's fingers gripped at his shoulders, her nails raking down his arms as they both got crazy. Somehow, she managed to slip away from him, and push him to his back on the bed. Then she rolled atop him.

"Oh, ye want to play that way, do ye? A little pussy and mouse game, I see." He brought his hips to meet hers now, and before she knew it, he had rolled them both over and was back on top again.

Their passionate acts of unbridled lust and love grew to extremes. And when neither of them could hold back any longer, they both cried out with release. Their movements stilled, and they separated, falling back onto the bed. Staring at the ceiling, they both remained quiet, just trying to regain their breathing.

They heard a little mewl from the floor, and then Midnight came flying at them. The kitten landed right atop Nash's chest.

"Bid the devil!" he cried out. "That scared me."

They both had a good laugh, and Nash finally accepted the cat. Together, in each other's arms, Kellina and Nash fell asleep, with Midnight right between them.

Kellina's last thought as she fell into a deep slumber was that this was her family now. Life was going to get better from this moment on. Never again would she let thoughts from the past haunt her. Nash was her husband and, together, they would make a new family. A good family. One that really mattered.

CHAPTER TWENTY

WHEN KELLINA MOUNTED her horse the next day, preparing to leave the marketplace, she noticed a small group of Sutherlands watching from the other end of the street. A shiver went up her spine. She held her hand over Midnight, who laid in a sling that Nash had made her and tied around her shoulders.

"Dinna worry, Midnight. No one is goin' to hurt ye," she said, petting the kitten's head.

"Ready to go?" asked Nash, making sure she was secure before he mounted his steed. Gavin and Cam rode their horses over from the stable to join them.

"I canna wait to get out of here," she told him, still eyeing up the Sutherlands.

"We have company," said Gavin, from atop his horse. He nodded to the group of Sutherlands watching them.

Nash glanced down the street and realized what everyone was looking at. A group of a half-dozen Sutherlands watched their every move from atop their horses. They were all armed heavily, and this didn't sit right with Nash.

"Dinna give them another thought." Nash pulled himself up atop his horse.

"Nash, I dinna feel guid about it," Kellina told him.

"If they are stupid enough to try anythin', my friends and I will take care of them. Dinna fret about it. Ye and Midnight are safe."

"Do ye really think they'll try to attack us?" Cam's hand wavered above the hilt of his sword as his eyes stayed on the small group of their enemies.

"There are too few of them," Nash stated. "They willna attack, and no' in such a busy place."

"What if they follow us back home?" asked Kellina. "I dinna want to bring them right into our camp without warnin'."

"Kellina, stop worryin'," said Nash, honestly a little more than concerned himself, but he didn't want to show it. "They willna give us trouble. I made the message clear yesterday to the Sutherland chieftain who tried to give ye trouble. Now, let's go, and stop with all the clishmaclaver or we'll never get back."

"I agree," said Gavin.

"Let's go," said Cam, leading the way. "I'm in the mood for thatchin' a few roofs."

Nash looked over his shoulder as he and the others rode away. The Sutherlands turned and headed in the other direction instead of following them. He let out a breath, feeling relieved. He would fight them if he had to, and wasn't afraid of that. What he was scared of was anything happening to Kellina. There had been too much death in the MacKenzie Clan lately and, by God, the last thing he wanted was to lose his new wife.

"WHAT THE HELL am I lookin' at?" shouted North from atop a roof as Kellina and the others rode back into camp. "Gavin? Cam? Is that really ye or am I imaginin' it since I'm so hot and tired that I canna see straight anymore?"

"It's us," shouted Gavin. "Ye're no' imagin' it, North, guid friend. We've come to help."

"Save some thatch for me," called out Cam, waving up at their friend.

Tomas was on the roof of the hut with him, and even Caitlin

and Jamie were helping with things on the ground. All the clansmembers bustled around busily. Kellina could see their camp looking much better than when they'd left.

"Kellina! Ye're back early!" Caitlin ran to her, with Jamie on her heels.

"Sister, we've missed ye," said Jamie. "Did ye bring me anythin'?"

"Stop it, ye fool," scolded Caitlin, hitting her brother on the arm. "They were celebratin' their marriage, no' goin' on a shoppin' spree for ye."

"I'm sorry, I didna bring ye anythin', Jamie," said Kellina from atop the horse.

"It's all right," said Jamie, kicking at a stone on the ground. "I didna need anythin'."

"However, I did bring something back that I think all of us can enjoy."

"Ye did?" Jamie's head popped up and his eyes widened. "Is it figs? Or did ye bring back hazelnuts? I love nuts."

"I have some special treats, but this one is no' food," she told him.

"Well, what is it, Sister? Hurry and show us," Caitlin urged her.

"Nash, will ye help me?" asked Kellina.

"Sure," said Nash, holding out his arms to help her dismount.

"Nay, with this." She carefully picked up Midnight, handing the cat to Nash.

"Is that a kitten?" Jamie ran over, holding out his arms. "Can I hold it?"

"Me, too," said Caitlin. "Och, it is so cute," she said, beaming at the kitten as Jamie took it from Nash. "What is his name?"

"Her name is Midnight," said Kellina, dismounting and handing the reins of her horse to a young boy who watched over the stable. "She is goin' to help chase away rats once she is bigger."

By now, North and Tomas had come down from the roof, hurrying over to greet them.

"Tomas, and everyone, these are Nash's friends, Gavin and Cam," Kellina introduced them as the men dismounted and joined them. "Oh, and these are my siblin's, Jamie and Caitlin," she told Nash's friends.

"Did I hear ye say ye wanted to help thatch roofs?" North wiped sweat from his brow with the back of his hand. "Because I'd like a break."

"No' if I'm goin' to get sweaty and stink like ye, I dinna want to do it." Cam waved his hand in front of his face.

"What?" North looked so disappointed.

Cam laughed and slapped North on the back. "Can ye show me what to do? Or is yer brathair the master thatcher in these parts now?"

"Nash, a master thatcher?" North blew air from his mouth. "He's just lucky no' to fall when he's on a roof. I am so much better at it than him."

"Ye are no'," protested Nash, never liking anyone to be better than him at anything.

"Aye, I am," said North, standing taller and jutting his chin out in the air. It was no different than the way Nash and North competed with each other as children.

"I think I'd better go with them and watch for trouble," Tomas told Gavin. "I dinna want anyone bein' pushed off the roof."

"Wait, I'll come with ye. I'm interested to ken just how these roofs are thatched," said Gavin.

"Do ye really plan on helpin'?" Tomas looked pleased.

"Why no'?" asked Gavin. "It couldna possibly be any harder than when I had to learn how to make shoes."

"North, I can already see that ye dinna ken how to use the leggett," Nash bantered with his brother, shading his eyes, looking up at the roof.

"Leggett?" asked Cam, walking with the group as they slowly moved toward the hut being repaired. "That sounds like a lass with shorter legs than the others."

Nash swiped a hand at Cam. "No' girls, ye fool. Dinna let

Yvaine hear ye talkin' like that."

Cam dodged Nash's swipe, laughing. Then he grabbed Nash's arm and looked down at it. "What are all those scratches?" he asked, making Kellina's heart skip a beat. "Did ye get those in bed?"

Kellina knew exactly how Nash had gotten the scratches. She gave them to him during their vigorous lovemaking last night. She held her breath, hoping Nash wouldn't tell them. If he did, she swore she would die from embarrassment.

Nash stopped and turned around, looking back at her. "Aye, I got them in bed," he told Cam. Kellina shook her head slightly, trying to warn him not to say anything, but it was too late now.

"Och, the cat is out of the bag now," said North with a chuckle.

"That's exactly right," Nash answered. "Ye see, these scratches are from Kellina's new kitten, Midnight. It happened when she jumped atop me in bed."

"She did, did she?" asked Cam.

"The kitten, no' my wife," snapped Nash. Then Nash looked over to Kellina and winked, before turning back and heading to the hut.

"Kellina, can I take the kitten over and show it to the rest of the children?" asked Jamie, cradling the cat in his arms.

"Of course, ye can," she answered, putting her arm around her sister.

"I've missed ye," said Caitlin, as soon as all the others had left.

Kellina laughed. "I was only gone for one day," she pointed out.

"It seemed like one year, I swear it did. I was afraid ye were never comin' back – like Mathair and Da, and Lorna and the girls." Caitlin looked so sad. "Or like Uncle Ciaran. I think I miss him the most of all."

"Caitlin," said Kellina, wanting to tell the whole truth about their parents and Ciaran to her sister. "There is somethin' I want to say to ye."

"What is it?" asked Caitlin, looking up with wide eyes. "Is somethin' wrong?" She looked so scared, and Kellina didn't want her to feel this way.

Several clansmen walked by, carrying things for the roof repair.

"We're makin' haggis," called out one of the women who was stirring a pot at a nearby fire.

"It'll be a celebration of Kellina and Nash's homecomin'," called out another woman.

"I'll get some wine," said a young boy, running to find it.

"Let's walk," said Kellina, not wanting the others around her to hear her horrible story.

"All right." Caitlin took Kellina's hand. "We can go up the hill and visit Mathair and Da, as well as our cousins, and aunt and uncle."

"Well, if ye'd like," said Kellina, seeing how much it meant to her sister. They climbed the hill together, stopping for a moment at their parents' graves, before Caitlin walked right over to Ciaran's resting place, and sat down on the grass.

"Sit," she said, patting the ground with her hand, waiting for Kellina. "Can ye smell all the heather in bloom? It's lovely."

Kellina sat next to her sister, wondering how to tell her everything she needed to know. She had just decided to tell Caitlin first that Ciaran might be her father, when Caitlin bent over and kissed the ground where the chieftain was buried.

"I miss him the most of all, dinna ye?" asked Caitlin. "I often wished he was my real faither."

"Well I – I miss all of our clansmembers who have died," Kellina answered.

"I miss Uncle Ciaran more than our parents, since I was too young to remember them before they died. Our aunt and uncle were always parents to Jamie and me."

"Caitlin, dinna say that," Kellina scolded.

"Ye ken it's true."

"Well, the chieftain isna yer uncle or yer faither," snapped

Kellina. "We called him Uncle, but he wasna related to . . . ye at all."

"Sister, why are ye soundin' so harsh? Uncle was never anythin' but kind to us after our parents died. He was especially nice to ye and even called ye Daughter sometimes. That should mean somethin' to ye."

"Ye have no idea," Kellina mumbled under her breath.

"What is it ye wanted to tell me? I'm sure ye'd like to hear it, too, Uncle, wouldna ye?" Caitlin spoke to the grave, running a gentle hand over the ground.

How in heaven's name could Kellina tell her any of this now?

"Caitlin, would ye still love me . . . even if I wasna yer sister?"

Caitlin laughed. "Dinna be silly! Ye are my sister. And if ye werena, I wouldna love ye."

"Y-ye wouldna?" Kellina's heart was breaking now. This wasn't at all what she wanted to hear.

"Nay. If ye werena my sister, I wouldna ken ye," Caitlin explained. "So how could I love someone I dinna even ken?"

"Oh. I see." Kellina could see this wasn't working and decided to try another approach to tell the story. "Do ye ever wonder just how our parents died?"

"Uncle said it was a battle with the MacKeefes."

"But dinna ye want to ken more about it? Like . . . how it really happened?"

"Nay, Kellina, I dinna."

"Nay?" Kellina didn't understand at all. Her parents and how they died had always been on her mind ever since she was a child. Wasn't it the same way with Caitlin, too?

"I didna ken our parents. No' really. I have no memories of them and I dinna want the only thing I remember was how they died horrible deaths."

"Oh. I understand. I think. But still, dinna ye even care to find out more about them? Who they really were?"

"No' really," said Caitlin, picking at a piece of grass.

"Why no'?"

"Well . . . what if they werena kind or guid? What if they were mean or . . . evil? If so, I dinna think I'd want to ken."

"But they are the people who gave ye life. Surely, ye must be thankful for that."

"Of course, I am, Kellina. But they are strangers to me and Jamie. We dinna remember them the way ye do. All we ken is the love of our aunt and uncle when they raised us and made us part of their family. Jamie and I were like their own children, and often we wished we really were. They gave us so much. We will always love them for takin' us in and givin' us the family we never really had. Besides ye, that is."

"Well, mayhap Lorna and Ciaran werena the people ye thought they were. If no', wouldna ye want to ken?"

"What are ye sayin', Sister?" Caitlin's brow furrowed. "Are ye sayin' that the man I regarded as my faither was somehow . . . bad?" The hurt showed in her eyes. Kellina suddenly realized that this wasn't such a good idea after all.

"I just . . ."

"What? Tell me!" Tears filled Caitlin's eyes. "If there is somethin' ye need to say, then do so already. Now, I want to ken."

"Nay, there is nothin'," said Kellina smiling and giving Caitlin a hug. "I just wanted to say that I am glad, too, that they took us in and raised us as their family."

"Are ye really?" asked Caitlin, wiping a tear from her cheek. "Ye were always so mean to Uncle. Oftentimes, I saw him watchin' ye from afar, and I could see such sadness in his eyes."

"I'm sure ye just imagined it, Sister."

"Mayhap," said Caitlin with a sniff, wiping away another tear. "I was always jealous, Kellina."

"Jealous? Of what?"

"I wanted the attention from Uncle that he really only gave ye. I felt like he loved ye the best out of all of us, and even over his own girls."

"Now, that's no' true."

"It is," said Caitlin. "I never told ye, but I overheard Uncle talking to Auntie one night when they thought we were all sleepin'. He told her that ye were the daughter he always wanted, but he could never tell ye that. It made Auntie mad, and she went to bed cryin'. Why did he say that, Kellina? Is there a reason that I dinna ken?"

This was her chance to be honest with Caitlin, but if she did, Kellina realized it would shatter her poor sister's heart. Caitlin would never be able to accept the things that Kellina had discovered lately, and neither should she have to. Caitlin was happy. She was content with no memories of their parents, and accepted the way Ciaran and Lorna took them in and made them part of their family. Who was Kellina to shatter the girl's hopes, her dreams . . . her memories of happier times?

Mayhap Nash was right. The dead were gone, and although they were not to be forgotten, there was nothing they could do to bring them back. Let her parents and even her uncle rest in peace, Kellina decided. It was time to leave it alone and, instead, look forward to the future. She was the one who could ruin Caitlin's life . . . or make it something special. The last thing Kellina wanted to do was to make Caitlin sad. They'd all seen too much sadness lately, and it was time for happier things to transpire. She would be a part of that instead, she decided, no matter what she had to do.

"There is no reason, Sister," she said, hugging Caitlin once again. "Our parents, as well as our aunt and uncle and cousins, were all guid people who didna deserve to die. Now, let's pick some heather and lay it on their graves, shall we?"

"Yes. I'd like that." Caitlin jumped up and hugged Kellina.

"It is wonderful, by the way."

"What is?" asked Caitlin.

"Ye asked me how it felt to make love to a man. Well . . . it is more wonderful than ye could imagine, and someday when ye find the right man, ye will ken, too."

"Oooooh, so that's why ye brought me away from everyone and what ye wanted to tell me." Caitlin's cheeks blushed. "Are ye goin' to tell me exactly what ye and Nash did?"

"Losh me, nay! Sister, some things are sacred between a husband and wife, and that is somethin' I'll never tell. Now, are we goin' to collect heather or no'? The haggis will be done soon, and I want to help Nash and the others finish thatchin' the roofs."

"The heather can wait," said Caitlin, looking back to their uncle's grave. "I think Uncle would tell us right now that we need to do what is best for the clan."

"And he's right," said Kellina, knowing now that she had made the right decision in keeping the secret. "We must always do what is best for the clan. And right now, that is finishin' the roofs so we dinna get wet when it rains."

"I'll race ye down the hill," said Caitlin, taking off at a run before Kellina could answer.

Kellina looked back at the graves of her parents, and her eyes settled on the grave of her uncle. It no longer mattered whose daughter she really was. All that mattered now was that she was Caitlin's and Jamie's sister and nothing . . . no one could change that. Not even the blood that flowed through her veins.

"It's all for the best of the clan, that ye're gone now, Uncle," she said. A small part of her now realized why he had never told her the truth, but it still didn't excuse him for his actions pertaining to her parents. Her uncle's evil acts shaped all their lives, and that is something she would never get over. "I forgive ye for keepin' it all a secret, but no' for what ye did," she said, feeling her heart thaw just a little. "I feel sorry for ye, ye poor, pathetic man. I may forgive ye for the sakes of Caitlin and Jamie, and even for poor Lorna and yer girls. However, I only do it for the guid of the clan."

She turned to go, and then looked back once more. "Dinna get me wrong. That does no' mean that I will ever forget."

◆•◇◆◇•◆

CHAPTER TWENTY-ONE

"NASH, THROW ME the lady leg," said Cam, two days later, standing at the bottom of the ladder, holding his hands in the air. Nash was at the top of the roof with his shirt off, working harder than Kellina had seen him do since he'd arrived.

"It's a leggett, ye fool, and the tools are no' to be thrown," Nash told him, picking it up, and handing it to Gavin who was near him. "Would ye mind handin' this to Cam?" he asked.

"Sure," said Gavin, turning and throwing it anyway.

"Nay!" shouted Nash, but his friends didn't care.

"Oops," said Cam as he caught the leggett but it slipped from his grasp, falling to the ground.

Kellina heard a thud and then some cursing. Even though from her side of the roof she couldn't see who the leggett had hit, she knew without a doubt it was North.

"God's eyes, what the hell are ye doin'? Quit tryin' to kill me. Och, that smarts!"

Then she heard a thud and an oof from Cam, and more cursing as Cam fell off the ladder.

"Are ye daft, North? Ye threw the beating tool at me and made me fall!" said Cam.

"Leggett," she heard Nash say as he continued pounding in a twisted spar at the apex of the roof.

"Well, ye threw the damned thing at me first," complained North. "It hit me in the head and nearly knocked me out."

"I didna throw it at ye," protested Cam. "It . . . slipped."

"Haud yer wheeshts, both of ye," Gavin ground out. They were all getting tired, hot and grouchy, having done nothing but thatch roofs for the last two days. "Ye'd think it would have knocked a little sense into either of ye, but it didna," Gavin continued.

"Well, the guid news is, we're done." Kellina stood at the top of the roof with her hands up in the air. She looked up at the vast, beautiful, Highland sky and took in a deep breath and released it slowly.

"Thank ye all for the help," said Tomas, making his way to the ladder. "Now that the roofs are finished, I'll write a missive to Storm MacKeefe, tellin' him that Nash has completed his punishment."

"Yes!" said Nash, raising his hands in the air over his head now. It made his naked, sturdy chest, biceps, and tight, toned stomach look so inviting. All Kellina could do was think about touching him and kissing him . . . and making love. "Now, I willna be an outcast anymore. I canna wait to get back to the clan."

The breeze blew, lifting up Nash's plaid. From Kellina's position on the roof, she was able to see his family jewels. She lost her footing and slipped, but Nash was there to catch her in his strong arms.

"Are ye all right, lass?" he asked, holding her tightly.

"Ye caught me," she said.

"Aye, of course I did. I wouldna let ye fall." He smiled, warming her heart and her soul. "I told ye, I'm as sure-footed as a goat."

"And ye smell like one, too," mumbled Gavin, getting away from him, heading toward the ladder.

"The food is ready," called out Caitlin, waving her arm to get them all to come to the outdoor fire.

"I'm famished," said Nash, helping Kellina to the ladder even though she didn't need his assistance. Still, she let him do it. If it made him feel like a good husband, then who was she to stop him? She rather liked all the attention he had been giving her ever since they went to the market together.

It was a beautiful day and the trestle tables and benches were set up outside for the meal. The clan seemed happy to have the MacKeefes here helping them. The work got done so much faster when everyone chipped in.

"We have rabbit stew with roasted vegetables today," said Caitlin, scooping out bowls of food while Jamie passed them out. Little Midnight wandered around the table, sticking its paw into one bowl and then another.

"Hey, get out of here. That's mine." North picked up his bowl and tried to shoo the cat away.

"She's just hungry," Nash told his brother, putting the kitten up to his bowl of stew, letting her lap at the juices. "Isna that cute?" He ran a finger over the kitten's head and smiled from ear to ear.

"Cute?" Cam looked up, chewing. "Did he just say that cat was cute?" asked Cam, shaking his head in disgust.

"He did," agreed Gavin. "I canna believe it either."

"What the hell has happened to ye since ye got married?" asked North. "I can see marriage makes a man lamebrained. I'll never let that happen to me."

"What did ye say?" asked Gavin, balancing his food on his spoon, looking up at North.

"Nothin'. I said nothin'." North all but stuck his face in his food as if he were trying to hide.

"Yes, ye did. Ye called us lamebrained," Cam said loud enough for everyone to hear. "Ye said all married people were lamebrained."

Now, half the clan was staring at North, and Kellina knew there would be trouble if she didn't intervene.

"They're brathairs. And friends," she told the clan. "They always talk that way to each other. They dinna mean anythin' by it."

"We're family," explained Nash. "The MacKeefes are closely-knit, and even if we talk this way it doesna mean a thing. Nothin' can ever come between family members."

"Speakin' of family," said Tomas, clearing his throat. "Kellina, where will ye and Nash be livin' after he is accepted back into his clan?"

"With the MacKenzies," Kellina said, at the same time that Nash said, "With the MacKeefes."

Everyone at the table stopped talking, and looked up at them.

"Nash, this is where I belong. I canna leave," said Kellina.

"Well, I'm no' goin' to leave the MacKeefes, lass," he told her.

"So, it looks like my sister will be livin' here while Nash will return to the MacKeefes," said Jamie, playing with the kitten.

"Nay, they canna do that," said Caitlin in concern. "It wouldna be right. They are married now and need to live together."

"I agree," said Tomas. "Nash, if ye'll stay here with the Mac-Kenzies, I'd like to make ye my right hand, and advisor. After all, ye are family now."

"Nash, Storm is expectin' ye back at the MacKeefe camp to help with the cattle again this winter," said Cam. "Ye've got people there askin' about ye. Ye have to come home."

NASH LOOKED UP, not knowing what to say. He'd made an alliance with the MacKenzies by marrying Kellina. However, it was never stated beforehand which clan they would live with when this was all over. Nash swallowed his stew, seeing Kellina staring a hole through him. Everyone was looking at him and he didn't know how to answer.

"Well, are ye stayin' here with the MacKenzies?" asked Jamie. "Or are ye goin' to take our sister away from us, too?"

"Please, dinna do that," begged Caitlin. "We've already lost our parents, our cousins, and aunt and uncle. We canna lose our sister, too."

"Well, speakin' to the fact, Kellina may no' really be –" Nash stopped in midsentence, hearing Tomas clear his throat. North was shaking his head, and Kellina had the look of fear in her eyes. He'd almost said aloud that she might not really be their sister but, thankfully, had stopped in time.

"What?" asked Cam. "She's no' really what?" Cam lifted the bowl and sucked down the last of the stew.

"Aye, what were ye goin' to say?" asked one of the women of the clan.

"Nash," Kellina whispered, shaking her head now.

"I was goin' to say that she may no' really be . . . interested in livin' with the MacKeefes, but she might change her mind if she got to ken us."

"Aye, that's a guid idea," agreed Gavin. "Ye can live with the MacKeefes for a while and then come back to the MacKenzies and stay here a spell, too. Just like Davita and I are doin', tradin' back and forth between places."

"That's no' the same at all," said Nash. "Ye're tradin' between Hermitage Castle and the MacKeefe camp in the Highlands. Ye are no' goin' back to live in her town."

"Nay, but she can visit her family whenever she wants," Gavin told him.

"Same with Yvaine," said Cam, looking around for more stew. "She could go back to the chandler's shop but she chooses to live with me instead."

"Only because her memories of the shop are so horrid," mumbled Nash under his breath.

"Ye have to choose, Kellina," said Tomas. "I canna have ye two livin' here sometimes, and then no'. I am chieftain now, and I will stick to my decision. Choose one place or another. Ye canna have both."

"Well, then I choose to live here," said Kellina, handing her kitten to her brother. "I will no' leave Caitlin and Jamie."

"No' even for yer husband?" asked Nash, feeling aggravated with Kellina.

"My husband can live here with us," said Kellina, being stubborn.

"Mayhap we can talk about this later," Nash mumbled.

"I dinna see what there is to discuss," she answered. "I have decided that we will stay here and there is nothin' more to say."

"I'll drink to that," cheered Tomas, lifting up his cup. "To my new right hand, Nash MacKeefe."

The clansmembers cheered, but Nash and his brother and friends did not.

"Is that really what ye're goin' to do?" asked North from one side of him.

"Tell her the way it's goin' to be," said Cam from his other side.

Nash looked over to Gavin who just shrugged.

"Nay," announced Nash, pushing up from the table. "I never agreed to live with the MacKenzies. I actually never agreed to the marriage or the alliance at all."

"Nash?" Kellina looked concerned. "What are ye sayin'?"

"I'm sayin' that I have been told what to do since before I got here. I didna have a choice in the matter when I was told to thatch roofs or plow fields, and had no choice in whom I was to marry. I will make my own decisions from now on, and no one will tell me what to do."

"Then go," said Kellina, pushing up from the table, and stepping away. "Go back to the MacKeefes if that is what ye want, but in doin' so, ye will have to leave me behind because I am stayin' right here."

"Kellina, stop bein' so stubborn." Nash felt a muscle in his clenched jaw tick.

"Me, stubborn? Hah! It is ye who is too proud to agree that stayin' here is the best idea."

"Why? Why is the best idea to stay here when everyone back home wants me to return?" asked Nash.

"Because this clan needs ye, Nash MacKeefe. I need ye," said Kellina with tears in her eyes. "Then again, I dinna suppose that matters to ye, since ye are the mighty Nash MacKeefe who doesna need a soul."

Kellina ran from the table, and Caitlin took off after her. Jamie picked up the kitten and glared at Nash. The whole MacKenzie Clan scowled at him now. The celebration for finishing repairing the roofs came to an abrupt halt. Suddenly, the whole alliance seemed like a farce. These people weren't his friends and neither were they his family. He was starting to feel like an outcast again, and being an outcast to two clans was just more than he could take.

"I'll be leavin' in the mornin', with or without my wife," announced Nash. "I'll sleep in the stable and leave at first light."

"Aye. Me, too," said North, following him.

"That goes for all the MacKeefes," said Cam, grabbing another bowl of stew and heading off to the stable with Gavin. Nash looked back at his friends following him, feeling their loyalty, but not being happy about putting them in this situation. Hell, he didn't like being in this predicament either. He never wanted to leave Kellina, but she hadn't given him much choice. She had spoken for the two of them, never discussing this in private first like married people should do.

He didn't feel married. Not really. He felt like a fool for more than one reason, and that didn't sit well with him at all.

"Nash, are ye all right?" asked North once they got to the stable. Gavin and Cam went to take care of the horses.

Nash looked out at the night sky and all the thatched roofs they'd helped build, feeling as if he were going to miss all this. Tomas wouldn't let him live in both camps, and Kellina had made it more than clear that she wasn't leaving here.

"Aye, I'm fine. Why shouldna I be?" asked Nash, staring up at all the stars in the dark, night sky.

"Because ye're about to leave here without yer wife, ye fool," spat North. "Nash, just stay here if it's what Kellina wants. It's no' important to come back to the MacKeefes. Just make her happy."

"It is important to me," Nash told his brother. "Kellina might be happy stayin' here, but I willna. No' since I ken the truth about what happened to our parents. Every time I go into the chieftain's hut, I'll think of what he did."

"He's dead!" spat North. "Let it go, Brathair. Isna that what ye keep tellin' Kellina?"

"I dinna ken," said Nash, flopping down into the hay on his back, covering his face with his arm. "I just want to sleep and no' talk about this anymore, Brathair."

"Sleepin' willna solve yer problem, Nash. Ye are goin' to have to decide by mornin', one way or another. And mark my words, if ye leave here without Kellina, ye'll regret it. It will break the alliance and the MacKeefes and the MacKenzies will be enemies once again."

Nash didn't answer. He knew his brother was right, but his pride was getting in his way of being able to make his own decisions. He loved Kellina, but was he willing to leave the MacKeefes and everything in his life to live with the MacKenzies? Would he be happy here? Or would it be too hard to look at the grave of the man who was responsible for the deaths of his parents? True, he'd told Kellina to leave the past behind and get on with the future. He hadn't thought at first that it bothered him as much as it did. However, when he was told he could never go back and live with the MacKeefes, it was just more than he could accept.

"Did ye hear me, Nash?" asked North, but Nash laid still and didn't answer.

Tomorrow, he would make the biggest decision of his life, and whatever he did would affect not only him but also his brother, his friends, and the future of both the clans.

Nay, Nash would get no sleep tonight, who was he fooling?

Chapter Twenty-Two

"I just canna do it," Nash told North the next morning, pacing back and forth in the cottage he and his friends shared while visiting the MacKenzies. They had planned to spend the night in the stable, but had been convinced by Tomas to use one of the cottages after all.

"I canna say I blame ye," said North with a yawn. "I wouldna leave the MacKeefes for a lass, no matter if she was my wife or no'."

"That's no' what I mean." Nash ran a weary hand through his long hair and plopped back down on the bed. "I canna leave Kellina. The lass has been through so much. She's lost nearly everyone in her life, and I will no' do that to her."

"Did I hear ye say ye're leavin' the MacKeefes?" Gavin got out of bed and started dressing.

"Nay, he'd never do such a daft thing." Cam sat on the edge of his bed and stretched and yawned. "Would ye, Nash?"

"Ye dinna understand. I love her." Nash groaned and buried his face in his hands.

"Well, after hearin' that profession of love accompanied by a groan, I really never want to fall in love or get married now," said his brother.

"I dinna understand why ye canna stay at both places." Cam got up and dressed. "Tomas is no' bein' fair at all."

"Aye, it would be guid to trade off where ye live, like Cam

and I and our wives are doin'," said Gavin.

"I told ye, it's different." Nash got up and started to pace again. "Ye two dinna have wives from another clan. If I dinna make the right choice, our clans could go to battle. I married the girl for an alliance, and I canna just leave her behind now. This is a lifelong commitment."

"An alliance that ye were forced into," North reminded him.

"Tomas is chieftain now," Nash continued. "He forbade us to live with both clans. We need to choose. One or the other."

"Then just convince yer wife to go with ye," said Cam, as if the answer were just that easy.

"She's already made it quite clear that she willna leave," Nash told him.

"Are ye really leavin' the MacKeefes, Brathair?" North looked so disappointed that it made Nash want to change his mind. He didn't want to abandon Kellina but, at the same time, he didn't want to leave his brother either.

Nash let out a deep sigh, sitting backwards on a chair, burying his face in his hands once again. He'd had no idea that when he served his sentence it was going to entail all these decisions, and possibly leaving the MacKeefes. This really isn't what he wanted at all. But neither did he want to leave his new wife. He loved her!

"God's eyes, I dinna ken what to do," Nash said with a groan.

"I'm sure ye'll come up with the right answer," said Cam, either being an idiot or having more faith in Nash then he did in himself.

"If there is an answer to solve all my problems, I dinna ken what it is."

"Well, whatever ye decide, ye'd better hurry," said Gavin. "We are leavin' for the MacKeefes soon."

"And we hope ye'll be with us, Brathair," said North, making Nash's heart ache even more, if that were at all possible.

"Hurry, Kellina, the sun is startin' to rise and I dinna want to miss it."

"Me neither," said Jamie, holding on to the kitten as he followed Caitlin up the hill to the gravesites.

Kellina followed her siblings up the hill, after they woke her much earlier than she'd intended on rising. Then again, this was the day the MacKeefes were leaving, and she needed to talk to Nash before he went.

"Look!" Jamie pointed at the orange ball rising in the sky behind the mountains of the Highlands.

"It's beautiful," said Kellina, glad she had come with them now. The sky looked magical. Orange hues lit up the horizon, and wisps of dark clouds made it stand out even more.

"It almost looks like fire," said Caitlin, picking a handful of heather to lay atop the graves.

"Dinna say fire," Kellina answered, feeling a shiver run up her spine. "There are too many bad memories involvin' that."

"We canna stay here long," said Jamie, putting the kitten on the ground and teasing it with a sprig of heather. "The MacKeefes are leavin' at first light, and I want to say guidbye to them. I really like them."

"Me, too," said Caitlin. "I'll miss them."

"Especially Nash," said Jamie. "Sister, is he really leavin' ye to go back with the MacKeefes?"

"Aye, I believe that is what he said," she answered, feeling her heart breaking.

"He's yer husband!" said Caitlin. "Ye should be together."

"I willna leave ye two," said Kellina, plucking a few sprigs of heather and handing them to Caitlin.

"Convince Nash to stay," whined Jamie.

"He has made up his mind, and so have I." Kellina gave the heather to Caitlin who laid it atop the graves of their parents and the others. "This is my home. I belong here with ye two, and I promised ye that I would never leave ye."

"Then take us with ye," said Jamie.

"What?" Kellina blinked, looking away from the sun that was rising quickly and becoming very bright now.

"Aye, we will all still be together, but just livin' with the MacKeefes instead," said Caitlin. "I mean, if they'll have us."

"Would ye two really be willin' to leave here?" asked Kellina, feeling suddenly excited. Why hadn't she thought of this solution?

"Why no'?" asked Caitlin. "We have no one left alive to stay here for. No' really."

"Except ye, Kellina," said Jamie. He picked up the kitten and gave it a kiss while it mewled loudly. "And ye, too, Midnight," he said to the cat.

"Well, I think that is a grand idea," said Kellina. "I'm sure Nash willna mind. That way he doesna have to leave his brathair or his friends."

"We'd better go and tell them before they ride out." Jamie took the kitten in his arms and started down the hill.

"I'll race ye, Jamie," said Caitlin, throwing down the rest of the heather and running after her brother.

Kellina looked over to the gravesites, and walked over to say her goodbyes. "Mathair, Faither," she said, talking to the parents she knew, and not her uncle. "I am goin' to take guid care of Caitlin and Jamie, so please dinna worry. We willna be livin' here, but I promise, we will be back to visit. I love Nash, and I dinna want to be apart from him. No' now, no' ever. Well, guidbye," she said, turning around, starting down the hill. That's when something shiny reflecting in the distance caught her attention. She looked out, able to see far from that height, and her heart almost stopped at what she saw.

"Sutherlands," she whispered, seeing so many of them on horseback heading right to their camp. "Nay," she cried, picking up her skirt and running down the hill so fast that she thought she'd fall. She had to warn her clan. She needed to tell the MacKeefes. They were about to be attacked again and, this time, they all might die in the battle.

◆•◦◇◦•◆

CHAPTER TWENTY-THREE

NASH WALKED WITH his brother and friends out to the stable to see them off. He had made his choice, but still didn't feel good about it. He'd chosen to stay with his wife, even if his heart was breaking that he would no longer be living with the MacKeefes. He especially regretted leaving his brother, since he was the only true family Nash had.

"Are ye sure ye willna change yer mind, Nash?" North asked for the tenth time since they left the cottage.

Nash thought he heard someone shouting, and looked around, but didn't see anything amiss. "Shhhh," he told his brother. "I thought I heard somethin'."

"That's probably Gavin," said Cam. "He ate a lot of beans last night." Cam started chuckling.

"Nay, I hear it, too," said Gavin, looking up and pointing at the hill. "Isna that Kellina?"

"What is she yellin' about?" asked North.

"Kellina," whispered Nash, taking off at a run toward her. He could tell something was wrong, but he didn't know what.

"Nash, Nash," she cried, running toward him.

"Lass, what is the matter?" He grabbed her in his arms, seeing how upset she was. She was out of breath and could barely breathe. "Did somethin' happen? Is someone hurt?"

"Sutherlands," was all she managed to get out, but that was all he needed to hear.

"Draw yer weapons," Nash called out at the top of his lungs. "We're about to be attacked."

"What?" Gavin pulled his sword from the sheath, holding it with two hands as he turned in a full circle.

"I've got ye covered," said Cam, doing the same.

"Someone get Tomas and the others," North shouted out, running for the stable. "We'll be able to fight them better on horseback."

Nash drew his sword and was about to run to the stable, but turned back to Kellina. "Get yerself to safety," he told her. "Watch over Caitlin and Jamie and that little kitten." He grabbed her and kissed her hard, just in case this was the last chance he ever had to do it.

"I WILL TELL Tomas," Kellina told Nash, turning and running to the chieftain's hut. She saw Caitlin and Jamie on the way.

"What's happenin'?" asked Caitlin.

"Why are ye shoutin'?" asked Jamie.

"Get yerselves to safety," said Kellina. "The Sutherlands are about to attack. Go fast, and tell the rest of the clan. Hurry."

"What about ye?" asked Caitlin, as her brother tried to drag her away. "Kellina, come with us to hide in safety."

"Nay," she said. "This time, I will kill any Sutherland who even tries to hurt a member of my clan."

"Did someone say Sutherlands?" Tomas rushed from the cottage before she could even get him.

"They're approachin' and there are twice as many as before. I saw them from the top of the hill," she reported.

"Get the women and children to safety," Tomas called out to one of his men. "The rest of ye, with me." He drew his blade. "Kellina, it would be wise if ye took cover."

"I willna!" she spat. "I am goin' back to my hut for my sword, and then I will fight with the others to bring down each and every Sutherland, until they are all dead. They will pay for takin' the lives of so many from our clan."

Kellina turned and ran, her hatred and anger for the Sutherlands so strong right now that she could think of nothing else.

⟫⟫⟫⟪⟪⟪

SURE ENOUGH, JUST as Kellina had told them, the Sutherlands arrived in droves. Nash and his brother and friends fought them on horseback, while Tomas and the rest of the men of the MacKenzie Clan fought them on the ground.

"God's eyes, they just dinna stop," said Nash, stabbing a crazed Sutherland who fell from his horse.

"There are too many of them," shouted North from his horse. "There is nothin' we can do to stop them."

"I hope to hell Kellina got her siblin's to safety," said Nash, right before he saw her. Kellina wasn't in the hut hiding like he'd instructed her to do. Nay, instead, she was on foot, fighting the Sutherlands with her sword.

"God's eyes, what is she doin'?" Nash knew he had to get to her before one of these bastards took off her head.

⟫⟫⟫⟪⟪⟪

"YE'LL DIE FOR what ye did," shouted Kellina, her sword clashing with that of the Sutherland chieftain with the scar. He was Iver, the same man who had threatened to kill her at the market.

"Ye never should have angered me at the market, Wench," spat Iver. "Now, no' only ye, but yer clansmembers and the MacKeefes helpin' ye will die. Then, everythin' here will be ours."

"Never!" she shouted, taking another stab at him, but the man was too fast for her. He flipped her sword out of her hand and up into the air. Then he pushed her down and held the tip of his blade right toward her heart.

"Before I kill ye, I'd like to see what's under those clothes." He used his blade to rip her bodice down the front.

211

"Leave me alone, ye bastard!" she spat, holding her arm in front of her so she wouldn't be exposed to this cur.

"I've never had such a pretty young one before, but ye, I'm goin' to enjoy." He reached for his plaid, pulling it up to show her his erection.

"Nay!" she screamed as he threw himself atop her, meaning to have his way with her.

"Ye bastard! Get off my wife!" Nash rode up, jumping from the horse, pulling the man off of Kellina. He punched him first, knocking the Sutherland to the ground. Then he thrust his blade right through the man's heart.

"Nash!" cried Kellina, running to him, throwing herself into his arms. Tears flowed from her eyes. She was scared, as well as angry.

"Why didna ye hide in the hut and protect yer siblin's like I told ye to do?"

"I wanted to help. Nash, watch out!"

He let go of her and turned on his heel, taking down another Sutherland.

"There are too many of them. We are outnumbered and will never be able to fight them all," she cried.

"Then I'll go to my death tryin' to protect ye, lass." Nash pulled her to him and kissed her hard, then released her just as quickly. "Go to yer siblin's now. They'll be frightened and will need ye."

"Nash, nay. I dinna want ye to die."

"Go!" he shouted. "I canna watch ye and fight off these bastards at the same time."

"I love ye, Nash MacKeefe," she said, turning and running to the hut. If she lost her husband today, she wasn't sure she would have the will to go on.

NASH AND HIS friends did their best to fight off the Sutherlands, but they were highly outnumbered and it wasn't looking good. Dead bodies from both sides littered the ground, making Nash sick to his stomach.

This never should have happened. This wasn't the way it was supposed to be.

"Nash, it's no' lookin' promisin'," called out North from the top of his horse as he rode to meet Nash. Nash had mounted his steed again as well.

"It was nice knowin' ye, Brathair," said Nash, spying a large group of Sutherlands pushing through the crowd. Just when Nash was sure they'd all lose their lives today, he heard the sound of a horn in the distance.

His horse got spooked and threw him, and he landed on his back on the ground. He dropped his sword in the fall. It was too far to pick up without getting to his feet.

"Die, MacKeefe!" yelled a Sutherland, lifting his sword above his head to kill Nash. Nash rolled to the side, and the Sutherland fell face first to the ground next to him with an arrow sticking out of his back.

Nash looked up to the hill with the gravesites to see Lady Spring with her bow in hand. With her was the Gordon Clan, all with their weapons at the ready.

"Sutherlands, drop yer weapons!" called out Shaw Gordon, chieftain of the clan.

"Ye canna stop us," called out one of the Sutherland Clan.

"Then mayhap the Gunn Clan can," came the voice of a Gunn member from the opposite direction.

"The MacKeefes are here as well," shouted Storm MacKeefe, leading his clan into camp, too.

"Bid the devil! They're all here," mumbled Nash, scooping up his sword and running to greet them. "Sutherlands, yer chieftain is dead," he shouted. "I just killed him. Surrender now, or ye will all die."

"Our chieftain is dead?" asked one of the Sutherlands and

they quietly talked to each other.

"We surrender," said one of the Sutherlands. "Drop yer weapons, men," he called out to his clan. "It is over." They all did as told, raising their empty hands above their heads, rather than die at the hands of the other four clans.

"Thank ye," called out Tomas, running over to Storm MacKeefe and Nash.

"What do ye want us to do with them?" asked Storm.

"I'm no' sure," said Tomas.

"I am," said Nash. "If I may?"

"Go on," said Tomas. "I trust ye."

Nash walked out into the middle of the camp, holding up his sword. "Sutherlands, ye will never bother the MacKenzie Clan again, or ye will be killed by the MacKenzies, the MacKeefes, the Gordons, and the Gunns. Do ye understand?"

"Aye," the Sutherlands answered, one after another.

That is no' all," Nash continued. "Ye will return all the livestock ye stole from the MacKenzies, and add half of yers to the mix as well."

"That's no' fair," shouted a Sutherland.

"Neither was it fair that ye killed innocent women and children the last time ye raided," called out one of the MacKenzies.

"Kill them all!" called out another MacKenzie.

"They deserve to die for the lives of our loved ones they took," shouted Alice.

"That's true," said Tomas. "They killed our chieftain's family, and should pay for it."

"Nay! Stop," yelled Kellina, running to join them, with her sword in hand. "Look around ye," she spat. "Too many have died already, and killing more isna goin' to bring back our loved ones."

"She's right," said Nash. "They can never repay us for the lives lost, but remember we took loved ones' lives from them as well now." He nodded at all the dead bodies littering the camp.

"We'll take no' only our livestock and half of yers, but ye'll also give us half of yer harvest, and seeds to plant for next year," said Tomas, adding to the deal.

"And thatch, to make up for burnin' our homes," said Kellina. "Ye'll send over whatever thatch ye possess for us to store for the future."

"Fine," growled the Sutherland who had stepped forward since their chieftain was killed. "Can we leave now?"

"Is there anythin' else?" Storm asked Nash and Tomas.

"I'm guid," said Tomas.

Nash looked over to Kellina and she shook her head.

"We also want a promise that the Sutherlands will never attack the MacKenzies again," Nash added as an afterthought.

"What about us?" asked one of the Sutherlands. "We have no promise that any of these clans will no' attack us."

"That's right, and that is just how it will be," said Nash. "Now do ye agree to the terms or no'?"

"We do," grumbled the new Sutherland chieftain.

"Guid. No' get the hell out of here," Tomas bellowed.

"What about our dead? We willna leave them behind," said the Sutherland.

"I've got this," Storm told Nash and Tomas. He looked up and spoke to the Sutherlands. "We'll help ye to load yer dead on a cart, and even escort ye back to yer camp to make certain ye bring back what was promised."

With that, everyone put down their weapons, and the proceedings continued until the dead Sutherlands were loaded, being led away by the Gunns and the Gordons.

Lady Spring stayed back to talk to them.

"Thank ye, for savin' my life," Nash told Spring, putting his arm around Kellina.

"How is it that all these clans were here to help us?" asked Kellina.

Storm MacKeefe was still there as well. Tomas, North, Gavin, and Cam stood close by. Jamie and Caitlin watched from behind Kellina.

"I had a feelin' the Sutherlands were goin' to cause trouble again," Spring told them. "We had scouts watchin' them. This mornin', they saw the Sutherlands travelin' toward yer camp, so we followed."

"And the Gunns?" asked Nash. "How did they hear about it?"

"The Gunns were my old clan before I married Shaw," Spring told them. "My brathair is married to one of them, and we have a close alliance. They agreed to help out as well."

"As for the MacKeefes," said Storm, "there were a few MacKeefes at the market who saw the Sutherlands and Kellina's encounter with them. When they came back and reported what happened, I kent we needed to come see for ourselves that ye were all right. And I'm glad we were in time."

"Thank ye," said Tomas. "We can never repay ye."

"Thank ye all," said Kellina. "Especially Nash and his brathair and friends. If they hadna been here, I have no doubt we would have lost many more before the other clans arrived."

"I'll always be here to defend ye, Kellina," Nash told her. "I've decided to stay and live with the MacKenzies now, since we're married. I ken that is what ye want."

"Nay, it isna," said Kellina.

"What?" asked Nash. "I'm confused."

"I canna let ye leave yer brathair and friends, Nash. Ye belong with the MacKeefes, so that is where I will go to live with ye, now that I am yer wife."

"But Kellina, I ken ye dinna want to leave yer siblin's."

"I dinna," she admitted. "That is why I am askin' if Caitlin and Jamie can come live at the MacKeefes with us."

"I would love that," said Nash, feeling like this problem was solved. "Storm? Would ye agree to lettin' Kellina's siblin's join the MacKeefes as well?"

"Why no'?" asked Storm. "After all, with Gavin and Cam and their new families, our clan is growin' every day. Aye, they are welcome to join us."

"And Midnight, too?" asked Jamie, running up with Caitlin, holding tightly to the kitten.

"Midnight?" asked Storm.

"The cat," Nash answered.

Storm chuckled. "Well, we could use a little help with the rats, just as long as it stays away from Aidan's squirrel."

"Then it's settled," said Nash. "Kellina, start packin'. We're leavin' for the MacKeefes today."

"What about a weddin'?" asked Spring.

"Lady Spring, ye ken we're already married," answered Kellina.

"But did ye have a proper weddin'?" asked Spring.

"Nay, we didna," Nash answered. "I would like a proper weddin' for Kellina, since she deserves it."

"And ye deserve this," said Tomas, pulling a parchment out of his pouch and handing it to Storm.

"What's this?" asked Storm, still sitting atop his horse.

Tomas answered. "It's a missive sayin' that Nash MacKeefe has concluded his punishment here. He has been a true help in rebuildin' the cottages and has become verra efficient at thatchin' roofs."

"So have I," North called out. "Does that count for somethin'?"

They all laughed.

"Plus, he made the alliance by marryin' Kellina," Tomas finished.

"Then, I'd say his sentence his over." Storm nodded, shoving the parchment inside his sash. "There is nothin' my grandda can say now about ye, Nash. Ye are no longer an outcast of the clan. Welcome back."

"What about me?" asked North, pushing to the front of the crowd. "Laird MacKeefe, what will my sentence be? I dinna want to be an outcast any longer."

"After Nash and Kellina's weddin' ceremony, ye'll get yer sentence as well, North."

"Then, let's quickly get back and get the blasted weddin' under way," said Nash. "I'm in a hurry to get my sentence over with . . . with Nash helpin' me as promised, of course."

"Of course," grumbled Nash, already regretting the promise he'd made his brother.

Chapter Twenty-Four

T HREE DAYS LATER, Nash was back at the MacKeefe camp with Kellina, ready for the marriage ceremony to begin. It felt better than ever.

"The MacKeefes really have a beautiful camp," Kellina told him, looking around at the way Caitlin had helped the other women of the clan decorate the area with arches woven with wildflowers.

"No' nearly as beautiful as my wife." Nash gathered her into his arms and kissed her, never wanting to let her go.

"Nay, ye canna do that until after the weddin'," said Caitlin, prying them apart. "It's bad luck. Ye arena supposed to even see her ahead of time."

"No' see her? We're in the same camp," said Nash. "It's no' like we're at Hermitage Castle. I'd have to walk around blindfolded no' to see her."

"Now, that sounds interestin'," said Kellina with a giggle. "I'm sure it can be arranged."

"Never mind." Nash let go of her. "I see the priest, and everyone is waitin'. Let's do this, Kellina. I canna wait any longer."

"I agree," she said, as they headed over to the crowd for the wedding ceremony to begin.

KELLINA STOOD UNDER the arch made of flowers, gripping a bouquet of heather in her hands. She didn't feel this nervous the first time they got married, but right now her hands were shaking and so were the flowers.

All of the MacKeefes stood around them, and even Lady Spring and her husband, Shaw Gordon, attended the wedding today. This was a special day for Kellina because, this time, she wasn't being forced to marry Nash against her will. Even though they were really already married, this time, she wanted to be the bride of Nash MacKeefe more than anything in the world.

When the priest was about to have them repeat the vows, Kellina stopped him.

"Kellina? What is it, lass?" asked Nash.

"I wrote my own vows and would like to say them," she announced.

"Really?" Nash looked over to the priest who nodded in agreement.

"Go on," said the priest.

"Nash MacKeefe," she started, feeling choked with emotion. She cleared her throat and started again. "I, Kellina MacKenzie take Nash MacKeefe for my husband. I would be honored to be his bride. I will stay at his side on the ground or even on the roof, in the air." That got a chuckle out of the bystanders. "In sickness and in health, I will stay with and care for him. I'll hand him leggetts and hammers without throwin' them, I promise. And I will never make a jest about him bein' sure-footed as a goat again. I'll love ye forever, Nash MacKeefe, and will be the best wife I can possibly be."

"That was beautiful, lass," Nash said with a smile, holding on to her hands. He looked so handsome in his white tunic with billowing sleeves, and his green and purple plaid. Kellina wore a skirt of the MacKeefe colors today as well, feeling proud and pretty. She truly felt as if she belonged here after all.

"It's yer turn to say yer vows now," said North, under his breath.

"What?" Nash turned and whispered to North. "Ye ken I dinna have any."

"Then make somethin' up," said North. "Be sure-footed like a goat, just like Kellina said." He chuckled, enjoying this way too much.

"It's all right, Nash," Kellina told him, seeing the helpless look on Nash's face. "I didna mean to put ye in such a position. Ye dinna have to make up yer own vows."

"Nay. Nay, it's fine," he told her, shooting a daggered look at his brother before beginning. He cleared his throat and talked.

"I, Nash MacKeefe, take Kellina MacKenzie as my bride. To have her and hold her, on the ground or on roofs, I promise to always keep her safe." That got a few laughs as well. "In spring or summer, or even autumn or winter. In guid times and bad, or in times that are neither, I will be by her side always, I swear. In the east or the west . . . the south or the –"

"God's eyes, that's enough Nash," growled North.

Nash turned and whispered to his brother. "Well, ye were the one who told me to make somethin' up."

"I didna say to write a book," North said in a hoarse whisper, but loud enough for everyone to hear and laugh again.

"All right, all right," said Nash, taking a deep breath, smiling at Kellina. "In sickness and health, till death do us part."

"That kind of sounded like the vows the priest reads, didna it?" she heard Cam saying to Gavin.

"Then, I pronounce ye two married," said the priest happily. "Ye can kiss the bride, Nash."

"Thank ye, Faither." Nash kissed Kellina passionately, making her feel randy.

"Nash, we'd better save this for later," she whispered when he brought her up and out of the dip he had her in.

"Let's drink Mountain Magic," came the crackly old voice of Callum MacKeefe. "Three down, and one to go."

"Aye, that's me," said North. "What's my sentence, Callum?"

"Easy, young one," said Callum, handing him a mug of whisky. "Just be glad I allowed ye to be here, and drink for the day. Because where ye'll be goin', ye will be far away, and ye willna like it, I am sure."

"Where? Where are ye sendin' me?" asked North anxiously.

"Brathair, calm down," said Nash with a chuckle. "Let's all drink to the bonniest wife ever."

"I'll drink to that," said Gavin, lifting his mug. His wife, Davita was next to him.

"Me, too," said Cam, doing the same. His wife, Yvaine clung to his arm.

"The bonniest wife?" Davita asked Gavin.

"Ye're drinkin' to that?" Yvaine asked Cam.

"We meant . . . we meant . . ." Cam started, looking anxiously at Gavin for help.

"We were drinkin' to our bonnie wives," said Gavin, taking a big chug from the tankard.

"Aye, that's what we meant." Cam did the same.

Davita and Yvaine started laughing, only having meant to tease their new husbands.

"We were only jestin' with ye two," said Davita.

"Let's go help the lassies set out the food," said Yvaine. She looked over to her four-year-old daughter holding the kitten, standing with Jamie and Caitlin. "Avianca, ye be careful with the kitten now, sweetheart."

"I will," said the little girl with a wide smile on her face as the black kitten licked her hand. Then, Davita and Yvaine headed away, chatting like the old friends they were.

"Congratulations, Sister." Caitlin ran up and gave Kellina a hug. Then she looked up and whispered. "There are a lot of cute MacKeefe lads here. I am glad we came to live here after all."

"Stay away from the boys," Kellina called out as Caitlin ran off with Jamie and Avianca.

"I think everyone looks happy here." Spring came up, cradling her baby. Shaw had his arm around her.

"We wish ye the best," said Shaw.

"And plenty of bairns," added Spring.

"No' too many too fast." Nash raised his hands in the air.

"That's right," said North, overhearing them. "After all, my brathair is comin' with me when I get my sentence. And from the sounds of it, it might no' be a verra nice place, or close by."

"Callum never said where it was," Nash said, looking over to Kellina nervously. "I'm sure it willna be that bad."

"I hope it willna be anywhere too dangerous." Kellina hugged Nash, never wanting to let him go.

"I'm sure my grandda willna be choosin' anywhere that is more dangerous than bein' up on roofs," said Storm, trying to ease the tension.

"Guid then," said Kellina. "Because my husband is a sure-footed goat when it comes to roofs, so he will be safe on the ground as well. Oops," she said, slapping her hand to her mouth. "I promised not to tease ye about that. Sorry."

"Baaaaa," chortled North, causing everyone to laugh as they walked away, leaving Nash and Kellina standing there together.

"Are ye sure ye dinna mind if I accompany North on his journey?" asked Nash. "After all, he did help me out a lot with my sentence, and that allowed us the time to go to the market instead of thatchin'."

"Would ye change yer answer to him if I said I did mind?" she asked, making him squirm again.

"Well . . . well, I . . ."

"It's fine, Nash." Kellina reached over and pecked him on the cheek. "A promise is a promise, and must be carried out no matter what it is."

"Like our marriage to form an alliance?" he asked.

"That, and also yer promise to the MacKenzies to help thatch all our roofs. Which, by the way, ye have succeeded in doin'."

"I kind of like it up there on the roofs," he told her, kissing her behind the ear and making her giggle. "After all, I found ye up there, and it was a guid surprise. Things look different from that high up. Better, I think. Bonnie."

"Of course, they do," she told him, snuggling up to him, knowing he meant her. It was a beautiful day and the clouds were white and puffy, looking striking against the bright blue sky. "Then again, bein' with the one I love on top of a roof makes life look better as well."

"I will miss ye when I go away with North," Nash told her, taking her hands in his. "I just hope it willna be for too long."

"I'll always be there with ye, in yer memories," she told him. "We will be back together soon, so dinna fret about it, Nash."

"What am I goin' to do when I start missin' ye too much?" he asked. "How will I survive?"

"Well, when ye miss me, ye'll feel my spirit with ye."

"How?"

"It's easy. Just look upward and think of me. Think of us on the roof together, and things will be different. Ye'll see me in yer memories, and that will hold ye over until we are back together again."

"I will," he told her, kissing her hand. "And if I have to, I will climb a roof to get that feelin' back. I love ye, Kellina. Ye are the light in my life, and will always be my personal *Highland Sky*."

I hope you enjoyed Nash and Kellina's story and will take a moment to leave a review for me. I found it fascinating while doing research, learning all the hard work that goes into thatching a roof. Someday, I swear I am going to build a little hut in my backyard just so I can experience putting on a thatched roof for myself.

As in many of my books, you'll find characters from some of my other series making guest appearances. In this book, there were several.

Aidan MacKeefe and his adorable little squirrel are from *Aidan – Book 2* of my *Madman MacKeefe Series*. His madmen friends, can be found in *Onyx – Book 1* and *Ian – Book 3* of the same series.

Storm MacKeefe, chieftain of the clan, and his wife, Wren, as well as Ian and Old Callum, can be found in *Lady Renegade – Book 2* of my *Legacy of the Blade Series*, as well as in many of my other books. Storm is the backbone of the MacKeefe Clan and you'll find him appearing over and over again, even in some of my later series such as *The Highland Chronicles*.

Lady Spring and her husband, Shaw Gordon, are first seen in *Highland Spring – Book 1* of my *Seasons of Fortitude Series*. Spring is the sister of the *Legendary Bastards of the Crown*.

Thank you for joining me on this journey. Next, and last of all to get his sentence, is North in *Highland Silver – Book 4* of the *Highland Outcasts Series*.

If you've missed Gavin and Cam's stories, you'll find them in Books 1 and 2. Here is a list of the entire series:

Highland Outcasts:
Highland Soul
Highland Flame
Highland Sky
Highland Silver

Thank ye,
Elizabeth Rose

About the Author

Elizabeth Rose is an Amazon All-Star, and bestselling, award-winning, author of nearly 100 books and counting! Her first book was published back in 2000, but she has been writing stories ever since high school.

She is the author of contemporary, western, paranormal, and her favorite – medieval romance. You'll find sexy, alpha heroes and strong, independent heroines in her books. Sometimes her heroines can even swing a sword. She loves adding humor to her work, because everyone needs to laugh more in life. Her ***Bad Boys of Sweetwater: Tarnished Saints Series,*** was inspired by people, places, and things in her own life. The location is the lake and small town of Michigan where she grew up visiting her grandparents.

Living in the suburbs of Chicago with her husband, she has two grown sons and one granddog – so far. A lover of nature, Elizabeth can be found in the summer swinging in her "writing hammock" in her secret garden, creating her next novel. Her secret garden is what inspired her series, ***Secrets of the Heart***, which of course centers around a secret garden too!

Elizabeth's current and upcoming books will be published by *Dragonblade Publishing* and independently too under *RoseScribe Media Inc.*

<u>**Social Media:**</u>
Elizabeth's Website: elizabethrosenovels.com
Newsletter Sign Up: bit.ly/3aK66i2
Eizabeth's Private Readers' Facebook Group:
facebook.com/groups/1069264379873015
Facebook: facebook.com/ElizabethRoseNovels
Goodreads: goodreads.com/author/show/89482.Elizabeth_Rose
Bookbub: bookbub.com/authors/elizabeth-rose

www.ingramcontent.com/pod-product-compliance
Lightning Source LLC
Chambersburg PA
CBHW070929190726
48292CB00004B/1158